The BACKUP Plan

EDEN FINLEY

The Backup Plan © 2024 by Eden Finley

Cover Illustration Copyright ©
Eden Finley
Photographer: Wander Aguiar

Edited by One Love Editing
https://oneloveediting.com

All rights reserved.
This book or any portion thereof may not be reproduced or used in any manner whatsoever without the express written permission of the publisher.
For information regarding permission, write to:
Eden Finley - permissions - edenfinley@gmail.com

Content Warnings/Disclaimers

This book deals with some triggering topics, such as toxicity in sports, homophobia and hate speech online, and anxiety disorders and mental health.

Chapter 1
Thad

When your boss calls you and says, "Pack a bag and get to the office as soon as you can," you hustle.

I have no idea where I'm going or what I'm doing, but it's my first assignment that has included travel since I started my internship at King Sports.

Whenever I was asked as a kid what I wanted to be when I grew up, it was always the same answer: ballplayer. I was going to be the next big thing in baseball. A Hall of Famer. I had big dreams, worked hard for it, and I got really damn close.

I wish I could say it was an injury or something out of my control that ended that dream, but unfortunately, it took me way too long to realize that I just wasn't good enough.

Ego, overinflated false sense of talent from my dad encouraging me and telling me I had what it takes, and all the money my parents sunk into private coaches who said the same thing set me up for failure.

This is why parents shouldn't dote on their kids. How dare they, honestly. Because when it comes down to it, my fall from the mediocre middle felt like jumping out of an airplane at ten thousand feet with no parachute. Though my heart was the only victim as it splattered all over the pavement.

So, this is my backup plan.

Thad

My second choice.

Becoming a sports agent wasn't where I thought I'd end up, but it's the reality I'm having to face. I wish I could say I've handled it all with grace, but I know I haven't.

I'm lucky to be where I am, and there are a lot of other people who would've killed for this internship, but I can't help that my heart is still broken over the sport I'm absolutely obsessed with.

Baseball will always be my one true love, and I think that's why I got this job in the first place. My boss, Damon King, was supposed to be the next big thing from the generation before me, but because of an injury, his dream also died at the collegiate level. Our stories were similar, and I know the manager in training on the West Coast also has a similar background. It's as if Damon has a soft spot for us misplaced baseball players.

I'm eternally grateful for him giving me a chance, even if I don't always show it. I'm trying to do better, but it's really difficult not to be bitter.

At least this way, I still get to be in the industry. I'm baseball ... adjacent. That's what I keep trying to tell myself.

When I get into the office, I head straight for Damon's office to see what my assignment is. Accompanying another agent on a scouting trip? Signing new talent?

I stop short in my tracks when I cross the threshold and see the last person in the world I'd want to see.

I've only met him in passing a handful of times, but I resent him. I know I shouldn't, but it's one of those things. He has a professional career, the talent, a multimillion-dollar MLB contract as a pitcher for Philly, and he takes it all for granted.

He's too focused on whether or not the public loves him to appreciate what he has, which is everything I've ever wanted.

Kelley Afton doesn't know how lucky he is. And to top it all off, he's probably the sexiest man I've ever laid eyes on. Because of course, the huge queer MLB star has to be drop-dead gorgeous. Couldn't make the super-talented baseball player have a huge nose or big ears or something to make his face not so perfectly symmetrical with flawless skin.

Chapter 1

His complexion and closely cropped dark hair suggests a Hispanic background somewhere in his heritage, or maybe he's the type of person who can get a tan and keep hold of it. During the summer, I usually have nicely tanned skin, but only because I'm outside a lot. During winter, I'm as white as a piece of paper.

One thing I've noticed about his light brown eyes, though, is they always look worried. It's probably the stress of caring what other people think of him that's aged the top half of his face, and I should feel sorry for him, but I don't because the crow's feet make him look distinguished and sexy. He looks older than the twenty-six years that is, but what would be a flaw on anyone else looks good on him.

How is life fair?

"Thad. You're here already," Damon says, looking surprised.

"You said to get down here as soon as I could."

Kelley still hasn't made eye contact with me.

"You've met Kelley Afton before, haven't you?" Damon asks.

I grit my teeth as I force a smile. "In passing."

Behind me, a fellow intern comes barreling into the room.

"I'm here, I'm here. What was so urgent?" Brady Talon spots Kelley on the couch along the side wall of Damon's office. "Oh, hey, Kelley, what's up?"

Kelley stands and greets Brady with a one-armed bro-hug.

"What took you so long to get here?" Damon mocks.

"You called half an hour ago."

"And your world does not revolve around my every command? It's official, you're my least favorite nibling."

"Pfft. Like you'd ever choose Freddie over me. He's a walking, talking emo boy who hates everything, especially sports."

"Fine. Second least favorite."

Brady grins. "That's better."

I've noticed they have a work relationship full of banter, and Brady is definitely the boss's favorite intern, but that makes sense with Damon being Brady's honorary uncle. It's how Brady already knows Kelley. He got to shadow Damon on a recent photoshoot for Kelley's coming out.

Thad

I wouldn't dare speak to my boss the way Brady does sometimes, but Damon is extremely professional when it comes to his employees; Brady is the exception to that.

Brady greets me with a cold up-nod, and I get the impression Brady hates me because of my bitterness toward ... well, everything. I thought out of everyone, he would understand. His fathers are the great Marcus Talon and Shane Miller, first same-sex couple to play on an NFL team and go on to win Super Bowls together. Brady's older brother, Peyton Miller, is currently kicking ass in his rookie years in the NFL, and then there's Brady. Not a football player but an agent.

The thing with him is, though, he chose to give up football. He wants to be here, and it's no company secret that when Damon King retires, Brady Talon will take his place.

If the man ever retires. I can see it now—he's going to be one of those people who work until they're in their eighties, finally retire, and then drop dead because their purpose in life is no longer there to throw themselves into.

"Kelley needs some help," Damon says. "As you're both aware, when Kelley came out, there was some backlash."

"No more than usual." What can I say, the industry hasn't changed much over the years. Coming out is still scandalous, and there are still those homophobic dickweeds who say sports are for real men and blah, blah, blah.

"But considering Kelley was hesitating to come out to begin with, it's hit him hard," Damon says.

"I love how you talk about me like I'm not here." Kelley's wearing a charming smile, and I swear I see his teeth shine off the light and make a bling noise like a damn cartoon character. Or maybe the lighting in here is making the diamond stud in his ear blinding.

"By all means, if you want to fill them in." Damon leans back in his chair.

Yet, when Kelley talks again, he still doesn't look at me. His only focus is on Brady.

Chapter 1

"You were right. When you told me things would be shit for a while after coming out, I was worried about it but prepared. Or, I thought I was prepared. I've been getting messages. Mostly supportive and amazing, but then there's the ones that start off great and say they're supportive of me and then follow it up with *'even if you're going to hell.'*"

Here's a novel idea. Don't go on social media. What? That's a thing?

"Then there are the ones that straight up say I should unalive myself."

Okay, that's not cool. At all. And even if I'm resentful of what Kelley has, no one deserves that.

"I'm trying to stay away from it all. I've deleted apps from my phone, I've put one of those child lock things on certain sites, but I can't stay away from it. It's as if a few hours go by, and my brain says, 'Maybe they're saying different things now.' So then I look and get anxious and depressed all over again."

"That's where you two come in," Damon says.

"Us?" I ask.

"At the photoshoot, Brady said I should become a hermit for a while. Go somewhere no one can find me, and that's what I want to do," Kelley says.

"I'm still missing the point." Am I being daft here?

"Kelley's going to take off to the Catskills for a while, and I want you two to go with him," Damon says. "To make sure that he actually stays away from the toxicity of the internet and gets the rest that he needs."

"How long for?" Brady asks, a whole lot more excited about it than I am.

"Two weeks at least. Then we'll reassess."

I thought I would be getting to do actual agent work when he called for me to come in immediately. Something that might advance my career.

Instead, I get to babysit a diva baseball player who doesn't know how good he has it. If I didn't hate him already, this would've sealed it.

Thad

Kelley Afton is the most ungrateful, oblivious son of a bitch on the planet, and if we even survive the next two weeks together, it'll be a miracle.

Let's hope I can keep my shit together because otherwise, I'll need a backup plan for my backup plan.

Chapter 2
Kelley

Okay, when my agent suggested this arrangement, I didn't realize they would be confiscating my phone.

Yes, I want to be on a social media ban, but this is a bit extreme. I can see where my phone sits in the middle console, in between Brady and Thad, who are in the front seats of the car, and instead of staring out at the winter scenery going by as we make the drive from Manhattan to the Catskills, all I can do is stare at my phone, hoping I develop telekinesis in the next two and a half hours before we get to our destination.

Thad mutters something under his breath about it being bullshit that he has to babysit a grown-ass adult. It's possible he's hoping I don't hear him, but I do. Either that, or he doesn't care if I know he thinks I'm blowing this all out of proportion.

The thing is, that's what my brain does. It catastrophizes everything, and a lot of people don't understand why I do that. It's taken a good amount of therapy to understand my anxiety, but that doesn't mean it's always easy to deal with. So I don't fault Thad for the way he thinks. Nearly everyone else in my life is the same. Compassion and empathy are the lost skills of society.

Thad is an intern, like Brady, but I haven't had any proper interaction with him. If I'm honest, he kind of intimidates the hell out of me.

He has these massively broad shoulders, light blue eyes, and

Kelley

dark hair that has a thin blond streak on one side. The few times I've seen him, his hair has had that permanent wet look. Whatever hair product he uses liberally keeps his hair slicked back.

But it's not his good looks or his bigger physique that intimidates me. It's the way he stares—no, more like glares—at me. Every time I've been into the King Sports offices lately and he's been there, his daggers are palpable from across the room.

I don't know what his deal is, whether he's that ornery with everyone or only with me, but it sets my skin aflame every time.

There's something about me that craves to be accepted by everyone, which is annoying and frustrating because I know that's an impossible feat. Especially as a gay athlete.

It's possible that's why Thad is unhappy about his assignment, but Damon King is not the type of person to hire a bigot. The whole reason I wanted to sign with him is because of what he's done for queer athletes. He started his company after making a name for himself as the agent for queer people. Sure, his firm represents people of all sexualities and orientations, including straight athletes, but the majority live under the rainbow. I knew he'd be able to handle my coming out and was naïve enough to think he was all I'd need.

Instead, here I am, on the verge of a panic attack because the online comments I knew were coming still happened. There was a small part of me that was hoping I'd be different. I'd be the outlier, and even the homophobes out there would say, "He's so good at baseball, I don't care where he parks his dick at night."

Deep down, I knew that was never going to happen, and I almost chickened out of doing that stupid photoshoot and article, but Brady was there with Damon, and he talked me into going through with it because, as he said then, doing it in the off-season is the best plan. This way, by the time spring training starts up, my news will have died down.

Would it be selfish of me to hope one of my teammates gets caught having an illicit affair during their break though?

I don't regret letting Brady talk me into coming out, but I wish the world was a different place.

Chapter 2

The reason I came out was to finally start living my life as my authentic self. I was looking forward to dating men, being out and proud, and having that freedom, and I thought I was ready for it, but it turns out I might not be. It's too late now though. I can't close that closet door now it's been opened.

"You doing okay back there?" Brady asks, looking at me in the rearview mirror.

"Yup. Just …" My gaze flicks to the back of Thad's head. "Thinking."

Brady smiles. "Overthinking, you mean."

"Well, yeah." I'm always overthinking, always in my head, and it's been that way since I was a child.

The only thing that has ever taken me out of my uncontrollable and runaway thoughts is being on that pitcher's mound. Having to focus on baseball and only baseball. Forcing my brain into thinking about technique, aim, and striking the next batter out. Baseball is my outlet. My reprieve.

"The next two weeks are going to be about relaxing and forgetting the rest of the world."

Easy for Brady to say. I can't forget the rest of the world, even if I try.

I've always envied those people who let everything roll off their back, the ones who don't give a shit what someone else thinks of them, but I am not that guy.

It's not that I want everyone to like me or I want to be popular or universally loved, but at the same time, there's something inside me that can't stand the idea of rejection. I wish my brain wasn't wired that way, but it is.

Which is another reason why Thad is intimidating. He hasn't said a word to me since we got in the car, and now that I'm thinking about it, I don't think he said anything to me in the office either. He talked about me, not to me, all the while only being six feet away.

I hope the next two weeks will get me out of my head, but I don't like my chances with Thad being around.

Kelley

We arrive at the estate, a huge property with cabins and a main house. It's obvious this is more of a summer destination, but that's why Damon picked it. The King Sports corporate retreat is held here, and he knows it's practically deserted in the winter.

I won't have to deal with the outside world for two whole weeks. I try to imagine not having to worry about what people are saying online, the speculation, the lies and projections turning into rumors and scandals, and the next thing I know, my team drops me, the world hates me, and I have to crawl into a hole for the rest of my life.

Nope, can't picture a day where I won't worry about that, but I do hope for a day where it doesn't make my chest heavy and my heart pound.

That panicky feeling is back.

I stay in the car while the guys go inside the reception area to check in. I would get out and go with them, but it's a little hard to breathe, and I don't want them to make a big deal about it.

My phone catches my eye again. They forgot to take it with them.

Anxiety is weird. Logically, I know that looking is only going to make me spiral more. Yet, there's that voice in the back of my head, the eternal optimist, that says maybe there are some more nice things being said about me. Maybe I'll read new messages or comments that show nothing but support, and then my anxiety will ease.

I bite my thumbnail—a terrible habit I never grew out of, even if my nail looks like a stump. When that doesn't work, I try other calming and grounding techniques my therapist taught me. From playing with the stud in my ear to pinching the hairs on my arm, nothing works.

Nothing takes my mind off the catalyst of my anxiety that's sitting right within reach. If I look and there is something bad, at least I'll only be depressed and no longer anxious, but if I look and I see something good, maybe I could breathe again.

Chapter 2

As if deciding for me, my body lurches forward to lean in between the seats. Before I can reach for the phone, my seat belt runs out of slack, and I jolt to a stop.

Shit.

I strain to reach forward some more, but the belt is tight. I go to release it when the front doors open, and Brady and Thad get back inside the car.

The look of guilt on my face and the way I throw myself back into my seat must give away what I was trying to do because Brady glances at the phone, then turns his head to me.

"You weren't trying to reach for this, were you?"

"Of course not," I lie. "I was trying to see if you two were coming back yet. You were gone for a long time."

"It was maybe two minutes, tops," Brady says. "You were the one to ask for this social media ban."

Technically, I asked for distractions from social media. The blanket ban came from them. I hang my head. "I know I need it, but it's a bad habit, and I've never been good at breaking those."

"Is anyone good at breaking those?" Thad asks. I still don't know if I can count it as him speaking to me directly when he's not even looking at me.

"Don't look at me," Brady says. "I'm the worst at letting go of bad habits. Okay, where's that map she gave us?"

"She said to follow this road to the end. We're near the river at the back of the property," Thad says.

"Okay." Brady reverses out of the parking space and slowly makes his way past some rustic cabins lining the drive. The gravel crunches under our tires, each cabin becoming bigger the farther we go until we hit the end and see the biggest one of all.

Not that being the biggest one means that it's in any way big. Or luxurious.

"This is what I call roughing it," I say as we get out of the car. I'm not opposed to it. It looks cozy, and the chimney with smoke coming out means they've already got a fire going for us inside, so it should be nice and toasty.

"Of course you'd think that." Thad storms past me toward the trunk.

Kelley

I spin and follow after him to get my bags out of the back. "What's that supposed to mean?"

"Sorry the accommodations aren't up to your standard, Your Royal Highness."

"Thad," Brady scolds.

"Did I say that?" What is this guy's problem with me, and why do I care?

"Practically," Thad mumbles.

"Dude, you've stayed here during a retreat," Brady says to him. "You know the cabins are rustic and cheap. He wasn't complaining; he was stating a fact."

Thad doesn't respond, just grabs his duffle bag out of the trunk and marches toward our cabin.

I step closer to Brady. "Why do I get the feeling he'd rather be anywhere but here?"

"Ignore him. He's ... going through a hard time at the moment."

"And why does that sound like the watered-down, politically correct thing to say?"

"Because I'm not sure it's my place to say anything at all."

"What, was it a bad breakup or something?"

He thinks about it for a moment. "Sort of."

"These two weeks are going to be fun, aren't they?"

"Don't worry. You'll have me around, and I'm delightful."

He might be joking about that, but so far, since coming out, he's the only person who's gotten me to calm down when I've gotten too panicky. Brady has a way about him that talks to my soul. My therapist could say something rational and logical, but my brain doesn't want to believe it. When Brady says it, for some reason, it sinks in.

"Lucky me," I say dryly.

He doesn't need to know I'm not being sarcastic.

Chapter 3
Thad

I await a phone call from Damon for days. The one telling me I'm fired for getting snarky with a client.

I shouldn't have let my own personal issues with Kelley interfere with my job because then he not only would have my dream, but he'd also take my backup dream away from me. But in my defense, could he be any more of a drama queen?

He's all, *"I need to get away from the world, but no, I can't live without my phone. I want to hide away where no one can find me, but eww, roughing it?"*

He was getting on my nerves, and surprise, surprise, I couldn't hold in my sarcastic comment.

Agents aren't supposed to talk to their clients that way, but I'm not even that. I'm lower than that. The lowest on the ladder: bitch boy. I mean intern. Same thing.

So since then, I've been trying to avoid Kelley as much as possible. Input what I can, which generally consists of getting groceries for Brady or Kelley to cook because after one night of my cooking, they banned me from the kitchen. Unless it's to clean up.

I'm good with doing menial jobs, the grunt work. As long as it keeps me away from Kelley's entitled attitude, I might be able to keep my job.

The sound of my ringtone blares through the small kitchen, and I jump. My hands are sudsy from washing up after lunch, and

Thad

I'm tempted to let it go to voicemail. Oh no, wet hands, can't reach into my pocket and grab my phone.

Getting fired over voicemail isn't ideal, but it's better than having to explain myself.

Kelley appears in the archway to the small kitchen, leaning against the wall. "You going to get that?"

I lift up a plate and let the soapy, hot water run down my arms. "Can't. Busy."

The phone stops ringing.

Then it starts again.

Motherfucker. I drop the plate back in the sink and go to wipe my hands on my pants when Kelley throws a dish towel at me.

"Here."

My eyes narrow because why is he being nice? Oh, I get it. He wants to be here for this phone call, no doubt. He ratted, and now he wants to see the fireworks.

I dry my hands and pull out my phone. I freeze at the name on my screen. It's not Damon. It's my mom.

I answer quickly. "Hey, Mom, what's wrong?"

"Does something have to be wrong to want to talk to my own son?"

"No, but you called twice in a row. Twice means there is."

"Everything is fine." Her voice sounds like it's about to crack.

"And I call bullshit."

She sighs. "It's your brother."

I will kill him. He's dead. "What has Wylder done now?"

"Well, we don't know for sure, but—"

"Don't be daft, Julie. We know it was him." Dad sounds as though he's right next to her.

"Know what was him? What's happening?" I ask.

My brother is ... a handful. Always has been. We're the complete opposite of each other, and I've always got the sense he's resented the family he was born into.

"We're missing money from our account, and when I looked, my card's not in my wallet," Mom says.

I run a hand through my hair. It would be typical of Wylder to

Chapter 3

do something like that. Where I'm the prized athlete of the family, Wylder was the little emo boy who hated sports, hated the world, but most of all hated us. Was I the best big brother in the world? No. But who can say that they were?

"Did you call the police or report the card stolen?" I ask.

"But if it was him, I don't want him to get in trouble."

Of course she doesn't. Dad wouldn't either, even if he's at the end of his patience with Wylder.

"Maybe him getting in trouble is what he needs," I suggest anyway.

He's twenty-one, only did one semester at college before dropping out, and now he mooches off Mom and Dad, who have worked their whole lives to give us what we need.

Mom doesn't reply.

"How much do you need?" I ask.

Like I can afford to bail my brother out, but I'll do whatever it takes to help them like they helped me. They paid for so much of my baseball crap, and maybe that's why I have issues being where I am now. Because they did it all for nothing.

I owe them.

"Enough to cover the mortgage this month."

"Jesus, how much did he take?"

Mom lowers her voice. "All of it."

Before when I threatened to kill him, it was hyperbole. Now, I actually want to do it.

"I'll transfer you the money into a different account so you don't have the banks breathing down your neck." And that is banks, plural, because they've remortgaged and refinanced their house so many times over the last twenty years I've lost track of what they owe to who.

Then all I'll need to do is find enough money to pay my rent this month. My roommates, all four of them, are going to be pissed.

I live with four of the guys from my baseball team at Olmstead in New York. Would I love to live on my own? Damn right, but when I found out the cost of living when outside of student housing, there was no way. Not on this intern salary. Once I become a

Thad

junior agent and start signing some clients, my wage will increase, but I have to get through my first year of being an intern until I can be promoted.

If Damon doesn't fire me. Which he probably will.

Fuck.

"We'll pay you back," Mom says.

I almost want to tell her not to bother because paying back a couple of thousand dollars will mean both her and Dad having to put off retirement even longer, but who knows? I'm probably going to need the money to keep me afloat until I find a new job.

"When Wylder gets home—"

"There ... was also a note," Mom says.

"A note?"

"He says he's not coming back. Said he wants to move to California and chase his dream of becoming an actor."

I rub my forehead. "Since when has that been his dream?"

"You know he's been lost ever since he dropped out of Olmstead."

I would argue it was before then that he started to lose himself. I don't understand where it went wrong. Wylder and I were close growing up, definitely not besties by any standards, and we would give each other shit all the time, but he was a happy kid. The only complaint he ever had was Dad trying to push him into baseball as well. Wylder was never sporty, had no hand-eye coordination, and would've preferred being on his computer or hanging out with friends than practice hitting until blisters formed.

"Do you think he'll come back?" Mom asks, hope still laced in her tone. No matter what my brother has put them through, my parents don't know how not to love him.

My sarcastic brain says, *"Yeah, he'll be back when he runs out of money,"* but I don't want to break her heart more than it already is.

"He will. And hey, who knows? Maybe he'll get out to LA and become a huge star and pay off all your debts."

"You're sweet to look at the positives that could come from this."

Only because I've been trying to teach myself how to stop

Chapter 3

with all the negativity surrounding my failed baseball career. Funnily, it's easier to do it with every other facet of my life except baseball.

"I'll send that money over now."

"Thank you, sweetie. Love you."

I look over my shoulder to make sure Kelley is gone, but he isn't. He's standing by the tiny kitchen island, watching me intently. It's not like I can't say it back to my mother though. She's my mom. "Love you too, but I gotta go. Talk soon."

I end the call and glare at Kelley. "Can I help you?"

"Sounded like someone was in trouble."

I cock my head. "Eavesdrop much? You don't see me prying into your life." Shit. There I go getting defensive again. I slump. "Sorry."

"Are you though?" A small smile breaks across Kelley's face.

"What do you mean?"

"What are you sorry for?"

"For speaking out of turn. I shouldn't talk to a client that way."

"But not sorry for what you said."

"What do you want, Kelley? I'm trying to be nice here."

Kelley scoffs. "That's being nice?"

"You're making it really difficult."

"What did I ever do to you?"

And there he goes, asking the question I often ask myself. Kelley has done nothing to me, but I have all this resentment toward him because of what is lacking in my life. Unfair or not, I can't get past it.

"Nothing," I mutter.

"Then why are you so—"

I grit my teeth. "I know this might be hard for the big, popular baseball player to understand, but the world doesn't revolve around you. I could be out there, learning how to recruit new clients, getting my first athletes to sign with me, and instead, I'm here, babysitting someone who doesn't know how good he has it because he doesn't know how to stop from looking himself up on the internet."

Thad

Kelley's mouth drops, but only the tiniest bit, as if he's about to say something, but it doesn't come out.

"Whatever," I say and turn back to finish off the dishes. "You're probably going to tell Damon how rude I've been to you, get me fired, and then all the new clients won't matter because I won't be handling them." I rinse a dish and put it on the drying rack with a clang.

"I'm not going to call Damon on you," he says. "But if you do want to retain clients, I'd suggest maybe learning a new tact to deal with athletes than berating them for something they can't control."

He can't control his screen time? Is he five?

He's right that I need to learn tact with him, but I also don't feel the same resentment for any other client on Damon's roster. That's a Kelley Afton–specific kind of grudge. Don't ask me why.

Kelley turns to go back to the living room but pauses and says, "By the way, you told your mom you'd send money right away."

Fuck, I'd already forgotten to do that.

I should thank—

And he's gone.

Chapter 4
Kelley

It's impossible to tell if Thad hates me or is merely an angry, stressed, and bitter man. The phone call with his mom opened up a sweet side to him. The way he spoke to her with soft tones doesn't match the way he barked at me directly afterward.

I still don't know his problem, and as much as I tell myself to let it go, my brain doesn't work that way. Which is why I'm sitting on the couch, pretending to watch *Friends* reruns, while I run through our interaction over and over again.

I'm antsy. I need to know what's been said online about me, but I'm trying so hard not to prove Thad right. It's obvious he's resentful of having to be here with me, and when put in simple terms like he did—that I need a babysitter because I have no self-control when it comes to public opinion of me—I sound like a spoiled brat. Two interns to make sure I'm not googling my own name? I'm a mess.

Brady comes through the front door to the cabin, shaking off the snow from his boots and beanie while slipping out of his coat.

"Where did you go?" I ask.

"Oh, I went to ask reception a question. How's everything in here? I was worried for a moment that you might have killed each other, but you're still here." He glances around the floor as if waiting for a dead body to jump out at any moment.

Kelley

"Hey, he's the one who has an issue with me, not the other way around."

"Still, I'd expect you to defend yourself if he came at you."

"Hey, you're back." Thad enters the room. "You mind if I go for a walk? I have a few phone calls to make."

"I've got it from here," Brady says, and Thad puts on his layers to go outside.

Once he's gone, Brady joins me on the couch. "So, how are you holding up?"

"Not great."

"It's like you're addicted to your phone, and now you're going through withdrawals. How long does that usually last?"

"You think I've ever lasted longer than a couple of days on an internet ban? The most I've gotten is maybe a few hours."

"Until here, right? Or did you smuggle in a cheap smartphone somehow, like in prison, and have been checking?"

"No, this has been the longest. All those people who say cutting off the rest of the world is cathartic are obviously the unstable ones. Not me. I can't stop thinking about it."

"You need a distraction. What do you want to do?"

I shrug. "I've been watching TV."

"Ugh. *Friends*? Save your sanity from all the homophobia in that show."

"What?"

"Have you never noticed it? Ross can't stand having a male nanny who's straight because he has to be at least bi to want to work with kids—what kind of fucked-up shit is that? Chandler is always offended when people think he's gay. He's embarrassed of his dad, the drag queen. Or trans woman. It's like the show either didn't know which Chander's dad identified as or didn't care to specify, so yeah, there's a lot of homophobic and transphobic moments in that show."

"And now I'm depressed again."

"Ooh, how about we play one of the board games they had stashed over here." He walks toward a cupboard in the middle of the living room. "Twister?" He pumps his eyebrows at me.

"Didn't you say you had a boyfriend?"

Chapter 4

He averts his gaze. "Uh, right. He probably wouldn't like me playing Twister with someone who isn't him."

For some reason I can't pinpoint, there's innuendo laced in there, but I let it go.

"Operation?" he asks.

I make a buzzing noise. "No. That whole noise is the reason I developed anxiety, I'm sure of it. Trying to do fake operating stressed me out to the point of panic."

"Ah. So this whole panic attack anxiety thing is not new to you."

"Nope. Always been this way. As long as I can remember."

"Sounds like a fun childhood," he deadpans. "Okay. Scrabble."

"As long as you're okay with baseball terms and swear words. I was never very good at English."

"Swear words and sports? You really think I'd say no to that?" He gets the game out, and we play for a bit, laughing each time one of us puts down something immature like *anal* or *cock*.

He questions my "fake-out," trying to tell me it's two words, but I fight tooth and nail for the hyphenated version. Which, turns out, isn't a thing. Stupid Google taking his side.

Thad comes back at some point but sees us occupied and goes right to his and Brady's shared room and closes the door behind him. I'm not surprised he didn't ask to join us with how surly he is.

I glance between the closed door and Brady. "When you say he went through a bad breakup—"

"Whoa, I never said that."

"Didn't you?"

"No. You said was it a breakup, and I said sort of."

"What does sort of even mean?"

"It was a breakup with baseball, not a romantic relationship."

Oh. *Ooooh.* "He played baseball?"

Brady glances back at the closed bedroom door and then back to me. "He really wanted to go pro, but he didn't even make the cut for the minors."

"I'm starting to understand his resentment toward me."

"I've tried to talk to him about being a bitter jerk about it, especially considering he should know you're not panicking over your career for no reason. It might be an irrational reason to some, but mental health is never rational."

I lick my lips. "Are we sure he knows?"

"It's in your file. He should've read it."

"Ugh. Does it have a huge orange label on it saying 'Head case'?"

Brady laughs. "No. All it says is that you need support due to anxiety disorders."

"Sss. Plural. That sucks to have that out there."

"It's only the people at King Sports, and we're here to help. We have strict NDAs in place, so no one's going to blurt your health status all over the news, and as of right now, your anxiety doesn't affect how well you play."

"To be fair, I haven't had to play since coming out yet."

"As my uncle likes to say, 'We'll burn that bridge when we come to it.'" He smirks.

"Isn't it cross that bridge?"

"Yes, but Uncle Damon likes to think he's funny."

"Damn, what was it like growing up with him as an uncle?"

"Chaotic. In the best possible way."

"Yeah, chaos sounds like a terrible time to me."

Brady doesn't lose his smile as he says, "Never would've guessed that." We go back to the game, but when the sky outside turns dark and we end another round, he says, "Do you mind if I take off for a bit? I'm thinking of going for a walk to, you know, prepare for all the whining I'll hear tonight, having to share a room with Thad. It's getting a bit much."

"Good to know it's not only me he has issues with."

"I'll tell him I'm going out for firewood, but I might be gone for over an hour to sit out in the silence."

"In the middle of winter?"

"I'll bundle up. Besides, are you forgetting I'm from Chicago? I'm used to the cold."

I watch as he heads for the bedroom to tell Thad he's going.

While I can understand better why Thad might resent me, I

Chapter 4

still think it's unfair of him to judge me. Yes, I have the MLB career he wanted, but it's not like I took his spot. I worked hard to be where I am.

My parents didn't have a lot of money when I was growing up, and the only reason I got the opportunities I did was because of baseball. Athletic scholarships to schools who would pay for my equipment, dedicated coaches and tutors to make sure I stayed on top of my game and my studies so I wouldn't flunk out and ruin any chance of making it to the majors. I often felt like I had to work twice as hard as anyone else on my team. And he resents me because why? Because I made it and he didn't?

Brady reappears and lets me know he'll be back later, reiterating he's going out to get some firewood.

I remain seated on the living room floor, but playing Scrabble by myself isn't as funny. Even when I get the word *ballsac*.

Fuck, is that one word or two?

Who cares, no one's here to dispute it.

When I get bored, I jump up to get started on dinner. We have the stuff to make spaghetti, but I always forget what's in the sauce, and because I'm not allowed my stupid phone, I can't look it up.

I go knock on Thad's door, and when he says, "Come in," he's on his bed, scrolling through his phone. Sure, they can have theirs, but I can't have mine.

I've been spending too much time around Thad, and his bitter mood has infected my brain.

"I need a recipe to make this sauce for dinner, so can I grab it off your phone, seeing as I'm not allowed mine?"

"You really think I'm going to fall for that?"

"Fine, can you please look it up and tell me what I need to do?"

"Ugh. Here, take it." Thad passes me his phone, already unlocked, and I take it out to the kitchen and search it up.

I grab out the ingredients and place them on the counter, but that annoying little sabotaging voice starts going off in the back of my head, telling me that the phone is still unlocked and one peek won't hurt.

I've listened to that voice many times before and have regretted

Kelley

it immediately. Yet, for whatever reason, I always, always, always think this time will be different. That if I start to see anything negative, I'll stop reading and go to the next comment.

I stare at the phone. It mocks me back. I pray for the lock screen to appear, but when it does, I let out a loud and long "No" and freak out. I tap the screen, hoping it's not too late to get it back, and it lights up, only having gone to sleep. One step before the lock screen.

Damn it. I wish it was the lock screen because then I would no longer be tempted.

What does it say about a twenty-six-year-old who is literally addicted to googling himself? That he's a narcissist? A masochist? Or is this my plain old anxiety and rejection sensitivity disorder?

No matter how many times I tell myself not to type in my name, my fingers don't listen.

The first time, I get as far as my first name before I delete it again. My thumb hovers on the lock button, and I hate that the voice telling me to click it is drowned out by the one telling me if I do, then I won't be able to check, and this might be my only chance the entire time I'm here.

It convinces me I have to take it, and the next thing I know, results of the Google search fill the screen.

The first article that pops up is one that was posted only a few hours ago. The headline asks why athletes feel the need to come out at all when it has nothing to do with the sport.

Well, Kenneth Oberman of the piece of shit daily news, if the straights didn't make it a big deal, we wouldn't have to come out. Normalizing queer figures in sports is our dream, but it will never happen while there are people who don't accept us.

And speaking of which, the comments on the article. I wish I didn't look.

From saying we should play in the women's league to then bringing up transgender issues in sports, the whole thing is a mess of phobic and ignorant comments that literally make me feel sick.

I pace the small kitchen while I close out that article and find another. This one is more congratulatory, but the comments are the

Chapter 4

same as the last. I go to the Philly baseball newsfeed, knowing they shared my news. The team management has been great about it. A lot of my teammates already knew—the ones I'm close to—so I'm not worried about backlash from them. I am worried about ticket sales.

Damon and Brady warned me before coming out that ticket sales might suffer.

While there are a lot more supportive comments on this thread to calm my broken heart, it's one comment in particular that stands out. In a sea of positivity, my brain still has to latch on to the one that has the potential to make me crumble.

It's not even what the commenter said: that one of my teammates, Cooper, and I would make a cute couple. That's sweet. Kind of. It's the reply to that comment from Cooper himself.

"Fuck off, u fucking troll." At first, I think he's defending me. He's not. I wish I'd stopped reading his message there. When in the next sentence he feels the need to use a slur to emphasize he's not gay, I get a very clear picture of what my teammate thinks of me.

My own fucking teammate. If I can't even get these guys who literally know me to have my back, how am I supposed to win over the public who know two things about me: that I'm gay and I play baseball?

Everything is hopeless.

Thad comes looking for his phone ten minutes too late. "What in the fuck are you doing?"

I can't breathe. I can barely move. "Don't mind me. Just having a setback."

And that's when I start spiraling.

Chapter 5
Thad

The wild look in Kelley's eyes actually concerns me. He won't stop pacing the kitchen, won't return my phone, and anytime I try to approach him, he goes into this rant about "Nothing will ever change" and "the future of baseball."

"I'm guessing you didn't use my phone to look up a recipe." I fold my arms. He can be pissed at the responses online all he likes, but how fucking hard is it to not look?

Kelley shakes his head.

"Why are you doing this?" I ask. "Do you like the attention?"

Kelley's wild stare is now trained on me. "Are you fucking serious?"

"You had one job. Stay offline. And the first chance you get, you're back on there? Is it an addiction thing? Do you want to see what the assholes out there say about you so you can whine about it and get sympathy? Are you really that conceited that you believe everyone should love you?" I'm responding in a way I know I shouldn't, and I was only lucky Kelley didn't run to Damon before. After this, I'm probably well and truly out of a job.

Self-sabotage much?

At this point, I may as well move to LA, find my brother, and try to become the next Hemsworth family of actors.

"Do you talk to all of Damon's clients this way?"

No, because I've never been in a position to. Not going to say

Chapter 5

that though. "Only the ones I have to babysit and confiscate their technology like they're a child."

"What is your problem with me?" he yells.

I throw up my hands. "This." My arms go wide. "This whole situation. Give me my phone back."

"So you don't think I have a right to be upset over this?" He taps on my phone. "I quote, 'I don't need my kid to idolize someone like that and think that it's okay.' Or 'Why can't men be real men anymore?'"

"They're assholes."

"The world is full of them! And I'm just supposed to take it?"

"No, but the best thing you can do for yourself is ignore it."

"Not all of us were born with that tool in our toolbox."

What does that even mean?

The sound of the main door to the cabin opening is music to my ears because I cannot handle this guy.

I rush out to where Brady's entered and mouth, "Help me."

He moves toward the kitchen, genuine concern on his face. "What's going on?"

Kelley still has his head in my damn phone. "Have you seen everything that's being said online about me?"

Brady glares at me. "How did he get access to the internet? We took his phone."

"You didn't take his." Kelley points at me.

Oh, so now he's going to blame me? "You asked if you could use it to look up a recipe, not go on social media!"

Brady, exasperated with us both, goes into agent mode. I'm not sure if it's because he's our boss's nephew, so he grew up with the great Damon King and learned his ways early, or if I don't have that agent mode yet, but I'm envious of the way Brady can slip between casual and professional so easily.

Hell, at this point, I'd settle for being professional at all. Not for the first time, I doubt if this job is for me.

Brady tells me to cook dinner—that's how I know he's desperate—and then drags Kelley out of the cabin.

At least Kelley finally put down my phone.

Thad

I pick it up off the kitchen bench and close down all his browser pages when I come to one of them and pause. A recipe for marinara sauce.

Shit. He really did take it for that. Originally. I wonder how long it took him to search up his name though. Right away?

I glance at the contents on the counter, and he only got as far as pulling out ingredients and pots and pans. He's going to regret this more than he already does. His punishment will be having to eat the worst spaghetti in the history of spaghetti.

I'm tempted to put everything away and order food from the small restaurant they have on-site, but this is his own fault.

I wish I could say that I didn't even try with dinner, but even my best cooking is still terrible. And by the time Brady and Kelley come back and we sit down to eat—silently because Kelley hasn't uttered a word to me since he left—we all force down forkfuls of bland pasta and a very tangy sauce. The recipe had to be wrong. Or I had to have read it wrong. I'd place my bet on the latter.

"It's getting late," Brady says after only eating a few bites. "Maybe you two should go to your corners and go to bed."

Escaping Kelley? Gladly. But there's something about the way Brady keeps looking at his phone and the way he's trying to get us to go to sleep this early. Because it's not late. It's 9:15.

"What, you got big plans?" I ask.

His face says it all. Guilty. "Of going to sleep? Yup."

Lies.

Kelley and I glance at each other, almost as if we're having the same thought.

"All right. We'll go to bed," I say.

Brady stands. "You do that, and I'll clean up, seeing as you cooked tonight."

I'm still suspicious as Kelley and I shuffle off into our separate rooms. The way the cabin is laid out, he's in the first room on the left when you enter, then there's the kitchen, then Brady's and my room straight ahead, with the living room being the center focus. There are sliding doors leading to a deck to the right.

I have no idea what Brady is up to, but I'm going to find out.

Chapter 5

While sitting on my bed, I strain my ears to listen to him cleaning up in the kitchen. The sloshing water, the plates clanging together—he's definitely doing the dishes.

After a while, I lie down and scroll through socials on my phone. Because Kelley searched himself before, the algorithms now think I want to know everything there is to know about Kelley Afton, and my suggestions page shows articles all about him and his coming out.

And okay, after the fifth post with every preview comment being something derogatory, I'm starting to realize how hard it must be for Kelley to see that day in and day out. But at the same time, I don't understand how he can't block all of it out.

It doesn't take long before I realize the kitchen is quiet, and before I get the chance to jump out of bed, there's a rap on the door.

"Thad? You asleep?" Brady asks.

I'm interested to see what he does if he thinks I am, so I get comfortable and close my eyes, pretending I've fallen asleep while looking at my phone, which is still in my hand and resting on my chest.

The door creaks open, and I hold my breath. Which I realize is a stupid idea because when you're asleep, you breathe deep and rhythmic.

I feel Brady's eyes on me, so I stir and roll over to my side as if he's disturbing me, and then a second later, the door closes with a click.

Without being too eager, I climb out of bed and wait until I hear the main door open and close too, but Brady must be some type of ninja because I don't hear it.

Maybe he's not planning to go out. Ooh, maybe he and Kelley are involved, and he's not so professional after all?

Before I can get my hopes up, I hear the sliding door to the deck open and then close.

There's a very good chance I'm reading into this, but there's something about the way he's been acting that's fishy to me.

Thad

And when I finally move into the living room, I find I'm not the only one who thinks so.

"You pretend to be asleep, too, so you can follow Brady?" I ask.

Kelley screws up his face. "I got up to get water, you psycho."

"Did you though? Or are you just upset that you had the same idea as me?"

"Hey, you're the one who has this weird grudge for no reason other than being bitter over having to give up baseball, which has absolutely nothing to do with me."

"You think that's why I resent you?"

He points at me. "Ah-ha. So you admit you resent me."

Oops. Wasn't supposed to do that. "Are you going to come with me to follow Brady or not?"

"What do you think he's doing?"

"I don't know for sure. Maybe he needs a break from all your whining."

"Or all your bitterness."

Touché.

I glance toward the sliding door where Brady disappeared. "It was weird how he sent us off to bed like that though."

Kelley nods. "Agreed. So we follow him."

"Layer up. It's frosty out there."

Kelley heads for where our coats and outerwear are on the coatrack just inside the door. "Careful, that almost sounded like you might care if I die of hypothermia out there."

"Of course I'd care if you died."

"Because?"

I can't help it. I break into a smile. "Because Brady will accuse me of killing you, and I don't want to face prison time."

Kelley surprises me by bursting out laughing.

By the time we get into our warm clothes and head outside, Brady's long gone, but it doesn't take us long to find him.

Voices filter from a cabin up ahead, and I put my arm out to stop Kelley from walking. Our boots make the gravel and snow under our feet crunch, and if we can hear Brady and whoever he's with, they'll probably be able to hear our feet.

I grip Kelley's puffer jacket and pull him down the side of an

Chapter 5

empty cabin beside us. I try to pinpoint where the voices are coming from. It's either the cabin right next to this one or the one next to that.

"What are we doing?" Kelley asks.

"I hear voices," I whisper.

"You should probably get that checked out."

"Shh." I put my gloved hand up to his mouth but am at least in control of myself to stop before I actually touch him.

"Rude," he says under his breath.

I can't tell if he means it or if he's still being snarky.

The voices die down, and the night fills with silence. Kelley and I hold our breaths, and I for sure think Brady has heard us, but a minute goes by, and then the low murmurs start back up.

As if connected by the same breath, we both let out a sigh of relief. We're standing so close, practically pressed against one another, and I notice the hitch in his breathing as his exhale comes out in a puff.

"Maybe we should go back," Kelley says, more softly than before.

"We will, but I want to see what he's up to first. What if Damon's here to check in on us and he's filling him in on how we hate each other? Or how you stole my phone and are going against your agent's advice."

Kelley's eyes widen, and I know I have him.

"One peek, and then we'll go back."

He relents.

I take careful steps to round the back of the empty cabin so I can get a look at the one that's next to it. The way each cabin is positioned, they're not directly in line with each other. The one Brady's at is situated slightly farther back than the one we're hiding behind, so there's no chance of them spotting us unless we poke our entire head around the corner.

But from where I am, I can see through the lattice siding of the deck railing that Brady is sitting on some guy's lap on the back deck of the cabin next to us. There's another guy on a lounger next to them, covered in all the blankets the cabin probably possesses.

Thad

I've never seen either guy before in my life.

"What is it?" Kelley peers around me. He's pressed against my back, and I hate the way my cock responds to the scent of his cologne or aftershave. Wherever that fresh, woodsy scent is coming from.

It's the scent. Not the man.

Definitely not the man.

"It's Brady," I say. "He's with two guys I don't know."

"Two?" He leans in further.

Fucking hell, it might be the man. Traitorous body.

I close my eyes and count to five, trying to think of all the reasons I don't like Kelley, but my dick obviously hasn't got the message. Yes, Kelley's a diva, but he's also really hot.

Damn him.

"They're getting up," Kelley says. "Do you think they've seen us?"

Brady and the two guys stand, but they're not looking our way. They're only looking at each other. All three of them have sex eyes. As they make their way inside the cabin, hand in hand in hand, it's obvious they're together. Like *together*, together.

"Huh. Good for him," Kelley says.

"*Lucky* for him," I add.

I step away from Kelley. "And show's over."

I start heading back to our cabin, and Kelley follows.

"I couldn't think of anything worse. Worrying about satisfying one man in bed is enough for me."

As if the mere mention of sex coming out of Kelley's mouth is an invitation, my cock practically tries to break free of my thick, warm pants. It's as if it's jumping up and down, screaming, "Yay, sex!"

Down, boy. We're not allowed to get hard for him.

Even with that self-warning, my mouth jumps on the dick train of thought. Of course it does. I hate myself.

"You worry about that?" I ask him.

I side-eye him because it's hard to fathom that someone as good-looking as Kelley Afton would need to worry about those

Chapter 5

things. I'd imagine he'd have men of all types throwing themselves at him and do all the work for him.

If we took baseball out of the equation and I had the opportunity to have sex with Kelley, I think I could come from just staring at him naked. I saw the photoshoot of his coming out article, and damn, even shirtless, he made my mouth water. Reluctantly.

Kelley doesn't look at me as he says, "It's why I haven't had a relationship in years. If you could even call my college relationships *relationships*. Situationships, maybe. But every time I went home with someone or hooked up, I was always worried about them outing me before I was ready. I didn't want my career ruined before it could start. And that's with only one person in my bed. Couldn't imagine two."

And now I'm thinking about Kelley and Brady in bed together and how hot it would be to join them.

"It's understandable Brady's keeping this a secret," Kelley says. "Though, one of them might be his boyfriend, and they have a third on the side or something. Either way, it makes sense to be on the DL."

"It does? It's not that big a deal." Am I missing something?

"Think about it from Brady's perspective. He has these famous dads, a brother in the NFL, and a well-known uncle in the sporting industry. The last thing Brady would want or need is to bring attention to his love life. Any scandal, anything that would play into all those accusations about queer people being sexual deviants, has the potential to not only affect Brady's career but his whole family's reputation."

"Having more than one partner isn't sexual deviancy, and neither is being gay or bi or queer or whatever label."

"Don't you think I know that?"

"Do you?" I ask. "You give so much weight to what people say about you it's almost as if you believe it yourself."

"If I had any control over how I react to those comments, believe me, I'd put a stop to it. You think I don't know when I'm being irrational? I do, but that's the thing with the countless anxiety issues I've been diagnosed with over the years: knowing it doesn't stop it from happening."

I blink at him. And then blink again. "You have anxiety issues?"

It makes sense that he'd have mental health problems with this whole being addicted to the negative comments about him, but now that I know it's not narcissistic personality disorder, it paints everything in a new light, and I'm realizing how much of an ornery, bitter asshole I've been.

Kelley frowns. "Brady said that's in my King Sports file."

Well, fuck. I guess I need to come clean. And apologize. And somehow make it up to him for taking my personal issues out on him when he didn't do anything to deserve it.

I hang my head. "I never read it."

Chapter 6
Kelley

I turn to face Thad. The night is crisp, and even though we're covered in layers of warm clothing, it's so cold my snot is forming into ice crystals. Lovely.

I sniff. "You haven't read my file? Like, at all? Are you sure you want to be a sports agent? I know you're only an intern, but knowing your client's basic information would probably be helpful."

Thad's gloved hand adjusts the beanie on his head. "I ... Ugh. I need to apologize. Will you let me explain back at the cabin over a nice hot cup of cocoa?"

It's impossible to know how to take Thad. His mood swings. Is he being genuine, or is he going to give me a cup of poisoned cocoa? Who's to know?

Also, me? Catastrophizing? Never. I continue to stare at him until he keeps speaking.

"I really do want to explain myself, but it's cold as balls out here, and it's not going to be as simple as 'I'm an asshole.'"

My lips twitch, wanting to smile, but I still don't know what he's actually going to say. "I'll hear you out. Mainly because we have another week and a half of living under the same roof, and I'd really like it if there was a chance you'll stop scowling at me." I turn on my heel and continue down the road to our cabin.

Kelley

Something tells me that Thad isn't the type of guy to apologize a lot. Or at all. With the way he looks, I doubt he has to. Men probably thank him for treating them like dirt and kiss his feet.

And now I really need to not think about men being on their knees for him before my body thinks it's a great idea.

When we reach the cabin, we strip off our outer layers, and Thad moves to the kitchen while I sit on the living room couch, not really knowing what to do. If I put the TV on, would that be inconsiderate because we're supposed to be talking? Wouldn't it be weirder if he came in here and I was staring at the wall?

One of the most frustrating things about my anxiety is that it doesn't only focus on worrying about my public image, but it makes me overthink every tiny social situation.

Over the years, I've learned to fake it at sponsorship parties, galas, press conferences, and things like that, but this? Socially, one-on-one, I'm still too uncomfortable to be myself around people I don't know well.

Brady was able to get me to open up quickly, and that's why I'm going to ask Damon for Brady to be my agent going forward. I'm currently signed with a guy named Merek, and while I like him enough—he has gotten me amazing endorsement deals and an okay-ish first-time MLB contract—he's all business. That's why I asked for Damon to be at my coming out photoshoot instead of Merek. Damon and Brady have that same aura of acceptance around them, and it's easy to talk to them.

Thad has been anything but easy to talk to so far, so I'm in that overthinking, elevated state that makes me tongue-tied and hesitant.

In fact, I overthink this situation so much that by the time Thad comes back into the living room with our drinks, I flinch at his appearance.

Smooth, Kelley. Real smooth.

"Okay, so while I was waiting for these to heat up, I read your file. Finally," he starts and throws himself into the armchair.

The shame I often feel over my mental struggles is like a weighted blanket. Those things are supposed to make you feel safe,

Chapter 6

but mine only makes it feel like it's forcing me to stay in one place and restrict my movement. It's one of those things that I know is irrational, and I shouldn't feel shame, but I do. Because just like society still has issues with gay men, it also has issues with people with rocky mental health.

It's one thing to say to myself that I feel like I'm going crazy, or my anxiety makes me batshit insane. It's another for someone else to say it with judgment. And I would never say it about someone else. Which is why Thad's attitude has gotten to me. I thought he was judging me for my diagnoses, but it turns out he didn't even know about them. Until now.

"I want to explain my poor behavior," he says. "But first up, I want to say I'm so sorry if I ever made you feel like your anxiety was ridiculous or over-the-top. I didn't realize ..." Now that he's not wearing his beanie or gloves, that hand reaches for his head again, this time smoothing the hair on top of his head.

At least I'm not the only one with nervous habits.

He continues but doesn't finish what he was going to say. "Has Brady told you anything about me? I don't know why he would, but—"

"He said you had an ugly breakup."

He pulls back and looks like one of those adorable puppies who cock their head when they're confused.

"With baseball," I add.

"Ah." He relaxes again. "Were you always gifted with baseball?"

"I had natural talent, yes, but that doesn't mean I didn't work for—"

"I'm not saying that," he says gently. "But I've always loved baseball, and yes, I had some of that natural talent as well. I worked my ass off, my parents spent their life savings on gear for me, on coaches, on everything, and then last year, during my final year of college, I thought I was heading for the big leagues. I had it in my head that I might not have been the best, but I was at least *good enough*."

Kelley

I remember back to when I was being drafted. I was a shoo-in. Everyone said so. But there was still that voice telling me I might not make it. If I'd thought for sure I was getting in and then didn't? I'd be heartbroken too.

"I've been kind of lost since then, and when I met you, you were coming off your amazing rookie year. You had endorsements, you had the stats, and from the outside, you had everything I wanted. And yet, all you would do is worry about your public image and hate that not everyone loved you."

I go to interrupt him when he keeps talking.

"I thought it was an ego thing, not an anxiety thing. And granted, I should have read your file sooner, but to my heartbroken, angry, and bitter self, you were just—"

"Being greedy."

"I know that's not actually what was happening now. You were self-sabotaging, and if you didn't pick up on the countless snarky remarks I've said to you over the past few days, I know a thing or two about self-sabotage."

I let his words sink in, let them settle over me. "You don't want to be a sports agent, do you?"

The bitterness toward me now makes sense, but I don't think he has an actual issue with me. I'm a mere trigger for a bigger problem.

Thad's lips purse as he thinks about the answer. Like, really thinks about it. "I do. I really, really do. This was my backup plan, even though I thought I was too good to have one of those. And I do want to grow to become the best agent I can be, but my heartache over the loss of baseball has made it hard for me to sink into my role at King Sports. I've tried to shake it off, and with all the other clients I've been around, I haven't had this ... this ..."

"Misplaced resentment?"

"Yes. That. For some reason, you bring out my bitter side more than the others."

"Wow, I'm swimming in that compliment," I say dryly.

"If you think about it, it is kind of a compliment."

"You hating me is a compliment?"

"I don't hate you. I wish ... I wish *I was you*. Or had your base-

Chapter 6

ball talent, at least. I resent you because I'm so goddamn jealous I can barely see straight."

Okay, that does kind of make me happy. My lips must show it too.

"You don't have to be *that* happy about it." This time, his snark sounds playful. Thad has a playful side after all.

"I'm not happy you're jealous. I'm happy you don't hate me because my brain likes to convince me of worst-case scenarios, and there's nothing I can really do about that." The coping mechanisms and tools my therapist has given me over the years only work to a certain extent.

Thad leans forward in his seat. "I know I'm not your agent specifically, but at least I have one thing to thank you for."

"What's that?"

"You've made me see that if this is a career I really want, I need to start making the effort to be professional and not make assumptions about the athletes under my care. Oh, and also for not having called Damon already to get me fired. That's a big thanks."

"I wouldn't have done that."

"You should have."

"No, I mean I couldn't have done that. I don't have a phone."

Thad bursts out laughing in a way that only makes me smile.

"I'm glad you had the opportunity to explain why you hold a grudge against me," I say. "After Brady told me that my file had all my health information, I was questioning how you got this job being a judgmental asshole, but I'm happy my hunch was right. You're not an asshole."

He holds up his thumb and forefinger close together. "I'm a bit of an asshole."

"Okay, I relent."

"Oh, and I had to twist your arm so much to do so."

Now that the truth is out there, I'm able to relax into the light-heartedness of the moment. "What can I say? Your argument was very persuasive."

He lifts his mug to his mouth with an amused smile. "Drink your cocoa before it gets cold." He takes a large gulp.

Kelley

If I thought Thad was hot while scowling at me, it's nothing compared to when he smiles in my direction.

I sip my drink but keep staring at him over the rim of the mug. Something crackles between us. A vibe. Something. Or maybe the minuscule nicety he's shown makes me think there's a spark between us.

Thad averts his gaze first and stares down at his cup before raising it to take another gulp.

"So, two partners is a fantasy of yours?" I ask.

He sprays hot milk all over the place.

Now that he's not so surly, I'm thinking Thad ... uh ... don't know his last name could be fun to hang out with.

"I can't believe you asked that," he says, trying to wipe up the brown milk stains off the coffee table with the bottom of his shirt.

"You're the one who said Brady was lucky. I figure now that we're not sniping at each other, the least we could do is talk about it."

"Aren't you supposed to have social anxiety that would prevent you from asking such things?"

"Ah, but that's where you're wrong. With some people, sure, I have anxiety over conversations we might have. And up until about ten minutes ago, you were on that list."

"And now?"

I shrug. "You've shown me a vulnerable side, and what can I say. My anxiety is a sucker for a sap with a broken heart."

While I'm telling the truth—that Thad opening up to me has helped drop my guard—it's still not like how it is with Brady or Damon, probably because I see them in a professional light. With Thad? Yeah, I don't think I'll ever see him that way.

My heart still thuds loudly in my ears around him, but it's no longer from worry that he's going to say something assholish. Somehow, when that angry mask came off, it showed me the truth of who he is.

Someone who's grieving and lost.

And for some godforsaken reason, I have the urge to fix him.

Chapter 6

It should also say in my file: has a penchant to run toward red flags.

I wouldn't question it.

Chapter 7
Thad

I want to hate Kelley. I really do. Or, did. But reading his file, seeing the struggles he has faced in this industry because of it, it was the stark kick in the ass I needed to remember that I have no idea what's going on in anyone else's life. I have no right to judge him or any other client because of what they have.

Am I saying I'll forever be cured of assholedom? No. I'm most likely going to need constant reminders to get my head out of my ass, but I'm hoping I will now be able to remind myself instead of waiting for a potential client to be so close to threatening my job.

"So, I was thinking," I say.

Kelley perks up. "Thinking what?" The way his voice sounds like sex, I'm guessing he's not thinking what I was. Not that I haven't been thinking about him in a sexy way, but that's not what this is.

"Brady has obviously gone to a lot of trouble to get his partners, hookers, or whatever those two men were here. And it's obvious he's not ready for people to know, or maybe if they are hookers, then he doesn't want that to get out."

"I'd never say anything, if that's what you're getting at." His interested gaze goes from sexy to angry so quickly. I wish I could say it's not a hot look on him, but it is. Then again, so is his vulnerable side. And his backside. Okay, and front.

Chapter 7

I shake my thoughts free. "No, I mean, we shouldn't even tell Brady we know."

"But if we told him he could go stay in that other cabin, he wouldn't have to come up with more elaborate lies like 'I'm going to go get firewood, and it's going to take an hour.'"

I huff. "He used the firewood line on you too, huh? Or did he tell you that I'm so overwhelming as a roommate that he needs a break from me, so he was going to lie and say he needs firewood?"

Kelley's face falls. "Do I even want to know why he said he needed to get away from me?"

"Nah, he wouldn't use your mental health against you. He mainly complained about us bickering and needing a break from it all, but I assume he told you I was the problem so you wouldn't think it was about you."

He nods. "He probably knows I wouldn't be able to handle thinking I was doing something wrong or stressing him out."

"And that's my point. Kind of. We should keep everything the same, so he's not uncomfortable about us knowing," I say. "We'll keep giving him the excuse he needs to keep sneaking away."

"You mean with the bickering? Why can't we tell him we're cool if he has people to see ... or do while we're here?"

"He's keeping it a secret for a reason, and what if we say, hey, we know, and it's cool, but all he sees is the pressure to tell his uncle before we do? I'm not saying I would do that, but I don't want to put Brady in a position where he feels like he needs to trust me."

Kelley cocks his dark eyebrow at me. "Not a trustworthy person, then?"

"I don't know how much I'd trust the bitter guy who appears to not want to be here at all."

"Fair point."

"I can't say I blame him." I sip more cocoa. "I think all the interns hate me because of my attitude. It's something I haven't had much control over."

"Your attitude or them hating you?" Kelley asks.

I snort. "Both? But no, I think if I analyze why I've been like that since I began this job, it might be more of that self-sabotage

Thad

thing. Like, I've already failed at baseball, and this is my backup plan, but ... what if I suck at this too? Then I will have failed twice. And I don't have a backup for my backup."

Kelley takes a drink. "Hot cocoa maker could be your calling."

"Ooh, yay. Paying off my student loans with that could be fun. Maybe I could find a place who'll let me sleep in their back room."

"Trust me when I say your fear of failing can ruin your career faster than anything else possibly could, so if you can get past that or find a way to deal with it, then you're going to be fine. Does writing out your goals help? If you can have a list of achievable and realistic goals set, it's not as daunting as only seeing your main objective."

"Are you therapizing me now?"

"Nope. I'm telling you what works for me. For instance, instead of looking at the big picture and saying, 'I'm going to be a great sports agent with a shit ton of clients and financial stability,' maybe start with 'I'm going to get myself a client' or 'I'm going to impress my boss during this internship so I can be promoted when it's done.' Start small and work from there."

He makes a lot of sense, and maybe by thinking in small steps, I won't be so overwhelmed by everything. I'm only an intern. I don't need to be thinking big. All I need to do is put in the work to show Damon that I have what it takes.

"I don't suppose you're in the market for a new agent? How's Merek working out for you?" I'm joking. I don't think I could work with Kelley without wanting to fuck him.

Only my joke seems to send him back into nervous squirrel mode. He looks terrified.

I laugh. "Calm down, I didn't mean that."

"No. I mean. But ... well ..."

Oh God, he doesn't actually want me to represent him just because I apologized, does he? Get some standards, man.

"I kind of asked Brady to take over as my agent when the time comes."

Ah. Weirdly, that hurts, even though it makes so much sense. If

Chapter 7

he was going to pick an intern, it could've been me, but again, I've treated him like dirt, so why would he ask me?

"Brady is a good choice," I relent. "He's going to take over the company one day. No doubt about it."

"It's not that I wouldn't want you, but—"

"Kell, it's okay. It makes complete sense. Besides, I'm thinking I shouldn't represent baseball clients anyway. I'm sure you're not the only one who will have the stats and rookie career I would kill for. And you're smart to get in with Brady before his client roster becomes too big and he can't take on any other clients."

Even if he's an intern like I am, he already has two clients, including Kelley.

It's weird that I'm unhealthily jealous of Kelley when Brady is the one who's actually doing my job better than me and getting ahead already, but at the same time, I wouldn't want the kind of pressure that Brady has on his shoulders.

He's the nephew of the boss. He has secret three-ways, famous dads, and basically lives in the shadow of his NFL quarterback brother. When I say he's the next big sports agent, it's because he has to be.

When I played baseball, I was happy I wasn't the best of the best. The best had way too much pressure on them. I'd strive for a happy middle, and I think that's what I want from this job too.

Maybe this is why I never made it in baseball. All the athletes I know have that competitive edge. That *need* to be the best. I don't have that. I want to be good, and I want to prove myself, and I loved being on a team that was number one. But that competitiveness? I only had it when it came to winning. Not me. The whole team.

"I went and made things weird again, didn't I?" Kelley asks. He shifts uncomfortably.

"No. You didn't. You just made me realize something is all."

"That you really do hate me?"

"No. And again, I'm sorry I ever made you feel that way. I'm realizing that to do this job, I'm going to need my clients to know that while I'm not the hotshot that Brady is, I do know how to put in the work and get them the deal that's right for them. I don't need to be the best. I only have to be the person they need, and I like that."

Kelley finishes off his hot cocoa. "That is a really healthy way to look at your position because I have no doubt that the intern bullpen is full of eager guys willing to stomp all over the others to get ahead."

"I might have been eager to do that with baseball, but not this."

Kelley blinks at me, as if he's trying to figure out if I'm being serious or not.

"Don't worry. I never kneecapped a bitch with a baseball bat. Even if I did, I think I'd have to kneecap about an entire team's worth if I even wanted to qualify for Triple-A baseball."

"Good to know. Even if I'm now a little scared of you."

I finish off my drink, too, and then stand and offer to take his mug back into the kitchen. "Just the way I like it."

I move to the sink and start rinsing the cups when Kelley follows me into the kitchen.

"You are intimidating, you know." He leans against the entryway, arms folded. "That might be something you could work on."

"I'm intimidating?" I put on an angelic smile.

"Argh. No. When you smile, you're plain scary. But the scowl is what I found intimidating the most."

I slump. "Okay, so I can't smile. Or scowl. And that leaves me with ..."

"Maybe you could be an over-the-phone agent."

I'm trying really hard not to laugh. "Is Kelley Afton calling me ... ugly?"

"No. Shit. The opposite. You're too hot to even be able to concentrate, and—" His eyes almost bulge out of his head. "Holy hell, that's inappropriate. I didn't mean—well, I did mean. You're hot as fuck, but I meant that ... oh my God, I'm gonna go to bed and pray an avalanche hits me." He turns to leave, but I'm hot on his heel. And hot everywhere, it seems.

At least in the eyes of Kelley Afton.

Chapter 7

I knew he was checking me out. "Why are you running off so fast?"

"To die of embarrassment."

"There's nothing to be embarrassed about. Just because you find me so incredibly hot and attractive. Soooo irresistible. But not when I smile. Or scowl."

He stops and turns his head toward me, almost hesitating before saying, "No. The scowl is very hot. But ... intimidating."

Even though he thinks my smile is scary, it's hard not to at that.

"Fucking hell," he mutters. "Your genuine smile is hot too. Can you go back to being an asshole to me so I don't find you this attractive?"

I move closer to him. "But where's the fun in that?"

Kelley's tongue darts out to wet his lips, and the urge to lean in and cover his mouth with mine is almost unbearable.

Telling him I'm going to be more professional and then trying to kiss him really could get me fired. But ... it's not like he's my actual client. I'm not his agent; I never will be his agent. So, is it really that wrong?

Apparently, it is.

Kelley steps back. "I should ... go to bed."

"We both should," I agree.

There go those deep brown eyes again, trying to pop out of his head.

I smother my amusement. "Separately. Of course."

Kelley swallows so hard I see his Adam's apple bounce. "Yes. Separately. That is also what I thought you meant."

"Good night, Kelley."

"Good night," he whispers.

Before he can disappear inside his room, I stop him for one last thing. "Thank you again, by the way. Not only for forgiving me for being a dick but for actually giving me some good advice."

"Anytime."

I might take him up on that.

Chapter 8
Kelley

I wake up at the butt crack of dawn to the sound of Brady sneaking back into the cabin. It's funny to me that he thinks he's being subtle, but like Thad said, we should pretend for his sake.

I don't blame him for wanting to keep it quiet.

When I think back to all the queer greats in sports, like Brady's fathers being the first queer couple to win a Super Bowl, it's unfathomable how much more difficult they had it. Even Damon King went through a lot to become the agent he is today. The industry has come a long way, there's no denying that, but it still has a long way to go.

I'm far from the first person out in baseball, and I won't be the last. Those players who were brave enough to come out at a time where it wasn't accepted at all had balls of steel, and I wish I could say it made a difference. But here we are, decades later, and I'm still facing the same kind of backlash they did.

It's complete bullshit and no one else's business but my own and whoever is in my bed.

Speaking of bed, I roll over onto my side, the warm blanket shifting with me, and I stare at the empty spot beside me. It's been so long since I've been with someone, and even then, I don't have the most experience. I was always too scared of being caught, of

Chapter 8

being outed. I don't even know if it's the orgasms I miss or that connection where skin is on skin.

I want to be held and feel safe while doing so.

Coming out was supposed to give me that freedom, but Thad's right about one thing. I've been too focused on the public backlash and what other people think of me to seek out the thing I've craved since puberty.

The way Thad looked at me last night, the urge to lean in and kiss him and take what I want ...

I really am desperate if all it takes for me to forgive asshole behavior to the point I want to rip his clothes off is one small apology and a smile.

And when he suggested we go to bed? Of course I had to think he was coming on to me. But there was something there; I can't have been imagining it.

Oh dear God, I was imagining it, and now he thinks I'm an even bigger loser than I am. I groan and cover my head with my pillow. Maybe if I press down hard enough, I can suffocate in my embarrassment.

I swear if I wasn't so good at baseball, my self-esteem would be at zero.

"You're up early." Thad's muffled rumble echoes around the cabin, and my casual morning wood becomes a raging hard-on instantly.

That's going to be a fun reaction whenever he speaks now.

"I didn't even hear you come to bed last night," he adds.

He's obviously talking to Brady, but I hear "come to bed" fall out his mouth and can't help picturing him saying that to me. With a sexy rasp. Looking at me like he did last night.

Come on, Kelley. Just because a boy gives you attention, that doesn't mean you have to get naked with him.

Even if I want to.

I really, really want to.

Though, I don't know what it would mean for his position. I'm sure sleeping with a client—any client of King Sports—is probably

Kelley

a no-no in the rule book. I couldn't ask him to risk that. Not for a night of orgasms in exchange for cuddles.

Out of everything I feel like I've missed out on in life, cuddles are what I want to experience most? I really am sad and pathetic.

Brady and Thad's muted conversation continues, and I should get up and go out there, but what's the point? I'm probably going to walk out there, trip over something, and then fall on my very hard dick.

There's a knock at my door, and I jump a mile high, the pillow falling off my face as I try to make sure the blanket covers my lap. It does, but it still has my heart racing anyway.

"Come in," I squeak.

"Hey," Brady says in that soothing way he has about him. "I was seeing if you were awake and wanted coffee."

"I'm awake, and yes, please."

Behind Brady, Thad scoffs.

"What, Mr. Diva can't even make his own coffee?" He says this under his breath, but almost like he wanted me to hear.

Okay, did I dream we put this shitty attitude behind us?

Did he wake up this morning and decide there was no truce after all?

But as Brady walks by him, shaking his head at Thad's poor behavior, Thad winks at me as soon as Brady's out of sight.

I smile.

Right. We're supposed to keep things as usual. To protect Brady and his secret. I still don't know why we can't tell Brady that we at least buried the hatchet, but keeping the status quo should be easy enough. Though this time, I don't think I want to back down or pretend I can ignore him like before.

I get out of bed and stretch. I'm shirtless, and my pajama pants ride low, showing off the bulge that's trying to escape. Normally, I'm not a tease—I haven't had the luxury to be one—but if I want to find out if Thad and I even have the smallest opportunity to hook up, I'm going to need to do something. Short of asking him, which no way in hell would my rejection sensitivity disorder let me, this is all I've got.

Chapter 8

Thad's gaze takes me in from top to toe, briefly pausing on the thick C and A tattoo with an arrow going through them on my rib cage. I wonder if he thinks it's someone's initials. A long-lost love.

I kind of wish it was instead of what it really is. The Charlotte Arrows. My college baseball team. All of us in my graduating class went and got them. I don't regret it, but it does bug my finicky brain that I don't have my other teams tattooed on me as well. Sure, I could go get them added or put somewhere else, but a team is never secure. I play for Philly now, but I could be traded at any moment like I was in the minors. By the end of my career, it's possible I could be on ten different teams. I only have so much skin.

I turn my back to him to reach for my shirt on the floor, and I happen to know I have a great ass in these PJs. They're basically what gray sweatpants do for dick imprints but with my ass.

A soft growl comes from the direction of the door, and when I glance over my shoulder at Thad, he's biting his fist.

Okay, I'm definitely not imagining that.

"Do you mind?" I snark for Brady's sake. "Trying to get dressed here."

I startle him, and he steps back, his face looking incredibly guilty. But like he did to me, I wink back at him.

He dramatically rolls his eyes, playing into the I-still-hate-you bit. "Calm your ego, dude. You're not my type."

Damn. He's either a good actor, or that's the truth. And it stings more than it should.

He walks away, and I'm left to dwell on whether or not he was playing or if I'm really not his type.

"Are you two ever going to stop bickering?" Brady asks.

"Nope," I call out.

"He's too easy to rile up," Thad says.

It's true. I am.

Brady lowers his voice, obviously not realizing sound carries in this place. "Careful. Kelley has enough on you to get you fired after this trip, so don't push it. And give him a break, okay?"

Kelley

Thad's reply, cocky and arrogant, isn't as quiet. "If you can't take the heat, get out of the kitchen."

Even that sounds like a genuine barb. I know it's supposed to, and logically, he's just playing the game of reassuring Brady that we still have beef. But the thing about mental health and logic is they often don't go hand in hand. As much as I like that Thad and I are on good terms now, I don't know how long I'll be able to keep up the charade of still being on the outs. Not when it makes me question everything he says.

Chapter 9
Thad

Toying with Kelley is fun, though not as fun as his striptease this morning. Okay, it wasn't exactly stripping, but with the way his pajama pants kept slinking lower and lower as he raised his arms over his head, it might as well have been. Miles and miles of tanned skin were bare to me. And that tattoo? Ungh, I wanted to run my tongue over each letter, making him forget whoever CA is.

He said he's never had a serious relationship, but why else would you tattoo initials with an arrow through them? Might not have been serious, but it looks like heartbreak to me.

All day, I push and push to piss Brady off, knowing he has somewhere to run to—into the arms of those hot men he has waiting for him. When he finally gets to breaking point, it's lunchtime, and he makes some bullshit excuse about wanting to go for a walk to get some fresh air, leaving Kelley and me alone.

Only when Brady goes and I throw myself on the couch next to Kelley and smile at him, he doesn't smile back.

"You okay?" I ask.

He averts his gaze. "Uh, yeah. Fine."

He's so not *fine*.

"Did I cross a line trying to get Brady out of here?"

"No. No, not at all. I knew what you were doing."

"But it still got in your head, didn't it?"

Thad

"Maybe."

"Okay, then we stop. When Brady gets back from his 'walk,' we'll quit the snark and be friendly. Tell him I had a lobotomy."

That gets me a smile. "It's honestly fine. There are the things I know to be true that my brain tries to tell me are not, so it gets mixed up in my head sometimes. As long as you haven't gone back to hating me."

I shake my head. "I shouldn't have even suggested we keep it up, and now I feel guilty for making you question it."

"Gah." Frustration radiates from his tight shoulders. "I really shouldn't react to it the way I do. I need to let it all roll off my back."

I press my lips together because I agree that's what he needs to do, but growing thick skin isn't as easy as acknowledging how thin it is to begin with. "Say the word and I'll happily drop the whole thing, but I could maybe help you with learning how to do that."

"Do what?"

"Not let it get to you. I'm not an expert by any means, but I'm the opposite of you. People can criticize me all they want about my sexuality, the way I look, the massive chest tattoo that is that little bit too big and peeks out the top of all my work shirts. But when it comes to baseball, my talent, or the fact I couldn't make it, that's when I have issues letting go."

"It sounds like we each have what the other needs," Kelley murmurs. "But short of actually giving you a lobotomy to try to steal that confident part of your brain, what are you suggesting?"

That's the last thing I expect to come out of his mouth, so I can't help but laugh. "I have the sudden urge to call Brady back in case you're about to bring out surgical tools."

He waves me off. "Eh. I wouldn't know which part of the brain to dissect anyway. You're safe while I don't have any internet to google it."

Again, I laugh. I like Kelley's sense of humor. A couple of days ago, I wouldn't have thought he even had one of those. Though, a few days ago, I was too blind to my jealous rage to really see.

"Could it be possible you might come around if you're desensi-

Chapter 9

tized to it?" I ask. "If there was a way for you to know for certain that I was not judging you or criticizing you, do you think you could learn to not let it get to you?"

"How do you propose to do that though? I knew this morning, and I still panicked, thinking everything you said last night didn't actually happen."

And now I feel even more guilty. I rub my jaw.

He continues. "I know it *did*, but that irrational part of my brain likes to question everything. I'm working on it, but it's a long road."

It must be difficult to know you're being irrational. Like, you know it. It's the truth. But your brain keeps telling you it could be a lie. I'll admit I have no psych experience other than all the sports psychology coaches have drilled into me over the years, but surely there would be something we could do to get him past it.

"I still think we should drop it, but if you want the help, I'm your man. I don't know if you know this, but I'm not always this happy guy. I've been known to be an asshole on occasion. Shocking, I know. Hard to believe."

Kelley fakes shock. "No, you? Really? Here I was thinking you deserved a humanitarian award for all the nice things you've said and done to me."

"It's a sacrifice I'm willing to make."

"How noble of you."

"I am very nobleous."

"Noble ... ous. Yes. Definitely a word. That you just said."

I smile. "Would you believe I graduated college with a 4.0 GPA?"

"Holy shit, really? That's like—"

"A lie. I didn't. No way. I was a standard 3.0 all the way. I did the bare minimum in the required courses so I could stay on the baseball team and excelled in all the sports management ones without really having to think."

Kelley playfully shoves me. "I totally believed you."

I rub where he shoved me, but not because it hurt. It didn't. It

Thad

... was something else. Him touching me. His smile. That spark again.

It shines in his eyes as bright as the sun outside.

I slink back on the couch. "Maybe we should work on your gullibility before toughening your psyche."

"I'll think about it. It would be nice to not stress over not knowing what's being said about me."

"Is that why you can't have a phone around you? It's not that you have to know, but you can't sit there and not know?"

Kelley nods. "It's so annoying, and I do hate myself for it. It's like I'm addicted to seeing it? Good and bad. Sometimes even the well-meaning messages and comments will set off my anxiety, and I know this. Yet, I can't stop myself from looking. It's a sickness. Literally."

"Have your therapists given you anything that helps?"

"I've been given tools to manage it, and mostly they work ... in public. By some miracle, I'm able to hold it together in front of others, but by myself? Alone with my thoughts? That's scarier than a haunted house on Halloween."

"Aww, are you scared of those kiddie haunted houses? That's a bit cute."

"It's not so much the ghouls and scary music. It's the fully grown-ass adults dressed up like demons or zombies who are able to stand so still you think they're a mannequin and then suddenly jump out at you. I, uh, might have punched one of them one time and then was asked to never return to the State Fair when I was seventeen."

Okay, that's a lot cute. "Note to self. Don't try to jump-scare you."

"Good plan unless you want a black eye."

"Ooh, you should give me a black eye, and then when Brady gets back, he'll freak out about leaving us alone and stress about telling his uncle what happened."

"And how will that encourage him to go out to see his boyfriendy people more?"

"It wouldn't, but it would be fun to watch him squirm."

Chapter 9

"Question. Do you like to emotionally torture all your friends?"

"It's not friendship unless it's toxic."

Kelley cocks his head, his lips pressed together. He can't tell if I'm being serious or not again. "You know, I have the number of a great therapist. If you need it."

I burst out laughing. "I assure you, I am joking. It would be fun messing with Brady, but you're right. We're trying to be nice to him, seeing as he's lucky enough to be getting fucked every which way 'til Sunday while we're here."

Kelley shifts, palming one leg of his jeans down as if needing to adjust himself without actually touching the part that's too ... tight. "I still don't know how the idea of sex with two people is appealing to you, but you do you."

I'd rather do you, my mouth wants to say, but I don't let it.

"He's got the right idea though. Spending the long hours out here in the middle of nowhere having multiple orgasms to pass the time ..." I really shouldn't be saying that, but I can't help myself.

And even though Kelley Afton has that deep, tanned skin, a blush is visible as it creeps up his neck, and I know I'm going to keep teasing him.

I want to move in and kiss my way across his pink-stained jaw, but I have to refrain. At least until he gives me the go-ahead. If he's even interested.

I should be focusing on my career and not the sexy client sitting next to me, but, well, I don't seem to have a professional side when it comes to Kelley. If I'm not insulting him, I'm wanting to have sex with him.

Or maybe I want sex because I haven't gotten any in a long while. Who knows? All I know is that I want Kelley.

Right here. Right now.

As I stare down at what I'm assuming is a really thick cock, if the way his pajamas showed it off this morning was accurate and his pants are tented, I can't help thinking he's on the same page. But having a bodily reaction and actually being interested are two completely different things.

Thad

"Are y-you ... are you implying ... uh, with ... me?" He can't make himself look at me as he asks.

"I was actually thinking Doris from the front desk might be up for a party."

His head snaps in my direction, and I laugh. He makes this way too easy.

"Fucking with you. Again. She's not my type. Gay all the way. Though good ol' Doris did have some masculine qualities about her, so maybe if I was desperate enough."

Kelley smiles. "You're fucking with me again, aren't you?"

"Old people deserve some love and sex too."

"I'm sure the groundskeeper, her husband, can do that for her."

"Damn, she's married? There goes my chance."

Randomly, Kelley asks, "Do you think the guys Brady's with are married? They seem older, and—"

"You're not, like, jealous, are you?" That's when it hits me. "Oh. *Oh!* Do you have a thing for Brady?"

"No," he says way too quickly. "I'm ... thinking about dynamics. How a relationship like that works."

"Well, I'm no expert. I can tell you how sex between three people works, but relationships? No clue. Actually, I don't know how relationships work between two people, so I can't help. I thought you said it would be too daunting to have to please two people, so why are you curious?"

He shrugs. "Exactly that, I guess. Wanting to understand. I'm not judging. More ... fascinated? I think I'd be too jealous to be able to share, but that doesn't mean I'm not interested in knowing more."

Damn, being so jealous he couldn't bring himself to share? That's hot. It shouldn't be, but oops. Finding toxic behavior attractive probably says a lot about who I am as a person.

"So, you're a one-man type of guy?"

Kelley licks his lips. "I will be. When the time comes."

"The time comes ..."

"Where I'll let myself have a relationship. You know, when I'm

Chapter 9

stable, have job security, a solid contract for financial security, and am not a total nervous wreck."

"Sooo, when you retire? What are you going to do until then? What about your needs?"

"I had my ways back in college. Discreet guys. My hand. Countless sex toys bought anonymously online and shipped in innocuous packaging. Those last two also helped a lot in the minors and this last year."

If I'm doing the math correctly, and I think I am ... "You haven't had sex since college? Is that, what, four years?" My words are probably way too loud, but luckily, this whole resort is practically vacant.

There's that blush again. "I-I've had orgasms. They count."

"They do, and there's nothing inherently wrong with not having sex for that long, but just like you not understanding threesomes, I can't understand four years without. I'd go insane."

"Hey, maybe that's why my mental health has only deteriorated since playing in the minors."

"Sorry. I didn't mean to imply—"

"It's okay. Technically, you're not wrong, but words like 'insane' or 'crazy' can get to me sometimes. Yet, I find myself still using them to describe myself. Go figure."

"Yeah, but that's you. You know your intention behind the word. You don't know others', but I didn't mean anything by it."

"You're getting really good at this apology thing."

"And you're getting really good at diverting attention from what's really important."

Kelley frowns. "What's that?"

"Sex. Duh."

"Trusting someone not to sell their story is more important to me than feeling the weight of a man on top of me."

Withholding for sex for that long purely because he can't trust anyone makes me feel sorry for him. Sure, sorry. That's why my cock is rock hard and begging me to make a move.

"What about the weight of a man contractually obligated to keep the details a secret?"

Thad

"What do you mean?" he asks.

I clear my throat. "All employees of King Sports have to sign NDAs for each individual client. There's a contract that literally says I can't talk publicly about you. And if I can't help you out with overcoming your social media anxiety, at least let me help you with this. Four years ..."

"You're sweet. I think. But I don't mind. I guess I don't have a high sex drive."

"Possibly. Or you could be on the ace spectrum or—"

"No. I'm not. I'm very sexual. I want it, but I don't *need* it. If that makes sense. And the thought of hooking up sometimes makes my anxiety worse because I'm scared of what happens afterward."

"You're scared of cuddling?"

Kelley's smile—damn that smile—is everything. "I'm scared of it going bad. Articles, tabloids, public backlash, sponsorship issues, loss of income, focus on baseball, failing—oh look, we've reached catastrophic level by having a simple one-night stand."

It's only in this very moment that I realize how much I've taken for granted in my life. Even the simple act of finding someone attractive, having sex with them, and then forgetting about it the next day.

Kelley doesn't have that. He's never had it.

"Let me be that guy for you," I blurt.

"What guy?"

"The guy you can drop your guard around. The guy who, no matter what you do to me, can't tell a soul."

"You could still tell people in the office."

"And risk getting fired? Fuck that. I can't speak publicly, or King Sports will sue me, and I can't tell anyone at work, or I'll get canned."

Kelley bites his lip. He's contemplating it, at least.

"You can tell me to back off, not to go anywhere near you, and say no. I don't want to pressure you, but I will point out that it's a win-win situation. You get to have anxiety-free sex and break your dry spell, and I get to have sex to pass the time in this hellhole."

There's a really long pause, so long I think he's going to chicken

Chapter 9

out, but then he says, "It wouldn't be completely anxiety-free. I might have had sex before, but I had no idea what I was doing, and it's not like I've been with many guys. What if I'm bad in bed?"

"If that's the only thing we have to worry about, we're good to go. I've got us covered."

"Cocky much?"

"Nope. I'm confident enough to know that you don't have much to compare me to, and chances are I can outfuck anyone who left any doubt in your mind that you could be anything but amazing in bed."

"But how do you know?"

I lean back more and put my arm out to run along the back of the couch behind his head. With my free hand, I rub over my aching cock. "Because of what you do to me just by being in the same room. You don't even have to touch me and I'm hard for you."

Kelley sucks in a sharp breath, and when I glance over at him, I know I have him right where I want him: desperate.

He's on me a second later.

Chapter 10
Kelley

It's as if someone else takes over my body as I fling myself at Thad. This is so unprofessional, way out of line, and I shouldn't be putting this on him. But there are only so many red flags a bull can resist before it has to charge as fast as it can.

It's as if the promise of an NDA, complete secrecy, has stripped away every worry I usually have when it comes to sex. Sure, I'm still worried about his experience, but at the same time, I'm so unleashed I don't have time to dwell on it.

Somehow, I find myself straddling Thad's waist, with my lips on his, his tongue in my mouth as I desperately swallow his moans.

He tastes like chocolate, smells like the outdoors, and makes sounds like a porn star.

My hips thrust and rotate, trying to get closer, trying to find the friction I crave. I want his dick against mine, rubbing and teasing.

I take back what I said about not needing sex. It turns out I do. And I need to have sex with Thad ... uh ... Still-Don't-Know-His-Last-Name. Like hell I'm going to stop and ask. Not when I'm like this.

I'm in this. Wholly and completely. The only word I can think to describe it is *liberated*.

I'm not in my head. I'm free to do whatever I want and everything that I crave without the worry of the world criticizing me for it tomorrow.

Chapter 10

While my mouth continues to devour him, tangling my tongue with his, my hands do their own exploring. He lets me run my hands over his chest, under his shirt, and when my fingertips brush over his nipples, which turns out are pierced, Thad shudders.

Up until now, he's let me do my thing. I've been in control. But I guess I've found his weakness because in the next second, he stands, me wrapped around him and his arm supporting my back. I throw my hands around his shoulders to steady myself while he carries me through to my bedroom and kicks the door closed behind us.

He lowers me to my bed, still kissing me, but when he tries to lift up, I wrap myself around him tighter.

Thad pulls his mouth from mine and places open-mouth kisses along my jaw and down my neck. "I want all your clothes gone, but I can't do that if you're permanently attached to me."

"I wish I could help you with that, but I can't."

"You can't, or you won't?"

"Won't."

Thad's smile lights me up inside as he stares down at me. "Just think, the sooner we get rid of our clothes, the sooner you can be inside me. Or me inside you. Your call."

My legs drop from around his waist, and my hold on him loosens. "Fine."

Thad snorts and stands tall, stripping layer after layer off, while all I can do is watch and drool as every inch of skin is exposed.

His chest tattoo, which is always covered by his shirts except for this tiny sliver, takes up most of his torso, and it's so intricate it creates an optical illusion of a hole torn in his chest. His heart, while roughly anatomically correct, has red baseball stitching through it. From the tear seam over to his other pec is an angel wing.

I sit up and run my fingers over it.

His nipples are pierced with silver barbells, and his muscles are insane. I'm not a small guy, and while I might not be as jacked as some players, I'm still heavy. I can see how he carried me so easily now though, with his bulging biceps and rock-hard abs.

Kelley

"I've noticed you haven't started taking anything off yet," he says.

"I'm too distracted."

"Distracted or getting in your head again?"

"Distracted because of all the hotness going on." My gaze runs from the top of Thad's head where his hair falls in thin wisps across his forehead to all the way down where he's no longer covering any part of his body.

His thick cock is long and angry-looking. He's so hard, the tight, velvety skin making my mouth water. And when he wraps his long fingers around his length and starts stroking himself, I almost short-circuit.

"I'm not touching you again until you're naked," Thad says.

I frantically undress and throw my clothes everywhere, trying to get naked the quickest way instead of what's probably the most efficient. All the while, I keep my eyes locked on Thad. At first, I don't dare tear my gaze away from his hand that's working over his cock.

A bead of precum dribbles out, and he uses it to smoothen his strokes.

"There," I say. "I'm naked. Now, touch me."

"Where?"

I throw my head back in frustration. "Anywhere."

"What do you want me to do?"

Everything. Anything. "Just fucking fuck me. Please. My mouth, my hand, my ass, I don't care. I need your cock, and I need it any which way you'll give it to me."

A split second later, he's back on top of me. Only this time, he captures my wrists and lifts them above my head, gripping both with one of his giant hands.

"Have you ever bottomed before?" he asks.

And while I say, "Yes," he must sense my hesitation about it.

"But ..."

"What?"

"I'm waiting for the but. What happened? Couldn't relax enough? Couldn't get off?"

Chapter 10

"That. The, uh, second one. It was fine, he was fine, but I couldn't—"

"Did you at least get to come after he did?"

I shake my head.

"Okay, we're going to fix that up first."

"Fix what up?"

"No matter what, we both come. Doesn't have to be together, and it doesn't have to be during anal, but either way, this will end happily for both of us. Got it?"

"I don't care how I come. I just want to fucking come."

"Good. That doesn't mean I'm not going to torturously drag this out though. If this is the only chance you get to have anxiety-free sex for however long, I'm going to try to give you everything I've got. I'll bring the small arsenal of tricks I've learned, having been sexually active since high school, and by the end, I'm going to make you scream."

"You already make me want to scream. Scream at you to hurry up."

Thad smiles. "I don't suppose you have supplies around here, do you?"

"Lube in the nightstand. Uh, no condoms though. Didn't think this would be happening here."

"I'm good without a condom if you are. Health-wise, I mean."

"Me too." I protect myself in other ways. Gone are the days of condoms being the only form of safe sex.

Thad reaches over me to the nightstand and feels around. "Did you put your sex lube on top of the Bible? Ooh, you're going to hell for that."

I pretend to pout because I know he's messing around. "You told me you wouldn't judge. What if I get off on Jesus looking down on me while I fuck my own fist?"

Thad grunts. "The thought of you doing that while I'm outside that door watching TV makes me want you to do it later tonight. When Brady's back. I'll be the only one who knows you're doing it. And Jesus, of course."

I laugh. "Eh, I doubt he'd tune in for that. Of all the sins organized religion pushes on people, I'm going to be going to hell for a lot worse than jerking off."

"True. It would probably be for something more like this." Thad sits up, resting back on his knees, and brings my legs up over his thighs.

For a moment, I'm worried he's going to push right into me, no lube or prep, but all he does is bring our cocks together. He lubes up both of his hands and wraps one of his large palms and long fingers around both of our cocks. Because of the angle, they're not completely in line, but when I shuffle down a bit further, it helps.

My ass is off the mattress completely, basically resting on his thick thighs, and when he reaches between us, he works his hand underneath my balls so his wet fingers can press against my hole.

He wasn't kidding when he said he has an arsenal of tricks, and we're only getting started. The way his hand feels against my shaft, while also having his hard cock pressed against mine, that's sensory overload enough, but with his fingers teasing my rim at the same time? I'm scared I'm going to blow before he gives me what I really want.

Am I nervous that he's made big promises and won't be able to deliver? Yes. If he can make me come through ass play, I'll be happy, but I won't lie, if it's still not as great as my past experiences, I might read into why that is and feel like something is wrong with me.

Logically—and there's that word again—I know that not everyone likes it, and like he said, if I don't come that way, he'll get me off another way, and I trust him to do that. But I think there's something about the social expectation about gay men and fitting a certain stereotype that I should be fighting. Instead, it's like I want in on the secret. I want great, unapologetic sex where I'm not in my head and I can truly let go and be myself.

I want Thad to fill me up.

As if reading my mind, he presses a finger inside me, sliding all the way in, brushing against my prostate. My toes tingle, and my breath catches.

"You're doing so good," he murmurs.

Chapter 10

"It feels good," I say. I'm not even lying. But the last time I tried this, it also felt good. I just couldn't get across that finish line. That guy was also closeted, so I could relax with him because he, too, didn't want anything to get out, but I was in college. We dated for a few months, and by dated, I mean we fucked a couple of times, but every single time I bottomed, which wasn't that many, I couldn't come, and it would end in awkwardness. I got the impression it was an ego thing for him. It wasn't his fault I couldn't come; it was mine. I guess it can be a bit disheartening if you can't bring a partner pleasure, but I never once blamed him. It was me. Even though I should've felt safe with him, I didn't. I never have.

This is the closest I've been to completely letting myself go.

"You're disappearing on me," Thad says. He releases our cocks and puts his hand next to my head while he lowers himself closer to me. "Are you getting in your head?" His finger is still lodged inside me, but he stops trying to stretch me with it.

"A little. I want this to be good for you. And for me."

His soft lips land on my cheek. "Don't worry about making it good. Focus on what you feel. If you feel good, I'm going to feel good. I promise."

I bite my lip. "I want you to fuck me."

"We'll get there, but I want you inside me first."

His finger leaves me, and then he reaches for more lube.

"Why?"

"Why are you fucking me first?"

"Exactly. What if I come way too early?"

"Then we flip, and I fuck you until I come. We don't need to keep score. We don't need to time anything. We can do what we want in any order we want."

I don't know where the expectation that you have to orgasm together came from, but a huge emphasis is put on men to outlast their partners. But Thad's right. What's to stop me from coming and then focusing on him? Absolutely nothing.

Thad pours more lube on his fingers and reaches behind him, his eyes fluttering closed while he fingers himself.

"Did you want me to—"

Kelley

"Have you ever prepped yourself?" he asks. "Used toys?"

I should be confident as I say, "Yes," but my voice trembles.

"Have you come while using toys?"

I nod.

"Okay, so the other guy you bottomed for either didn't know what he was doing, or you were too uptight to come because you were too anxious. So while we do this, you need to focus on me, and I'm going to constantly remind you that you can let go and take what you want."

I might be in my head a bit, but I'm not anxious. At least, not when it comes to Thad telling the world.

"If you want me to fuck you, I want you to prep yourself for me," Thad says. "I want you nice and relaxed and stretched further than you think you need. That way, when you are ready for me, you won't be worried about anything but feeling me move inside you."

He's not saying anything deliciously filthy, but his words sound like sin to my ears.

He places lube in my hands and then climbs off me, getting on all fours—well, three of four while he reaches behind him and continues to prep himself. I watch his face as I do the same to myself, feeling like every time I push a finger inside my body, he reacts to my touch. Which makes no sense, but because we're doing this in tandem, it feels as though I'm doing it to him, not myself.

I'm an expert at making my hole wide enough for the singular thin toy I have hidden in my house, but I'm going to need to really stretch it if I'm going to be fucked by Thad's thick cock.

"How are you holding up?" he asks, his voice breathy. "Because I gotta tell you, I need you filling me soon. Please, Kelley. Fuck me."

I don't even care if I'm not ready yet; he is, and that's all that snaps into focus when he asks me to fuck him.

I'm not nervous. My anxiety is low. So when I get behind him and line up my cock, I don't hesitate to push inside. His heat

Chapter 10

surrounds me, his long moan fills my ears, and it's as if something deep down inside me unlocks.

I do as he tells me to and focus on what I'm feeling while I move inside him. I feel everything. I tune out the worry of how good it is for him because, like he says, after this, I can make him come another way. I let myself go. With each thrust, I make it harder, faster.

I pay attention to his reactions, how he fists my comforter in his hand, how his breathing becomes erratic.

Warmth builds in my gut, and an impending orgasm threatens to flood my body, but this is too good to end it now.

"Fuck," Thad chants over and over again. "Kelley, if you still want me to fuck you, you have to slow down. I'm so ... I'm so close."

As tempted as I am to keep going and to feel him fall apart on my cock, I want him inside me more. So I slow down. I pull out of him to the tip and then slam back inside. Over and over again.

The change of pace makes my skin break out in goose bumps. My skin is flushed, I'm sure I look out of it, and it feels as though I'm drunk.

Drunk on sex.

Drunk on Thad.

I slam back inside him one more time and then stay there for a moment. I run my hands down his back, exploring all his muscles, and then I lean over him and kiss his shoulder blade. "That's all you get. It's my turn, and I know exactly how I want you. Roll onto your back."

He does, and then I straddle him.

"Are you sure you're prepped enough?"

I arch my back. "Why don't you check for me?"

He reaches behind me and sinks two fingers inside my hole. "Mm, you might need more. Ride my fingers before you ride me."

With him making sure I'm comfortable, that I'm ready, and with the way he's bossing me around but also letting me take what I want ... I've never trusted anyone in the bedroom the way I have trust in him.

His fingers feel so good, but I crave more.

Kelley

"Give me more," I say.

He adds another one, and while the sting of stretching is there, it's in a good way. So fucking good.

"I need you," I rasp. "I need your cock."

Never before would I have said any of this to someone, but it falls out of my mouth with Thad.

Thad removes his fingers and then grips his cock, guiding it to my hole. As I sink down on him, I feel so full. So stretched.

Thad grips my hips tight and waits for me to start moving, and the second I do, he thrusts up into me. Every pass, every time I rise up, he grips tighter and then slams upward. We meet over and over, and I have to hold on to his chest for leverage.

A warm flush travels from my face down my back, and it lands in my groin.

"You going to come?" Thad asks. So in tune. He can tell I'm close.

I keep going. "I need ... Need ..."

"Tell me," he says.

"My cock. Touch my cock."

He does, and then it only takes a few strokes for me to spill over. I keep rotating my hips, keep taking his dick deep, and as I empty onto his stomach, my ass pulses around his cock.

Thad lets go of my cock, and his cum-covered hand goes back to my hip. "Fuck, Kelley." He thrusts up once, twice, and then the third time, he stills. He grits his teeth to the point a vein in his neck sticks out.

I didn't know sex could be like that.

Thad lifts his hand and cups my cheek. "You okay?"

I smile down at him. "Never better."

Chapter 11
Thad

Damn, I needed that.

Technically, that was for Kelley, but as I lie on my back, covered in cum, trying to catch my breath, I have to admit I did this for me as well.

I wasn't lying when I said I wouldn't tell a soul and he can trust me, but I'm not conceited enough to think this was completely altruistic of me.

Again, damn. That's the only word I can think as I begin to come down from what very well could be the best sex of my life.

Kelley was so hot, so uninhibited. He took what he wanted, asked for what he needed, yet was happy to exchange that power role. From pliant to dominant, he has it all locked up inside him, and I'm so happy he trusted me enough to share it with me.

And now, as he lies in my arms, I wait for regret to come. It doesn't.

Have I possibly screwed my entire career for it? Yes. But there's no way he's telling anyone, and my lips are sealed.

Saying the phrase "Would you like fries with that?" a thousand times a day holds no appeal, and while there's nothing wrong with being in fast food—hell, I probably couldn't last a day without telling someone off for being rude to hospitality workers—I've always wanted more for myself. I wanted to be the guy who took care of his family after they spent so much time, money, and effort on me. I'd

Thad

love to take that burden away from my parents, so I need to make sure this job sticks. It's not going to be nearly as much as what I would've made in Major League Baseball, but it will still be more than I'd ever need. I will have enough to pay my parents back and let them finally retire. I'll be able to keep my brother out of trouble. Hopefully.

So yes, even though Kelley just gave me the best sex I've ever had and I want to do it again, we probably shouldn't. He's broken his dry spell now, so we're all good. I should get up and leave before Brady comes back. If he comes back. If he didn't come back, then we'd—

Hell, I just told myself not again, and I guess my brain—or, more likely, the brain in between my legs—is already trying to find loopholes to my own rule.

Though, we probably could stretch this thing out while we're here in the middle of nowhere and Brady keeps disappearing on us.

"What's your last name?" Kelley's random question is random.

"Huh?"

"I don't know your last name."

"Do you need to know it? For, like, legal documents for the sexual harassment case you've decided to file?"

Kelley turns his head toward me, his warm brown eyes crinkling. "What?"

"It's a really random thought after having sex with someone you shouldn't have."

"So you jumped to I'm going to sue you?" He rolls onto his side to face me properly. "You're not having regrets, are you?"

"Definitely no. But I—"

He presses a single finger to my lips. "That was perfect, and I in no way have any complaints. We both wanted that. It might have been unprofessional, but I don't want you to worry about me ruining anything for you."

"Ditto. I meant my word. I won't tell anyone."

"Weirdly, even though you've given me no real reason to, I trust you."

Chapter 11

I relax. "It's St. James."

"Thad St. James. Sounds like an important name. You know, like, there should be a third or fourth attached to the end."

"Especially when my full name is Theodore St. James the Seventeenth."

"The seventeenth?"

"I'm joking. There's no important number next to my name."

"Ah. Thad the First."

"Technically Theodore, but the first all the way. And despite what my uppity last name might imply, I'm not from a wealthy family."

"Oh, I wasn't meaning—"

"I know." I roll over to my side now so we're facing each other. "It's a thing with me. Growing up, people assumed we had money because of how much my parents sunk into my baseball career, but they worked hard for that. I worked hard to be everything they expected me to be, and ... I failed them. So when other kids would come to my house and saw that we were more lower-middle class than the rich kid they expected me to be, it was as if I could see their disappointment. I don't know if it was that they were planning to use me for my nonexistent money or if that's the only reason they were friendly to me or what, but I learned to be upfront about it. Especially if people assume I'm important because of my last name."

"I can relate. Sort of. My family had no money growing up, and I got where I did on scholarships and fundraisers, basically. Had a few girls in high school and college who tried to be my girlfriend in a very obvious way where they only wanted me because they knew I was future MLB material. It's not exactly the same, but I do get it."

"Oh yeah, had lots of those kinds of 'friends' in college too."

"Did we ..." Kelley mock gasps. "Just figure out we have more in common than our love of baseball? No. What?"

I love his playful side. "We probably have a hell of a lot in common. It's why I resented you. You know, what does he have that I don't have? Why was he lucky enough to be blessed with enough talent to take him all the way when I wasn't?"

I can tell he's about to cut me off with the way his brow scrunches and lips part.

"And I'm not saying you didn't work for it. I know you did. But there has to be something about natural ability that got you across that line. I pushed myself to breaking point to make it, and then there came a time where I had to admit I don't have what it takes."

"I'm sorry," Kelley says softly.

"You have nothing to be sorry for. It's not like you kneecapped me with a baseball bat to take my spot in the majors."

"I would never Tonya Harding someone."

I laugh. "Neither would I. Mainly because I know there were way too many people ahead of me. That would be a lot of kneecapping, and who has time for that?"

"What does it say about me that your laziness for violence based off of the amount of effort needed is comforting?"

"That maybe sex has made your self-preservation instincts weak?"

His eyes light up at that. "Hey, it's usually the opposite. I call this a win."

I reach for him and run my hand down his back, stopping at the curve of his spine. "I'd say this was more than a win. I'd say it was a home run at the bottom of the ninth with all the bases loaded."

"Mmm, talk dirty to me," he deadpans.

Okay, I'll hand it to him, Kelley never came across as this playful guy before. He really knows how to be himself when he lets go. When his anxiety is not gnawing at him.

"You're funner than I thought you were," I admit.

"I could say the same. Because what we just did would be considered fun." Kelley rolls closer to me, almost closing the small gap between our naked bodies. "And you know what they say about fun needing to repeat itself."

"Actually, I don't think I know that saying at all."

"You know, anything worth doing should be done all the time."

Chapter 11

Kelley inches closer, his lips tantalizingly close to mine, and as much as I'm telling myself to pull away, I don't think there's a force in the world strong enough to make me do it.

As if proving me wrong, the main door to the cabin opens, and there it is. The force is scary enough to make me pull away and jump a mile high. Brady's back.

"Shit," I say under my breath and practically fall to the ground as I roll off the bed and try to scrounge for my clothes.

Kelley gets up, too, and throws on his pajamas.

We stare at each other, breathing heavily, neither of us sure on how to explain this away.

He breaks first, shoving me toward his window. "I'll tell him I was napping while you … you were…"

"Taking a walk barefoot and without a jacket? Do you think he'll believe I went for a walk because hypothermia sounds fun?"

"Is there any excuse under the sun to explain us naked in here other than we had sex?"

"Anything. We got locked outside and needed to share body heat when we managed to get back in. We were sticking our asses out the window to sun our assholes because it's therapeutic. There has to be something."

"Those … are not things. He'd see right through those."

He's right, but ugh. I really don't want to go out there when all I have on me is jeans and a base-layer shirt. "Can you at least give me a pair of socks so I don't get immediate frostbite?"

"Kelley?" Brady calls out. "Thad?"

"Go, go," Kelley whisper-yells. "I'll distract him."

Before he reaches the door, Kelley throws me a pair of his thick socks. They'll help, but not much.

I somehow need to get out of here and around the other side of the cabin without being seen so I can sneak back inside through Brady's and my bedroom window and pretend I'd been there the whole time. My feet shouldn't freeze that quickly. Hopefully.

As soon as I'm finished wrangling with the socks, I unlatch the window as quietly as I can and push it open. Noise in this place travels so easily, and it wouldn't surprise me if Brady already heard

Thad

everything we've been whispering back and forth, but on the small chance that he hasn't, I have to be careful getting out of here. There's a bit of a drop to the ground because the cabin is on stilts. There's no way to jump out of here gracefully, but at least the snow should help break my fall.

As soon as I jump, I realize I'm wrong. Not snow. Ice. It's fucking ice, and now that I've possibly broken my ankles and fallen to my side, my clothes are wet, I'm in pain, and I still have to get around to my bedroom without being caught.

"What was that?" Brady asks loudly.

At least, I hope it was loudly, otherwise there's no chance of him not hearing us already. My uncoordinated jump slash fall was louder than us though. So ... still have to push through, I guess.

"Oh, did you hear something?" Kelley could use some acting classes.

I can't go around the front of the cabin because if I go that way, I have to walk past the front porch and down the side that has the sliding doors on the back deck, so I have to sneak down the other side and past the kitchen windows. They're smaller and easier to avoid detection.

With it being snowy and icy and wearing socks means my footsteps are silent, which is a bonus. I don't even dare look inside as I sneak past the kitchen, and it's only when I get to my bedroom window that I slow down to peek inside. The room is empty, but that's when I run into my next challenge.

The window is latched from the inside.

Options run through my head. I can't smash the window. There's no point in that because of the noise. Then there's the issue of actually pulling myself up to climb through the window once it's open. It's not impossible, but quietly? Yeah, I don't have that much faith.

Okay, so here's the plan. This is what I'll do.

I'll walk up to the sliding doors and get Kelley or Brady to let me in, where I'll explain that I was in my room and I thought I heard a bear. So I went to the window to see and then started to worry about bears breaking in and if they can climb through the

Chapter 11

window, so I thought I'd try to see if I could climb through even though bears are like three times my size, but that's not the point. If I couldn't climb through it, then a bear wouldn't. But it turns out my parkour skills are not great, and instead of climbing in and out, I fell, and that's why I'm outside. In the snow. With hardly any clothes on.

Honestly, who *wouldn't* believe that story?

All right. Here I go. I can do this.

I turn and walk up to the back deck, my heart hammering, but when I get to the sliding glass door, Brady and Kelley are on the couch, deep in conversation.

Brady's back is to me, and Kelley barely acknowledges me, but he does run his arm along the back of the couch and summons me by waving me in.

Cautiously, I open the door, and Brady turns to look at me, but it's as if he's looking right through me.

"Where have you been?" It's not an accusation, more a cordial question he doesn't care to have the answer to.

Because as soon as I start my amazing, brilliant bear story, all I get out is, "I thought I heard a bear," and he's cutting me off.

"Oh, cool." He turns toward the TV. "What are you watching?"

That was ... easy. A waste of a perfectly good story, but okay.

Also, the screen is off. Does he not realize the TV isn't even on?

I point to Brady and mouth to Kelley, "Is he okay?"

Kelley does a subtle shake of his head. "What do you want to watch?" Kelley asks.

"Whatever you want."

There's something down about Brady's tone, and his attitude is all ... off. If those guys he was with hurt him, I'm gonna be pissed.

"I'm going to go, uh, get changed," I say.

"Okay." Brady's still staring blankly at the off TV.

"I'll make hot cocoa." Kelley stands, and instead of going to my bedroom, I follow him into the kitchen.

My feet are freezing, so I take off the wet socks, letting my feet sink into the heated flooring. "What's his deal?"

Thad

"I don't know. It's almost like he's here, but he's not really here. Do you think something ..."

"Something happened with those older guys? I'll kill them." I turn to prepare to leave the cabin and give those fucks a piece of my mind when Kelley stops me.

"You can't go to them, or Brady will know we know."

At this point, I don't care. I'm growing kind of protective of my colleague. "Can I go yell at them, at least?"

Kelley smiles. "No, and we don't even know if that's what's wrong."

"True, but what else could it be?"

"Why don't we find out?"

"You mean ... ask? That seems too easy."

"Hey, I got you to open up with cocoa—"

"That I made," I point out.

"It's not who makes it, it's what's in it. It's like truth serum."

"Sounds scientifically legit too."

Kelley nods. "Just think, the sooner we get the info out of him, and if it does have to do with the two guys, we can fix it, he can go out again, and then we can ..." He glances into the living room and then back at me. "Finish what we started."

"Funny. I remember already finishing. Hard."

"We still have another week here." Kelley blinks up at me, and I give in. Just like that.

"I'll help you make the cocoa."

Chapter 12
Kelley

Whatever daze Brady's in, it's gone by the time we bring him cocoa. Thad's changed into dry, clean clothes now, but he still looks uncomfortable, which of course means my brain immediately jumps to thinking he regrets what we did, that we almost got caught, and he never wants to mention it again.

But then I remind that negative voice that when we were in the kitchen, Thad was all for this plan of getting Brady happy again so he can leave to be with whoever those two random dudes are.

"So, what happened while I was out?" Brady asks.

"I napped," I say again. I'm getting the impression he was completely zoned out when he got back, and hey, I'm not going to complain.

"I thought I saw a bear," Thad says. For the second time. I was hoping he wouldn't bring that up again because it's almost as absurd as his asshole-sunning excuse.

"A bear? No shit." And yep, Brady seems as though it's the first time he heard that too.

"Are you okay?" I ask. "You're a little ..."

Brady slumps. "Okay, fine. I snuck my boyfriend here, and I've been slinking off to see him."

Boyfriend. Him. Singular.

Maybe we misread what we saw the other night. Or they're open.

Kelley

"Why aren't you with him right now?" Thad asks, obviously sticking to the *we know nothing* plan. "If you're worried we'll tell your uncle, we won't. There's nothing to do around here, and if I had someone to have sex with, I'd be trying to sneak time away with them too." Thad's blue eyes meet mine, amusement shining in them.

"He's gone," Brady says, and it almost comes out like a petulant child.

"Okay, when you say gone, please tell me you mean back home and not in a 'you got in a fight, and now we have to bury a body' kind of way?" Thad's joke is funny—well, I think so anyway—but Brady doesn't laugh.

"Long distance sucks." Brady grunts and slinks back on the couch, using the backrest as a pillow.

"From here to New York?" Thad says. "It's a couple of hours. Calm down."

Brady shakes his head. "I knew the—him from college. In California. He could only get away from work for a couple of days."

It's almost visible the way Thad's heart sinks. I wonder if I'm as transparent. I also didn't miss the way Brady almost said *them* instead of him.

"So, that's what you meant by he's gone?" I ask. "He had to leave?"

"I'll get over it. I always do after he leaves. It'll just take a while to get out of my funk. I might actually go have a warm shower to reset." He stands, but before he leaves the room, he turns to us. "Please don't tell Uncle Damon that I brought a boy on a work trip or that I'm even seeing anyone to begin with? This whole long-distance thing is hard enough without my entire family finding out and pressuring me to introduce them and wah, wah, wah. We're not even technically together. We're ... see you whenever we can and fuck anyone else when we're not together type thing. Not that I do ..."

"We won't tell anyone," I say.

"You can trust us," Thad adds.

Brady narrows his gaze at Thad, as if he's hesitating to trust

Chapter 12

him. That look alone should tell me that having sex with Thad and trusting it won't get out is naïve of me, but I'm trying not to freak out, and if I let those kinds of thoughts run free, I'll be breaking down by dinnertime.

"Seriously," Thad says. "If you get fired, Damon will start paying more attention to the other interns, and I'm hoping to skirt through this internship without any drama or spotlight brought on me."

Maybe this is why Thad never made it in baseball either. He wants to ride the middle. He doesn't have the drive to be the best, just *good enough*.

I can't tell if it's a good mindset to have or if it's what's holding him back. Not that I can talk about having the most supportive mindset. All my brain tries to do is sabotage everything good in my life.

Brady disappears into the bathroom, but Thad and I are silent until the water's running and we're more confident he can't hear us.

"Well, that puts a wrench into our plan," he says.

"Does this mean Brady's going to be around us twenty-four seven again?"

"If the walls weren't too thin, I'd say I could sneak into your room after Brady's asleep, but he's a light sleeper, so even the sound of me getting out of bed would wake him up."

"So, that's it, then?" It's a question, even though it comes out as more of a statement. The one time I've been able to have sex the way I want, free and uninhibited, I get told it won't happen again.

Damn.

This sucks.

"Probably for the best anyway," Thad says. "I can't jump out that window again." He shifts where he's sitting, wincing at the same time. Is that why he's been looking like he'd rather be sitting anywhere but here?

"Shit. Did you hurt yourself?"

"Mostly my pride, but yeah. I think I've bruised my hip and possibly sprained my ankles. I don't think they're broken because I can still walk, but—" He lifts up the legs of his pants, and his ankles are both swollen.

"Ouch."

"They're not too bad."

It's inappropriate, but I can't help laughing.

"My pain is funny to you?"

"No, not your pain. Just ... it's all a bit dramatic, isn't it?" I laugh some more.

"Dramatic?"

"Getting caught post-orgasms, sneaking out a window like we're having an affair. Hurting yourself. Lying about seeing a bear." It sounds ridiculous.

Thad finally thinks so, too, because his laughter joins mine, and then it's one of those wild-ass roller-coaster rides where it's impossible to stop, and every time we lock eyes, we lose even more control of it.

I'm in tears by the time Brady is out of the shower.

"What are we laughing at?" he asks. He's only wearing a towel, and while his body is impressive, it's nothing compared to what I saw a mere hour ago.

And what are we laughing at? Something about windows and orgasms.

"Kelley here has realized that while you're going through real heartache, he's over there fretting about online trolls. He's gaining something called perspective, and he thinks it's funny."

Man, I wish that's what was happening. I wish I could accept the ridiculousness that is my anxiety sometimes. I also wish it didn't hurt when Thad calls me out like that, but I know not everyone can understand what I experience.

It's hard to describe, and to someone who can't relate, it does sound a bit ridiculous. I hate it.

I will say, though, Thad certainly found a way to shut my brain off to all of it. To get out of my head, I have to think with my other one.

"Perspective is always nice," Brady says and goes to his and Thad's room, closing the door so he can get changed.

Chapter 12

"Sorry," Thad whispers. "It was the first thing I thought of."

Okay, so maybe he does understand. I force a small smile. "Hey, at least you didn't say we were laughing at a bear. In the middle of winter. Let's hope Brady doesn't click that bears are all hibernating."

Thad shrugs. "Maybe I'm just a dumbass when it comes to bears and I actually saw Bigfoot. Or the groundskeeper. But I also think Brady's not thinking about it too deeply. He's too distracted."

"Yeah. I haven't seen him like this before." I lean in. "Is it bad that I kind of like he's not this completely put-together early twenties phenomenon? He was starting to give me a complex with how in control he seems."

"Oh, tell me about it. I think he has to be though."

"Because of who his family is," I agree.

"At least we don't have to worry about that," Thad says.

"Hooray for growing up poor?" I lift imaginary pom-poms.

"You know what I mean."

"I do, but could you imagine the amount of pressure both Brady and his brother had growing up? I just wanted to make it so I could take care of my family. I didn't have the added pressure of living in someone's shadow."

"Damn. The world really is ending. I think we have something else in common." Thad's smirk is so fucking sexy.

We don't have long left here before we have to go back to our real lives, where I'll have to be responsible for myself and won't have anyone confiscating my phone or internet from me. I want more of that freedom Thad gave me. I want more of that distraction where I'm so blissed-out that I physically cannot think of anything else but his dick.

I don't care how it happens, we have to find a way to ditch Brady so we can hook up again. I would do anything to escape the hundreds of little thoughts that are constantly running through my head.

Thad is the only person who's managed to achieve what years of therapy hasn't. And I'm not delusional enough to think his dick is a magic cure, or even that it's him, but it's the first real break I've had from it all in a really long time. I hope one day I can find someone who will make me feel as secure in myself as he does. I want the safety of being able to let go without any of the worry that comes afterward.

I want to find my person.

I know Thad can't be him, but he's perfect for what I need at this point in my life.

He might not be Mr. Right, but he's the perfect Mr. Right Now.

Chapter 13
Thad

I like Brady. He's an amazing coworker, and I respect the hell out of him, but I swear on the ghost of Babe Ruth that haunts the Yankee Stadium—true story—that if he doesn't find somewhere else to channel his lonely energy, I might have to find a way to bury a body after all. *His.*

Because since his boyfriend slash boyfriends slash none-of-my-business left, he hasn't moved from Kelley's side.

And because we don't want him to get suspicious of what happened between us, Kelley and I haven't really interacted.

I have stopped with the taunting him, though, because I meant what I said. I don't want to make him uncomfortable. If he ever does want me to help try to desensitize him to those types of comments, I'll do it, but I'm not going to force him into that, especially if we don't know if it'll work or if it could even make him worse.

So instead, we're cordial. We say good morning, ask if the other wants a cup of coffee or cocoa if we're making one, and that's about it.

I've had to jerk off in the shower like I'm a damn teenager again because I can't get the way his ass felt around my cock out of my head, and I can't jerk off when Brady is in the twin bed next to mine.

Thad

I'm desperate for some alone time with Kelley.

"I'm glad you two are finally getting along," Brady says while he and Kelley play more Scrabble.

I sip my coffee and swallow the retort that we'd get along a hell of a lot better if we could fuck each other again.

"Thad apologized," Kelley says.

"Kelley lies. I had nothing to be sorry for."

Kelley laughs.

Brady doesn't. "I shouldn't have said anything."

"Nah. We're good," I say. Could be better. We could be alone and naked.

It might seem like I have a one-track mind, but in my defense, I do. There's nothing else to do out here in the dead of winter but have sex and play Scrabble, and I hate Scrabble.

My phone next to me on the couch armrest lights up and vibrates. When I see "Mom" on the screen, my gut drops. I don't want to answer for fear of what she's going to say Wylder has done now.

But I answer anyway because of course I do. "Hey, just give me a sec?" I tell her and head for the kitchen so Brady and Kelley can't hear this conversation. "What's up?"

"It's Wylder."

"He's back?"

"No. He, uh, took more money."

"What?" I growl. So much for not letting Brady and Kelley overhear me. I lower my voice. "I told you to cancel that card."

"We were going to, but it's the account work pays us into, and your father didn't want to deal with the headache of having to change it with them and then all of the direct deposits that come out of it for our bills—"

"But now you can't even pay your bills. Cancel the card, Mom. Yes, it's a pain in the ass, but he'll keep doing it. You know he will because he never has to face the consequences of his actions."

"Your father is refusing, and I don't know how—"

I grit my teeth. "I'm only away for work for a few more days. I'll come to you and go through it all with you."

Chapter 13

"Thank you," she says softly.

"Is Dad there? Can you put him on?"

"Brad. Theodore wants to talk to you."

"Hey, son."

"Did you really not cancel your bank card?"

"Our pay was due to go in there only a couple of days after Wylder took off. What were we supposed to do, you know?"

Call the bank, call your work, figure out what payments were going to come out, and change the damn details.

I don't say any of this though. My parents should be close to retiring, and they're nowhere near it. Because of me. And now Wylder. Because he's a selfish piece of shit. I'm allowed to call him that because as I, too, am a selfish piece of shit when it comes to our parents and wasting their money, I can recognize the problem.

"I'm going to come by and help you cancel it and reset everything back up, but I'll be a few days. In the meantime, how much do you need to cover what he took?"

"We can't ask you again. We know you're tight on money, too, with taking the internship."

It hurts to hear him say internship like it's a dirty word. Like it's a note of my failure to be good enough for my dream and having to settle for ... this. But it's the only way I can set myself up, and them, for a financially stable future. I could've tried for a higher-paying job for now, but then I would forever be paying off debts. Once I'm an agent, and if I can sign big clients, I'll be able to support my parents to retire immediately. I'm playing the long game.

I was already going to be short on rent this month, so I guess I'm not eating now either. I'll figure it out. Worst-case scenario, I ask my roommates for help. Though, they're as broke as me, mostly.

I glance back out into the living room, where Brady and Kelley are playing. I could ask Brady for a loan, but that's probably even more unprofessional than sleeping with a client.

Brady's not my friend. He's my coworker.

If I was going to ask him, I may as well ask Damon for an

Thad

advance on my meagre salary, and no way in fuck is that going to happen. Like I told Kelley, I don't want attention on me. I just want to get the job done, get paid, and then keep my private life and work life separate.

"How much?" I ask again. I'm scared to hear the answer.

"We'll talk about it when you're here," Dad says.

Maybe make that two months without rent or food.

I have no idea what I'm going to do.

I'm frustrated, and not only about the Wylder thing. Sure, that's the source of it, but along with stressing about money, I also can't get anywhere near Kelley again because Brady is always here.

It's like my skin is too tight for my body and I'm going to explode. I'm fidgety, can't sit still, and doing absolutely nothing out here isn't helping. Kelley's need to look at his phone has died down, and as cocky as it is to say, it happened to coincide with the amazing dicking down. Coincidence? I don't believe in those. But my point is, I don't think he needs two babysitters anymore. Yet, I don't have the guts to ask if I can go home early because how will that look? To Damon and to Kelley.

Having sex with Kelley was never going to turn into anything, but if I leave now, I just know Kelley is going to think it's about him or what we did, or hell, he might even jump to the conclusion that I'm eager to sell the story to a tabloid. And if I tell him about my money situation, he'll think I'm trying to blackmail him.

So, I do the only thing I can think to do in this moment, which is get out of this cabin.

"I'm going for a walk," I announce like it's big news. "I can't sit around here anymore. Is it hot in here? It feels like it's hot." I pull at the collar of my shirt and head for the coatrack where all our jackets, scarfs, and warmer layers hang.

"Are you okay?" Brady asks. They're still playing Scrabble, which isn't helping my sense of helplessness and time wasting.

Chapter 13

"Need some fresh air."

"In this weather?" Brady asks.

There's been a cold front moving in, making outside as cold as the Antarctic.

Brady and Kelley look at each other with the same furrowed brow.

"Is ... is this about the phone call with your mom?" Kelley asks.

He shouldn't have because it sets my frustration even more on edge, and I fear I'm not going to be able to contain it much longer.

"That's my business," I snap.

I hate myself for it the second the words fall out of my mouth.

Brady slumps. "And just when I thought we were all starting to get along."

"Not my business," Kelley says, surprisingly confident. "Got it. Have fun freezing to death for some fresh air."

His snarky remark makes me pause because it was so unexpected. Hell, it even makes me smile.

I have no clue what that says about me, but with one clapback, some of that tension building inside me fades. I turn to him. "Want to come freeze to death with me? I promise not to push you into the river."

"Yeah, because he can't," Brady says. "It's frozen over. I wouldn't trust it though. He could throw you into a bear cave."

"Come on, all of us could go. We could make it a bonding experience." Yes, my tone is laced with fake, sarcastic enthusiasm, but I'm hoping at least Kelley will know I really want him with me and that I won't throw him in a bear cave or drown him in a frozen river.

Outside in the snow might not be the alone time we wanted, but I can make anything work. Maybe an orgasm will at least settle my frustration until I can get back to Trenton to deal with my family drama. If we can't find a place for that, even talking to Kelley might help. The more I learn about him and vice versa, the more we find in common.

He'd understand if I were willing to talk about the money situation, but it's not something I want to put on him or make him

Thad

question my motives. A lesson we both probably learned when we were young is people think you're asking for money when all you want to do is vent about not having any, but I don't want to risk his anxiety telling him differently.

"I really wouldn't trust him now," Brady says, louder this time. "But if you two want to go do that, I should really check in with the office. Give Uncle Damon the update of an impending murder and all that." He grins.

"You want to call your boyfriend, don't you?" Kelley asks and then dramatically sighs. "Fine. I know where I'm not wanted."

I don't miss that he didn't even let Brady answer him.

"It's a sad day when I'm the option you choose to go somewhere you're wanted." I'm testing the waters. Is he going to play, or will he go crawling back into his shell?

"Right? No love here at all."

I let out a breath of relief that he's still his energetic, playful self I've only seen glimpses of so far. If I can bring him out of that shell as many times as possible while I'm here, maybe I have the chops to be a sports agent after all.

It wouldn't be the most conventional method of being there for a client, but maybe I could ask Damon if he needs a fluffer, like they have in porn. I have sex with all the clients while other people reap the benefits.

With where my thoughts are headed, I really should get that fresh air before I resort myself to whoring. I'll make that my backup plan to my backup plan.

I get my boots on as Kelley finishes layering up.

"Where we walking to?" he asks.

"I just need to move around. Is it possible to get cabin fever in only a week and a bit?"

We walk outside and are welcomed by a blast of icy air to the face.

"Jesus fuck," I whisper.

"This was your idea," Kelley points out.

"I know."

Chapter 13

We walk through the snow, ice crunching under our boots.

"So what's really going on?" Kelley asks.

"I was hoping to drag you out here so I could have my way with you, but it's so cold out I don't think my balls are outside of my body anymore. Is it possible for a dick to be an innie? Like belly buttons? Mine's heading that way."

Kelley laughs. "We should've kicked Brady out and told him to go for one of his 'walks.'"

"Only problem is he admitted he wasn't really walking."

"True. Damn it."

The snow-covered path that leads between all the cabins acts like a damn wind tunnel, but as we come to the side of the main house where they serve breakfast and you can order food, the breeze dies.

"Let's stop here for a second," I say.

Kelley smiles. "Because it's so much warmer?" His teeth are practically chattering.

"Yes."

"Seeing as there is no possible way to get our dicks out here, want to talk about whatever has you so uptight?"

Yes. "No. It's nothing. More brother drama."

"Ah, so it's your brother who is in trouble. Last time I tried to ask about it, you practically bit my head off. All I caught was that you needed to send your mom some money."

I scoff. "Yeah, same shit, different day, but I don't want to put any of that on you. You already have enough to deal with up here." I tap the side of my head. "You don't need my baggage added to it."

"You know one good thing about my anxiety?"

"What's that?"

"When it has nothing to do with me, I can actually empathize with people. Hell, it makes me feel not so alone to see others struggling with their own issues. Sure, sometimes it can make guilt creep in—that I'm getting upset over things like online comments when others are going through real problems—but all in all, it gives me a good ear if you do want to talk to someone about it."

Thad

He's surprisingly sweet, so much so that it catches me off guard when my eyes start to water.

Nothing's going to plan, and worse, it's all going to shit. I thought the pressure of baseball was hard enough; now, I have the pressure of doing a good job in a position I originally didn't want.

I keep waiting for that resentment toward baseball to subside. For me to fall in love with the game again through my clients. I'm not sure I can do it.

But I have to. Especially now because Wylder has put all this financial pressure on Mom and Dad, which I feel obligated to cover because the reason their house isn't paid off by now is because of me.

"You have no idea how much that means to me," I say.

"But you're not going to take me up on the offer." It's a statement because he knows it's true.

"Just like me hating you for having baseball, this is something I need to get over myself."

"Having sex helped with that. I don't suppose that would help with your family problems too?"

"Having sex with you or having sex with my family? Because I might need to ask if you're okay now."

"With me. You're the one who took it to a gross place."

I screw up my face. "A very gross place. And if we had somewhere to get naked, it would be a no-brainer. I have no idea if it would help with my family problems, but it can't hurt to try."

"So let's find a place." Kelley steps closer to me and looks up at me through his full lashes.

I move in closer too, determined not to touch him, only tease, but I almost slip on some ice, so that plan goes out the window, and he ends up backed against the side of the main house with me closing him in. "Mm, this isn't what I intended to do, but I can't say I hate where we ended up."

Kelley pats my chest. "Here is definitely not the place."

I want to argue it's out of the wind, and the whole resort is deserted, so no one's going to see if we have our hands down each other's pants, but as if the universe is determined to prove me

Chapter 13

wrong at every turn, the sound of footsteps coming around the corner makes me pull away.

"See?" Kelley turns and starts heading back up the road.

"Where are you going?"

"I told you. To find somewhere."

I trail after him like a puppy.

Chapter 14
Kelley

Short of paying for a room—which I can't pay for because all my money is on my phone—I run out of ideas really quickly. But Thad and I are also running out of time to make each other come again.

Having it only be that one time could make it special, but fuck that fairy-tale bullshit. I don't want to be the person holding on to a memory of one night with the perfect man. Give me the perfect man as many times and in as many ways as I can get it.

Which is how I find myself desperately pulling Thad inside the boathouse down by the river, which is packed with summer equipment, kayaks, and river toys that haven't been touched in a long time.

Me too, buoys, me too. Not counting the other day with Thad.

I have years to make up for, and it's not going to happen with Brady overseeing every move we make. And after my kitchen stunt where I took Thad's phone, I don't think Brady would trust me asking to be left alone with him. I can't exactly say, "Don't worry, it's because I'm desperate for his dick, not his phone."

Hell, I'm desperate for any part of him. His hands, his mouth—I'd love to have another turn of his ass, but that's not going to happen in here.

He glances around the small shack. "I think this is the most romantic place I've ever had the chance to orgasm. Ooh, look, a

Chapter 14

smelly bucket that smells like fish guts. I'm the luckiest man in the world."

"Sorry, should I have brought you flowers that aren't in bloom and light candles that I don't have in a wooden shed?"

Thad gets this look in his eyes, and I've only seen it a couple of times, but it takes my breath away. It's like he has this inside joke that only I'm in on. And even though I have no idea what it means or what that inside joke is, all I know is it gives me a warm and fuzzy swoop in my gut. It's not like he's laughing at me but laughing with me. At a joke I don't understand.

"This is perfect," he says.

He backs me up until I'm pressed against some shelving, and we find ourselves in the same position as we were up at the main house. He's blocking me in where I can't move, but I don't want to anyway.

"I wish I had the patience and the supplies to turn you around and fuck you against these shelves, but it's also way too cold." He lifts his hand and bites down on his glove, pulling it off and then shoving it into his jacket pocket.

While it's a hell of a lot warmer in here—the space is small and unventilated—he's right when he says it's still cold. Or it could be that we haven't warmed up enough yet.

Either way, wherever he's going with this, I'm on board. I just want him to touch me.

My hands stay by my side, even if I'm itching to reach for him, to wrap my arms around him and pull his body against mine completely. My desire to see where he's taking this is stronger though.

He unzips my jacket but leaves it on so I can stay warm. Then he moves on to the button on my pants and slowly unzips my fly. I have long thermal underwear underneath, so he pulls my pants down over my hips and ass. My shirt rides up, and the small of my back hits the metal shelving. I wince, pushing my hips forward to get away from the cold, but that only makes my cock brush against Thad's hand.

He chuckles. "Impatient?"

"No. Well, yes, but no, the back of my shirt rode up and reminded me how cold everything is."

"What, you're not willing to risk frostbite for me? I'm disappointed."

"Maybe if you showed me what I'm risking it for, I might be more inclined to ignore the pain."

Thad's fingers trail under my shirt, splaying out over my abs and completely ignoring my dick, which is trying to escape my underwear.

His hand dips lower and lower, palming my erection over the warm material. "You're already leaking for me."

I swallow hard, suddenly experiencing a last-minute bout of self-consciousness. But with the words that come out of his mouth next, it disappears as quickly as it came.

"I want to taste you." Thad drops to his knees, and I have to grip the shelf behind me to steady myself.

My legs threaten to buckle as I hover above him. The sight of him on the floor, his mouth so close to my cock, I'm not so sure I could survive a blowjob from Thad. I sure as fuck am gonna try though.

Because that mouth ... His bottom lip is plumper than the top one, disproportionately so, but all it makes me think is how sexy they'll be wrapped around my cock.

Thad doesn't take his eyes off me as he lowers my underwear so the waistband sits under my balls.

The frigid air doesn't exist in here anymore. Not with the heat radiating from Thad. From his skin to his warm breath, I no longer feel the cold. Only the fire from his lust.

He licks his lips, and it's as if time has slowed right down because I swear I've had my cock out for at least five minutes now. In reality, it's probably been fifteen seconds.

Thad makes me impatient.

When he finally closes his mouth over me, just around my tip, and he licks over my slit, my legs tremble even more. For a moment, I think I've come, some weird ninja orgasm sneaking up on me, but I'm still hard as a rock and needy for more.

Chapter 14

Thad groans, and when he releases me, a string of precum follows. "You have the best cock I've ever had in my mouth."

I want to take that as a compliment, but all it does is make me think about how many other cocks he's had in his mouth, which makes me think of comparing and not measuring up, and fuck. Oh fuck, no. Don't start getting in my head now.

I close my eyes and silently chant to myself to get back in the moment, but it's either not that silent, or I'm obviously so checked out mentally that it's physically noticeable because Thad doesn't go back to sucking my dick.

His long fingers wrap around my shaft, and he says in the sexiest rasp I've ever heard, "Kelley?"

My eyes fly open, and I gaze down at him.

"Keep your eyes on me and trust that I'm everything you need right now."

I'm locked in his stare.

"I'm your safe place. Somewhere you can be yourself and take what you need. So, what do you need?"

"You."

He keeps stroking me with his hand—a painfully slow but sensual stroke—while his shoulders shake with small laughter I can't hear. Not that I can hear much over the heartbeat echoing in my ears. "You might need to be more specific."

"I need your mouth."

"Do you want it soft, or do you want me to take you deep to the back of my throat?"

Jesus Christ, I can't think. Not like this. I throw my head back.

"Nuh-uh. Look at me," Thad orders.

The first time we hooked up, we switched between being in control and being the follower, but I guess Thad wants all the power this time. Who am I to deny a man what he wants?

Our eyes lock, and for a moment, I'm frozen, staring into icy blue eyes I have no reason to trust but do anyway because he's right. He is the only person I can trust with this. The only person who lets me take those self-preservation walls down and let go.

I should probably feel guilty for using him like this, but it's not like he's not getting anything out of the deal. It's the perfect exchange.

He's perfect.

And just when I think he can't get any more perfect, he says something I've only ever heard in porn.

"You want to fuck my face?"

I swear I almost come on the spot.

Chapter 15
Thad

Kelley is the sexiest when he's flustered. Not the kind of anxious fluster he gets when he's reading stuff he shouldn't be online, but like this. His hairline is about to eat his eyebrows, but I can see the affirmative glimmer in the way he's still staring down at me. His hands white-knuckle the shelf behind him, and his lips are parted, but no sound is coming out.

I stroke his cock some more, loving how with every pass, Kelley's eyelids flutter. "You want my mouth? You want me to deep-throat you until my eyes water and I can barely breathe?"

Kelley's lip trembles, like he's trying to say yes but isn't confident enough.

The other night, he had no problem asking for what he wanted. But that was when it came to things he wanted me to do to him. Not this. Not asking to do something to me.

"You don't even have to say yes," I tell him. "Just grip the back of my head and let me do this for you."

Pfft. For him. Sure. Technically, it is, but I wasn't lying when I said he has the best cock I've ever had in my mouth. He's long but not too long. Thick but not too thick. He's the perfect size to blow him confidently without worrying about getting lockjaw.

Some guys don't like giving blowjobs, and while I love when I'm on the receiving end of one, giving is a whole other experience.

Thad

It's a trip being in such a submissive position but holding all the power.

It's my mouth that can drive a man to the point of orgasm only to back off and make him come when I want him to. Watching that fraying thread of control get thinner and thinner until something snaps is the hottest thing ever in my eyes. I associate the taste of desperation with the salty taste of cum, and knowing I can drive someone to become so desperate, so needy, that they come down my throat, it's so easy to get too worked up over it. I swear my cock is the most sensitive after I've given a blowjob.

Kelley looks like he's about to snap, and I don't even have my mouth on him.

"Do it," I encourage.

He still doesn't give me the words, but he does release one hand from the shelf and run his fingers through my hair. It's gentle, but when I lower my head, moving my lips closer to his cock, his grip tightens, and he pulls my hair back.

My scalp stings in the best possible way. I don't have a pain kink. In fact, I usually hate all other kinds of pain during sex. Not into spanking or paddling. Some guys like the sting during anal, but nope, not me. If I'm not prepped fully, there's no way a dick is getting in there. But this? A hand wrapped in my hair to control my head while they face fuck me?

I whine and have to press down on my aching cock. Somehow, he's given all his desperation to me, and now I'm practically begging for it.

My mouth is open, waiting, ready, and he's taking his sweet-ass time.

Kelley finally surges forward, the swollen head of his cock reaching my lips but Kelley holding me back just enough that I can't close my mouth over him. He grips the base of his dick and guides the tip over my bottom lip.

Nrgh. I'm supposed to be driving him wild, not the other way around.

As if getting the courage, or perhaps he simply can't hold out anymore, he pushes inside my mouth, and it's as if we both lose the

Chapter 15

tension in our bodies. I melt in relief, even though I'm still so pent up.

Kelley pulls back out to the tip and thrusts forward again, this time deeper. He keeps doing that, sinking further and further each time but not pulling out as far, and then with one last surge, he buries himself to the root, and his tip greets my tonsils with a warm hello.

He stays there, pausing for a second, and I remind myself to breathe through my nose and relax my throat.

His body says it wants to unleash on me and go wild, while his eyes say he doesn't want to hurt me. Or maybe screw it up somehow. I don't want to pull off him to tell him to go for it, but I don't want him drowning in his head either.

So for the first time since getting to my knees, I break eye contact with him, rest my head on his lower abdomen, and reach behind him to grip his ass cheeks through his base layer. My fingers dig into the material and push him forward, forcing him to move inside me. It only takes a few times of me doing that for us to get a rhythm that works and for Kelley to take over.

That's when it happens. When he lets go of his insecurities and becomes his true self. This unrestrained, confident guy who fucks like a beast and doesn't hold back.

His thrusts become so fast and shallow that I have to keep grip of his ass in fear of him pushing me over with the force of his cock.

That would be the worst superhero side effect ever. "I'm so strong, every time I get a blowjob, I break their neck with my cock."

Poor superheroes.

Kelley's breathing kicks up, and with every thrust, every bump to the roof of my mouth and throat, I'm confident he's ready to spill over, but he doesn't. He keeps going, and the longer he holds out, the more desperate I become. I'm tempted to shove my hand in my jeans and jerk off. I'd probably beat Kelley to coming. But I'm too preoccupied with his cock and the way he grunts while he fucks my face with hard, shallow thrusts.

Just when I think I won't be able to take any more before touching myself to relieve some of the neediness simmering under

Thad

my skin, he tenses all over and fills my mouth with the heady flavor that turns me on so much.

I drink him down, licking and sucking while he slows down and draws out his orgasm by moving in and out of me slowly with longer strokes. He's completely clean by the time his cock falls from my mouth.

I look up once again, his warm brown eyes hooded in that way only an orgasm can bring. Like he's blissed-out and completely relaxed. It's a good look on him. One he should try to have more often.

I stand and bring my face close to his. I want to kiss him, but not everyone is into that—tasting themselves on someone's tongue.

"I'll be able to return the favor in a minute," he breathes.

"Cute you think I'm even going to last a minute. All I need is right here." I run my finger under his shirt and up the shape of his cut abs, where the V forms along his hip to his groin.

I undo my jeans, and unlike him, I'm not wearing thermals underneath because I'm a fucking moron.

"You're going commando? No wonder you're cold."

"Dumb move on my part that turns out to be really helpful in this particular situation."

"Want my hand?"

I press against him, my cock hard against his bare skin in that V, and I roll my hips. "Don't need it. You have no idea how close I am just from blowing you."

He pushes his hips forward, creating more friction between our bodies, and I shudder.

"You liked it that much, huh?"

"Loved it." I move against him fluidly now, my hands on his hips and using them to hold our bodies together. "You're so hot, and your cock ... Fuck, your cock. You have no idea. No idea how amazing you taste."

"Show me," he whispers in that unsure tone once again.

"You want me to kiss you?" I thrust against him at a frantic pace.

"Please fucking kiss me," he says more forcefully. Confidently.

Chapter 15

The second our mouths meet, I spill over and cover his abs in my cum. But we don't stop kissing. Don't stop holding each other.

Even when my pulsing dick has calmed down and my warm release starts to go cold, he doesn't stop kissing me.

I didn't plan for this to happen. Especially not with Kelley fucking Afton. But as our mouths keep exploring long after our bodies have come down from their high, I realize I might actually like Kelley.

A lot.

And it really sucks that in only a few more days, we'll leave here and never speak of this again. We can't. Not if I want to keep the job I so desperately need.

As desperate as I am to get Kelley back out into that boat shed or kick Brady out for an hour or two, the chance doesn't happen again. There was talk of extending our stay, but Kelley has obligations he shouldn't put off any longer, and I really have to go fix this Wylder issue with my parents.

Kelley's anxiety has been more settled this last week in the cabin, and he even stopped asking for his phone or trying to sneak mine, so it's time to go back. Even if I don't want it to be.

Somehow, Kelley calls shotgun before I can get in the passenger seat to make our way back to the city, so now I'm in the back, dreading every piece of small talk Kelley and Brady share but not wanting to tune them out because then I'll be left alone with my thoughts. Deciding to have a fresh mindset toward work and clients is a hell of a lot easier than putting it into practice because if I let myself think about where I could be financially had I made it in pro ball, I'd be happy and not forced to hide the bitterness creeping up my spine.

Slowly, I'm understanding Kelley more. He can't control his irrational thoughts the same way I can't keep my bitterness off my

Thad

facial expression. I don't mean for my face to display inside thoughts for everyone to see, but I can't help it.

The two weeks spent with Kelley in the middle of nowhere helped me gain perspective, but suddenly having perspective doesn't mean intrusive thoughts are no longer intrusive. I don't want to hate everything in the world, but there are moments where I just ... do.

Like knowing that once we get closer to Manhattan, I'm going to have to ask for them to drop me at Penn Station so I can go home to Trenton, something I'm not looking forward to.

It's difficult not to feel like a piece of shit when it's my fault my family is pushing bankruptcy. Would Wylder have grown up to be this selfish had Mom and Dad not sunk all their money into me and my potential future? Probably not.

And the guilt I have to carry around because of that makes my body heavy.

"You're quiet back there," Brady says. "Nothing to add?"

Turns out I tuned them out anyway. "Uh, yeah. Weather. It's been so unpredictable, right?" At least, I think they were talking about the weather last time I was paying attention.

Brady laughs. "I don't know how I feel about eating weather for lunch, but if that's what you want—"

"Oh, lunch? I have some things to take care of, so if you two wanted to drop me at the nearest train station, I'll head off and let you two get lunch. Talk business. Whatever."

Kelley refuses to look at me. He even turns away as I talk.

"What do you have to take care of?" Brady asks.

"Personal shit. Family stuff." That's about as detailed as I'm willing to get.

"You're from Trenton, aren't you?"

Fucking Brady. Why does he have to have a good memory?

There's a reason I didn't bring up where I'm from, and it's because—

"You're from Trenton? I can give you a ride home. My car's in the city."

—that.

Chapter 15

Trenton is on the way to Philly, and as much as I'd love to have more alone time with Kelley because road head would be super fun, I'm too in my head trying to come up with a money solution. Plus, I don't trust myself not to blurt everything all over him. This is my problem, not his.

"All good. I really should be getting home as soon as possible."

Now I feel like a dick because he probably thinks I'm blowing him off. I'm not. But babysitting is over, and we need to go back to our real lives now.

Our real lives where he's a famous MLB player and I'm an intern on a meagre salary. We might have a lot in common, but there's a divide when it comes to how we grew up as opposed to how we live now, and it's something I don't want to get into with him.

"So, what am I doing?" Brady asks. "Dropping you at the train station and getting lunch or heading for the city?"

Kelley says at the same time I do, "Train station."

I guess that's that.

I knew it was coming, and it's for the best. It just sucks.

Chapter 16
Kelley

It's nothing against me. We're cool. We're leaving everything casual, and whatever happened at the cabin with us was pure distraction for me. Him refusing to spend more time with me alone has nothing to do with me. Absolutely nothing.

Nothing.

While we were away, Thad's parents called a few times, and each time seemed more dramatic than the last. I couldn't get the full story, but it was always something about money and his brother. It could be that his parents need money for his brother, like maybe medical expenses or something, but he seemed angry at the situation. Not so much at them, but at the context of whatever is wrong.

It's none of my business and all sounds very melodramatic, and yet, I still can't accept that Thad not wanting me to give him a ride to his parents' place has nothing to do with me.

I want to help him the way he helped me, but I can't if I don't know what he needs.

Since being in the Catskills and for this whole car ride, I haven't thought about the internet once. Driving home, by myself with my phone in my possession, I'm worried the desire to look will creep in again, and I've just learned how to ignore that.

Maybe I was offering more for me than for him, but he's made it clear he's not interested.

Chapter 16

So when Brady pulls up to the station, and Thad says, "I'll see you back at the office," to Brady and barely looks at me, all I can do is give him an up-nod goodbye as he slips out the back seat.

Goodbyes are stupid and overrated anyway, and it's not like I'll never see him again. In the year I've been signed to King Sports, I think I've crossed paths with him three times.

I watch Thad's retreating back and realize that a pass by in the office once every four or five months isn't enough. Getting away from real life, escaping Philly, that's not the only thing that has helped me these past two weeks. Thad has helped me more than possibly anything else in the last five years by allowing me to be myself. Allowing me to put my trust in him and not once making me doubt that trust—you know, outside the usual amount of paranoia.

I turn to Brady. "Can I ask you something personal?"

"If you want to know why Thad is an ornery jackass, you'll have to ask him. He doesn't give anyone much other than being bitter over the baseball thing."

"That isn't what I was going to ask, but really? How long have you worked together?" I know more about him than that, and I've only spent two weeks with him.

"He's a first-year intern like myself, though he's full-time. I'm still studying to get my law degree. He chose to skip that step and go straight to working."

"You can choose between those?"

"Yep. I'm following in Damon's footsteps. A law degree isn't required to be an agent, but it does mean you have a good grasp of contract law, and it means you'll start out on a higher salary."

Yet, Thad chose to go full-time, and it sounds like he, or at least his family, has money problems.

"How much does an intern earn?"

Brady scoffs. "You don't want to know. Seriously, if I wasn't living in one of my uncle's houses, I wouldn't be able to afford rent in the city. Actually, my dads would pay for it if I asked. Let me rephrase: if I wasn't born into my family and I was like Thad, I wouldn't survive in New York."

Kelley

"How does Thad manage it?"

Brady purses his lips. "I haven't thought about it. I figured he went to Olmstead, so he probably has money already."

A common misconception, as Thad told me.

"Though, now that I think about it, whenever the team goes out for drinks, he never comes. Everyone thinks he's antisocial and angry at the world, but now I'm wondering if he can't afford to take a turn ordering a round for everyone."

"That's a rule in the office? Even with the interns?" It reminds me of college, where it was the same deal. All these rich kids who had their parents' credit card, and little ol' scholarship me, feeling like I was mooching off my friends.

Luckily, being a sporting school, a lot of my teammates were on scholarships, so they understood, but not everyone did.

"It's not a rule. Just … a courtesy, I guess? Like, when we're going out, it's always 'Teacher's pet gets first round.' Guess who teacher's pet is?"

I smile. "The firm's owner's nephew?"

"Exactly. So, why are you asking?"

Uhhhh. "Like you said. Trying to figure out what makes Thad tick."

"If you get answers, I wouldn't mind knowing too. He's like a book with the pages glued together. You get snippets, but the important parts are hidden, and if you try to rip them open, you get a million paper cuts, and it falls apart to the point you can't read anything anymore."

"That's … an oddly specific analogy."

Brady shrugs. "That's the impression I get. I probably shouldn't be bitching about another coworker to a client. Maybe let's not tell Damon about that."

"I get the impression sending you and Thad with me on what was technically my vacation wasn't exactly normal sports-agent-to-client behavior. I think some bitching is warranted. Especially when Thad's so … so …"

"Like I said, ornery?"

"Yeah," I agree, but that's not him at all. He's private and keeps

Chapter 16

to himself. He is mad at the world, but I think it's more than that. It's like he's mad at himself for not making it.

I can understand that disappointment. I'm terrified every day that my anxiety will start messing with my career. To get this far and then have to say goodbye, I'd say he has a right to be ornery. I would be a wreck.

By the time we've gotten something to eat and reach the King Sports offices where I left my car in their secure parking lot, I've decided I'm going to help Thad. How? I have no idea, but my first order of business is to see Damon King and tell him how amazing both his interns were for me on this trip.

So long as I can manage to do that without it sounding like I've seen one of their dicks. Or fucked his face. Had his dick inside me. None of those things.

Shit, can I do this?

I think of Thad, of how he's helped me, and it no longer matters if I can. I have to.

"You coming up to the office or heading right home?" Brady asks as we get all our crap out of the company car.

"I'm coming up. I want to talk to Damon about having you on my team permanently."

Brady puts his duffle bag over his shoulder. "You don't have to do that now. I'm still an intern, and—"

"I want to. I also want to reassure him that he's raising some great future agents."

"Including Thad? Or are you ratting him out?"

I snort. "I'm not ratting him out. Yes, he was an ass to me in the beginning, but I think we found common ground." *Each other's dicks.* "And weirdly, his blunt nature helped me a lot too. It's like he's the voice of reason I don't have. The one telling me I'm being dramatic and should be more grateful."

"Kelley, you are grateful. Just because you question what you have sometimes, it doesn't mean you're taking it for granted. He's an angry guy—"

"I know I'm grateful. I'm one of the luckiest people in the world to have the career I do. I've worked hard for it, yes, but there

Kelley

are a lot of people who work hard and don't achieve it. On the other side of that though, sometimes I get so far in my head it's easy to forget how grateful I am. And Thad helped me with that."

Brady shuts the trunk. "Maybe don't tell Damon Thad's form of support is tough love. He might not like it. He's more of a 'you have to appease your clients' kind of agent. Though, he'll follow that up with 'even when they're being unreasonable and childlike.'"

I smile. "He was talking about your dads with that one, wasn't he?"

"Definitely. He uses them as an example for a lot of agent issues. Them and hockey players. Hockey players are the worst."

"Good to know."

"Once, Damon had a file labeled NHL Nightmares, and it was all the hockey scenarios that he's had to deal with over the years. Like one client, he had a three-way in an alley, knowing there were surveillance cameras. Because he wanted attention from his PR manager."

"Really?" Who in the fuck is confident enough to pull that off?

"Yup. So Damon and that PR manager had to step in and squash the story. And, to make matters even cuter ... or worse, depending on how you look at it, that PR manager ended up marrying that hockey player."

"What?"

"Yep."

We ride the elevator to the top floor, where it spits us out at reception.

"Oh, and speak of the devil, here's that PR manager now."

I watch as the man I know as Lane Pierce walks by, head in a binder. His dark hair has streaks of gray but has nothing on Damon, who's turning into a full-on silver-daddy type.

"Hi, Lane." Brady waves.

Lane lifts his head. "Hey, Brady."

"Didn't know you were in New York."

"Quick visit to go over some things with your uncle." He spots me. "Kelley. Did we have an appointment?"

Chapter 16

"No. I'm here to see Damon before I head home."

"Oh, right. The, uh, the thing. Catskills thing."

"Yeah. The Catskills thing." Also known as the *Kelley can't be left alone in fear of sending himself into a downward spiral* thing.

"Let me know if you need anything," Lane says. "I just left Damon's office, so

he's free if you need him."

"Thanks," I say.

Lane keeps walking, and I turn to Brady.

"His husband is a hockey player?"

"Yup. Retired now, but he was supposedly this huge playboy with a bad reputation. Lane whipped him into shape."

"Why can I not help thinking you mean literally?"

"After all the things I know about Oskar Voyjik, it wouldn't surprise me if that's how he did it."

"I like the way you're honest with me."

Brady's face falls. "Shit. Now I'm gossiping about actual employees that you need to work with. Maybe Uncle Damon's right. I'm not ready for this job. You shouldn't ask him to—"

"I wasn't being sarcastic. I actually mean it. Yes, Thad has that strong hand, but you ... you manage to put me at ease. You're real with me. And now, when I have to go see Lane, I'll no longer be intimidated by him because what you said makes him more real. Does that make sense?"

"Just don't tell my uncle I'm giving you office gossip."

"Deal."

On the way to Damon's office, Damon exits and pauses when he sees us. "You're back."

"We are," I say. "I was actually hoping to talk to you before I head home."

His eyes narrow, and then he sends a glare at Brady. It's subtle, like a parent scolding a child who is talking or running around during a serious moment, but he's pleasant as he turns his attention to me. "Sure. Come on in."

"It's all good. I promise."

Kelley

Damon holds out his arm for me to go in first, and then he follows. "How was the trip?" he asks.

"Amazing."

"Really? The Catskills in December are amazing?" He leads me over to the couches in his office instead of the desk. I get the impression the desk seats are for employees who are in trouble, and these couches are for clients. More comfortable and inviting.

I sit across from him. "That part was fucking freezing, but the trip was good for me. Mentally."

"Do you think you're ready for real life to set back in? Public appearances, charity benefits, getting ready for spring training?"

"I hope so. I feel good right now. I don't have the urge to ruin my positive mindset by reading horrible comments online, and I'm refreshed."

"Great. So, what did you want to talk to me about?"

"There's a couple of things. The first is that I want you to know that both your interns were great with me while we were away."

"I should hope so."

"Brady is really great. I think he's going to make an amazing agent."

"Okay." There are those narrowing eyes again.

"I want him to be my agent. When he's ready. He said he currently has a client but has to run everything by a senior, and I was hoping he could be the same for me."

Damon lets out a loud breath. "Thank God. I thought you were going to say something like you slept with him, and then I am legally obligated to tell his dads, and then you'd get an over-the-top visit from them, and it would scare you off, and you'd fire this agency. It would be a big mess."

"I can see where Brady gets his dramatics from."

"Brady was dramatic?"

I wave him off. "Nah. Good dramatic. I promise. But yes, I want him to be my agent. I feel like he understands me better than Merek does? Don't get me wrong, though, Merek is a great agent, and he has scored me some incredible contract deals, but ... I'm comfortable with Brady."

Chapter 16

"That's no problem at all. I can throw Brady on your account with Merek supervising."

"Thank you."

"And the other thing?"

"Huh?"

"You said there were a few things you wanted to talk about?"

The voices in my head are yelling at me not to cross personal lines with Thad. Not to bring attention to him in the office. But I want to help, and he's not going to let me in, so this is my only option.

"I just wanted to say that Thad also did an excellent job. While he could never be my agent because, well, his delivery of advice isn't as sugarcoated as I'm used to—"

"I love how diplomatic you're being here, but if you have a problem with him—"

"I don't," I cut him off. "I'm just saying his managing style won't fit me. He's going to become a great agent for someone who's stronger than I am."

"You're not weak for having anxiety, Kelley."

"I know. Theoretically. My brain won't let logic win though. And my point was, is it at all possible for me to give Thad, like, a tip? Or a bonus for doing such a good job while dealing with my breakdowns?"

Damon rubs his chin. "A tip? He's not a waiter. We take his salary out of the commission you pay us."

"I know. I ..." I have to come up with an excuse, and for some stupid reason, all I can think about is the ridiculous he-saw-a-bear excuse. I can't use that here. "I don't want him to feel like he did a poor job because I've put Brady on my team and not him. That's all."

Damon leans back. "You singing his praises is probably more beneficial to him than money is."

Coming from a poor family myself, I can guarantee that's not the case.

"If it's against company policy or whatever, don't worry about it. I was just hoping to do something nice for him. He was really good at getting me out of my head and giving me perspective. I think the reason I've stopped reaching for my phone from muscle memory is because of him."

Damon leans back in his seat and thinks about it. "There's nothing in the company policy that says you can't."

"But you're uncomfortable with it. It's okay. I get it."

"I can't stop you from leaving him something, but it has to come from you and have nothing to do with our firm. I don't want future agents or staff to think if they suck up to clients—which they should be doing anyway—they get bonuses."

"Thank you. I'll do that. I'll leave it and say it was from me. As a thank-you."

"No worries at all."

I stand to leave because I need to find an ATM.

"Can I say ..." Damon stops me.

I look back at him.

"You do seem a lot more relaxed."

Yeah, I can thank Thad for that too.

Orgasms release tension. Who knew?

Chapter 17
Thad

ONRI:

Rent's due.

OUT OF ALL MY ROOMMATES, ONRI IS THE PEDANTIC ONE. His type A personality makes him need to pay bills as soon as they come in, and when it comes to rent, he's adamant it has to be paid the day before, not the day of.

JOSH:

I can get it to you this afternoon.

GUS:

I left it on your dresser this morning.

SEAN:

Transferring it to your bank right now.

Of course, I'm the only one who's going to let them all down.

ME:

I'll have it by tomorrow. I promise.

I still don't know how, but I have to because I can't ask them to cover for me again.

The point of coming into the office this early was to avoid having to tell them I don't have the money. Doesn't make sense,

Thad

considering I'll be back at the loft tonight, but I don't know what I'm going to do. At this point, I might have to sell my ass on a street corner. Though I don't think I could earn enough to cover rent. Who'd pay seventeen hundred bucks for a turn of my ass?

My phone dings, and I expect it to be Onri full-naming me and asking why I like to stress him out, but it's not. It's one of my other roommates in a private message instead of the roommate chat thread.

> GUS:
>
> Need a loan, bro? I had a good week at the club and can cover you.

Gus is a bartender and has the flirting ability to make men and women throw their money at him. Most times, he has to work seven days a week to cover rent, but on the rare occasion, like obviously this week, he has some extra cash to burn, and I could really do with the handout, but my stupid pride has me hesitating. I can't keep taking money from my roommates, who are also struggling financially.

Josh made it onto a high-A Minor League Baseball team in Brooklyn, which is amazing for him, and I probably could have made that league as well, but it seriously pays less than my internship.

Onri is in a similar position to me, an intern at a big corporate company, but for sportscasting.

And Sean, he's a bit lost with what he wants to do with his life, but he's lucky enough to have a small trust fund to live off. He has about enough money to last a year, and he's calling it his gap year, but we're about five months in, and he hasn't done much but play video games and try entry-level jobs at places where he lasts a few weeks before crossing that career path off his murder board. Okay, so he actually calls it a vision board, but I dunno. Looks like one of those crime scene boards detectives use to solve crimes.

I'm still staring at my phone, contemplating taking Gus up on his offer, when Damon walks in and scares the crap out of me.

"You're in early, St. James."

I drop my phone to my desk and probably look like a kid

Chapter 17

getting caught with his hand in the cookie jar. "Early worm and all that."

Damon smiles back at me. "Good work. Can I see you in my office for a moment?"

Oh, fuck.

It's the first time I've been back in the office since I went home to help my parents. It took nearly the whole Friday afternoon to get it all straightened out, and so I stayed that night and didn't come back until Saturday afternoon. We sometimes have to come in on a Saturday because there is always work to be done, files to be filed, and all that runaround bitch work, but we're usually notified ahead of time. I don't think I was supposed to come in on Saturday, but maybe I missed an email.

"You're not in trouble," Damon says, and I swear he's trying to smother a chuckle.

I stand and follow him into his office, more relaxed now but also confused.

"Kelley Afton came to see me on Friday," he says, and I almost trip over my feet. I try to cover it by casually slinking into the seat in front of his desk, but he's still wearing that amused expression that he's trying to squash.

I'm hopeful Kelley didn't break and tell Damon exactly what happened between us, but I'm assuming if he did, Damon wouldn't have said I'm not in trouble. Or maybe he would so he could lull me into a false sense of security because maybe he's a secret sadist and likes to inflict emotional pain on his employees.

Damon takes his seat opposite me and leans back in his seat. "So, I heard he was a bit of a handful in the beginning."

Oh, shit, did Kelley end up filing that complaint about me?

"Uh, he—"

"You don't need to worry," Damon says. "He only had good things to say about you. Well, mostly good."

I swallow thickly. "Mostly?" My heart starts racing.

"He did say that you and him wouldn't be a good fit to work together, but only because you differ in management styles. Players

Thad

like Kelley Afton need a soft hand, and you're more of an old-school kind of agent."

I frown. "Old-school?"

"Tough love," he clarifies.

I rub the back of my neck. "I'd like to think I wasn't entirely a tough-love kind of person to him, but I understand where he's coming from."

"Something you'll learn as you get further into this business is that not everyone is going to be a fit for you. Personality differences can be a major snag in building relationships with clients, but I guarantee that you'll find the right clients for you. It's a matter of figuring out your particular management style and selling that to potential clients. You've been around athletes, so you know that some can have an ego and be sensitive, but I'm sure you also know there are those of us who thrive on being pushed, and if you're going to be that type of agent, you will have plenty of clients to choose from."

Okay, so if I'm understanding this correctly, he's telling me I have the potential to be a good sports agent, just not for Kelley. I'm totally okay with that because Kelley and I already had that discussion, and after the first few days together, it was obvious I could never work for him.

"The other thing Kelley left me with was that he wanted to give you a bonus check for all the help you did give him."

A what?

"Bonus cash, I should say. It's not a check."

"A bonus? Is it normal for clients to do that?"

"It's not usual, no, and I had to inform him that we need to tell you it is from him and not from the company. Under normal circumstances, it might be different, but Kelley Afton isn't a typical client, and if you were his agent, babysitting him for two weeks would never have been part of the deal, so I'm giving some wiggle room here."

It would be wrong to accept this. I don't even know how much cash there is, but it's ethically gray to take it. Even though I'm fucking desperate for money.

Chapter 17

"You don't have to accept it," Damon says, and even though he says that and my gut tells me not to, the thing is ... I think I have to.

"Not going to lie. It makes me somewhat uncomfortable, and I'm not sure why he'd do it when he said himself I'm not a good fit—"

"He did say you helped him immensely. I got the impression he was feeling somewhat guilty over choosing to ask Brady to join his team instead of you."

"He has nothing to feel guilty about. I understood that. But ..." I bite my lip.

"But what?"

"I don't like bringing personal stuff into work. My parents have had some money issues lately, and I've been helping them out, so ... even though it feels wrong, I could really do with that money."

Damon unlocks the top drawer of his desk and pulls out an envelope. A thick-ass envelope. "You can take this. It's yours, and if you're worried I'll think any less of you for taking it, you're wrong. Many others in your position would have taken it, no questions asked. Hell, back when I was an intern, you wouldn't believe the things I did to get ahead."

"Murder other interns?" I ask.

He laughs. "No. Nothing like that. But I once agreed to fake date a guy in exchange for a meeting with his brother-in-law, who happened to be a famous hockey player."

That makes me smile. "No way. What happened?"

"You've met my partner, Maddox, haven't you? He happened. He was my fake date."

Aww, that's actually a really sweet story.

Damon pushes the envelope across the desk. "Take it, and take care of that family of yours."

Hesitantly, I reach for it. "Thank you."

"And if your family is in a lot of trouble, I'd much rather you come to me and ask for an advance on your income or even offer you a loan you can pay back once you're a junior agent. We can work something out."

I don't know why I'm so intimidated around Damon King.

Thad

Sure, he's built this entire sporting empire, but he's an amazing man to work for. "I didn't realize that was a possibility." It had passed through my head, but I didn't want to be looked down on. He's doing anything but judging me right now.

"I'd much rather you put in the extra hours here or sign away some of your future commissions than have to go out and get a second job and get distracted from your goal of making it as an agent."

I nod. "Hopefully, it won't come to needing to take you up on your offer, but I'm grateful for it anyway." I stand. "And thank you for this."

"I'm not the one who needs thanking. I was just the messenger."

Right. I need to thank Kelley somehow.

Damon thinks the money is because of guilt over Kelley not wanting me as his agent, but all I'm thinking about is the way he overheard me talking to my parents. He knows I'm in financial trouble, and if this is some kind of handout for that, I don't want it at all.

Will I take it? I don't really have a choice at this point unless I want to burden my roommates with my issues. But it doesn't mean I like it. Even if I'm touched he wants to help.

Ergh. This money has me all jumbled. It's wrong, but I need it. I don't want it, but I do at the same time.

I get back to my cubicle and open the envelope.

Holy shit.

Holy. Fucking. Shit.

I thought it was so thick because it must have been small bills, but no. They're all crisp hundreds and fifties.

Paranoid, I quickly glance around the still-empty office. I have no idea how much is in there, and no way am I taking it out here to count it, but it's too much. Way too much.

Seeing as Kelley isn't my client, I don't have his contact information on my phone already, but it will be in the database.

I have to more than thank him for this. Or at least send half of it back.

Chapter 17

I pull up his file, and while he has an email address, I'm not so sure who has access to it. It might be the publicist for Philly who checks them.

So I grab the phone number off my screen and just hope it'll be him who answers.

With it still being early and no one in the office, I don't bother going outside to call. It rings out, and I'm frustrated, but it's Kelley. I'm sure he's used to not answering phone calls from unknown numbers. I could use the work phone as he'd know King Sports' number, but it's a bit icky to me and unprofessional. Even though I'm calling him about a professional matter—this bonus is, after all, supposed to be for the help I gave him—I don't feel right about it.

So I settle for text instead and hope that it's his direct number.

ME:
> I don't know whether I should be offended or flattered about the "bonus" you gave my boss to give to me.

I really want to say it makes me feel like an expensive whore, but again, I can't be sure this message is going direct to him. Also, I wouldn't mean that in a negative way. Turns out, I might have found that someone who would be willing to fork over seventeen hundred dollars for my ass and then some. I really should be more offended than I am.

When my phone starts ringing a second later with his number, my gut swoops, and my heart flutters.

I can't help smiling as I hit Answer.

Chapter 18
Kelley

I knew I shouldn't have left the money. Or so much of it. But I wanted to help, not make him feel bad. I panic when I read his message, and now, as the phone rings, my heart is in my ass. And as soon as the phone clicks over, I don't give him a chance to speak.

"I'm sorry, I'm sorry, I'm sorry."

There's a small laugh, and thankfully, he doesn't sound too pissed. "You don't need to be sorry."

"Wait, what?" I sit up in my bed, where I haven't bothered to get up for the day yet. I have this charity thing I have to go to tonight, and I really don't want to. When I came out, I was hoping to do this stuff with a partner or at least a date, but I'm still not comfortable with the scrutiny that will come with taking a man to one of these things.

Thad's voice is soft and warm as he says, "I appreciate the gesture, I really do, but it's way too much."

"It would have been more if my bank had allowed me to take more in one transaction," I mumble.

"I don't want to accept it—"

"Please do. You have no idea what you did for me while we were away."

The smile on his face is evident in his tone. "I have a pretty good memory of exactly what I did for you." He hesitates before

Chapter 18

lowering his voice. "And I thought about it all weekend. Do you know how awkward it is being hard around your parents twenty-four seven?"

Parents? He was there all weekend, only half an hour away from me? It kinda hurts he didn't let me drive him there on Friday, but I assume he had his reasons, and I keep telling myself it wasn't because of me, even though deep down, I think it was.

"I don't know what's going on with them or with you, but you should keep the money to help them. I know they're in some kind of financial difficulty, and you don't have to tell me what, but please let me help you." I can't believe I have to beg someone to accept ten thousand dollars. "I know what it's like to go without. Growing up, my family struggled. I relied on scholarships and handouts to get where I am. Let me—"

"If you let me finish ..." Thad laughs again, his voice like silk. "I don't want to accept it, but I'm not really in a position not to. Maybe one day, when I make it to junior agent, I'll be able to pay you back—"

"It's not a loan. It's a gift."

"I'd feel more comfortable if it were a loan. If it's a gift, it makes me feel like a whore."

"Shit. I didn't think of that. Oh God, I am literally treating you like a whore." I gasp. "I'm the worst."

"Don't think like that. You are not the worst. You're actually really sweet and thoughtful, and you have no idea how much I appreciate this, even if I don't like it."

"Okay, it's a loan, then." I'll do anything to make him feel better about it. "Pay it back to me whenever you can. There's no rush and no interest."

"When I sign my first big client and I get them a deal where my commission can cover it, you're getting it back."

"Deal."

The line goes silent for a beat, like it always does before someone says, "*Anyway, nice chat, talk later, bye.*"

I cling to the desperation of keeping him on the line, so I, being the really smooth person that I am, say, "Did you get that rain in

Kelley

Trenton on the weekend? It was that annoying drizzle where it wasn't enough to make the excuse to stay home but was miserable if you were out. Which I was. I had a press conference thing for this event that I'm going to tonight."

"Yeah, it was raining at Mom and Dad's too. Thought it might have been trying to snow but just couldn't get there."

More silence.

And I've run out of things to say. Which is so ridiculous, considering I've talked to Thad about things I haven't ever spoken about to anyone. Though those conversations were more about the type of sex I was too scared to have for fear of it getting out. Not everyday shit.

I'm about to give up and tell him I have to go, even though I don't want to hang up the phone, when he beats me to talking first.

"My younger brother stole money from our parents to fund his lifestyle where he doesn't have to work a proper job. He's changed his number, fucked off to California somewhere, and because my parents are the sweetest people on Earth, they refuse to call the cops or to cancel their card, so I've been keeping their head above water financially."

I don't think I took a breath the entire time he was speaking. "That's ... shit. That's heavy. They really won't cancel their card?"

"I managed to convince them while I was there to do it. They say they didn't want to cancel it because they have bills come directly out of it, and they're getting older, so technology isn't nice to them, but I know they feel guilty about Wylder."

"Guilty why?"

"Because when we were growing up, Wylder was the artistic one, and I was the sporty one. Mom and Dad worked their asses off to get me everything I needed for baseball, and Wylder was overlooked. They feel guilty for neglecting Wylder, I feel guilty for wasting all their money after not even making it to the minors, and Wylder feels guilty for nothing, evidently. Not even stealing Mom and Dad's money. I don't like talking about it because it makes me relive that failure and guilt over and over again. That's why I was snappy when you tried to ask about it."

Chapter 18

"I'm sorry I pried. And I'm sorry you're going through that. Do you need more money? I can send—"

"Don't you dare throw more money at me. What you've given me is more than enough to cover what I gave them and then some. I can pay back my roommates for the times they've helped me out, and I might even be able to get a few months ahead on rent. I'm guessing. I don't actually know how much is in there. I'm scared of getting mugged in the office."

I hope he's joking. It sounds like he is.

Thad giving me this, something real about him, it makes me want to see him again. But how would that even work? He's in New York, I'm in Philly. I'm not comfortable being seen with men in public yet, and he works for the sports agency I'm signed with.

But that doesn't mean we can't be friends. Right?

"Do you visit your parents often?" I ask.

"Not as much as I should. Why's that?"

"I was thinking next time you were in my part of the country, maybe we could go out. Or catch up. I mean, see each other." I grunt. "Why does this sound like I'm asking you on a date? I'm trying to hang out. Uh, with you."

"You miss me already? I thought you would've been glad to be rid of me. According to Damon, I gave you too much tough love. But after what happened in that boat shed, I think we can agree it was the other way around, wasn't it?"

I groan and have to push down on my growing cock. "I take it back. I don't want to hang out with you."

"Aww, why not?"

"Because you're way too good at turning me on," I say quietly.

Thad sighs. "And I really wish the office wasn't filling up with people right now."

"It's probably best we don't see each other again."

"It could make things messy," he agrees. Damn it. I was hoping he might have said screw it, let's fuck again.

"Just clarifying, messy is a bad thing, isn't it?" I really need to make sure.

"It is. I need to focus on work and becoming an agent so I can pay a certain baseball player back. You need to be the person you came out to be. You should be dating and embracing being an out public figure. Wait, how's your social media addiction going? Because you shouldn't be taking those steps if you're still checking your phone."

"I can proudly say that I've been cured of my curiosity." Sort of.

"Why don't I believe you completely?"

"I didn't realize I was that transparent. I haven't looked. I've been tempted, but ..." I don't know if I should admit this or not. "When I think about what those comments could possibly say, I think about our time at the cabin." How good he made me feel. How secure. "I didn't need validation from the outside world. I didn't need validation from anyone. I got to be myself. And you did that for me."

"So what I'm hearing is, I'm basically your hero, and you're obsessed with me. The money makes so much more sense now."

"Then you go and say something like that. I'm glad we've decided we shouldn't see each other again. I'm not sure you could hold your head up with how big it is."

"You're the one with the ego here," he teases. "I'm actually *that* awesome."

I laugh. "I've heard delusion is good for mental health. Must be why you don't need a therapist."

"That's the thing about delusion. The people who have it don't realize they need therapy."

"Ah, ignorance. I wish I knew what that was like."

"It's fun. I'm perfect."

Somehow, I think that might actually be true.

"I should get to work, though, before my boss begins to think otherwise."

I still don't want to stop talking. Especially knowing we've agreed not to pursue this any further. Apparently not even friendship.

"I'll let you go," I say. Reluctantly.

Chapter 18

"But hey, if you ever need someone to talk you down from going online, I'm your man. Or Brady, if you need a softer hand."

"If I'm ever in need of some tough love, I'll go directly to you."

"Take care," he says and ends the call.

There's a text that must have come through while we were talking, and it's from the team's publicist, asking if I have a date lined up for tonight, even though I told her I wouldn't.

I wish I could ask Thad but know it's not a possibility.

Thinking about what he said though—that I should start living the life I came out to have—I think I do need to find someone. Rip off the Band-Aid. Get a date out of the way.

I hit Reply to Solene and say:

> I don't. You wouldn't happen to know any cute, single gay guys, would you?

As soon as I hit Send, my anxiety spikes to an eight. Anything over an eight, I can't come back from, but this? This I can manage.

Worst-case scenario, we go, he's a horrible person, everyone slams me in the media and comments, and I have the worst night ever.

Best case? I might meet someone who interests me half as much as Thad does.

I can only hope.

Chapter 19
Thad

As winter turns to spring and I sink into my role further at King Sports, I take notice of the full-fledged agents I'm shadowing. I proof their reports and contracts, fetch their coffee, and observe how they are with their clients. Nearly all of them adjust their persona, or tact, to suit each need of that specific client.

Damon says that I must have an old-school technique because of how I treated Kelley, but I'm learning that if I want to be successful in this industry, I'm going to need to set my personal opinions aside and be a chameleon. Like Damon said, I will find plenty of clients who will like my way, but there will be those who don't fit. And if I can't budge or adapt even at all? My pool of possible clients becomes smaller than those who can adapt.

Like Brady.

We're both still interns and will be for a few more months until summer's here, and that's when we're supposed to find out if we're good enough to become junior agents or not. He's a shoo-in, not only because he's the boss's nephew but because he's already scored himself two clients.

He reps a practice-squad quarterback for Chicago and Kelley.

I wish I could say I'm happy about our talk and that I felt good leaving things the way we did, but I don't. Not because those things aren't true, but because the second we decided not to take things further, he shows up to a fundraising event that very night

Chapter 19

with some guy on his arm. And not any random guy but a recently out NASCAR driver who's small and petite and as pretty as a fucking flower. And okay, maybe he wasn't super small, but he was compared to me. Next to Kelley in the press photos for the event, they actually looked really good next to one another.

They fit.

Stupid good-looking motherfuckers finding each other.

I'm not bitter about it at all. I have wondered—ever since the event happened—if he already had that date planned and was testing the waters with me to see if I'd be pissed. Even if we spent two weeks together and shared orgasms, I wouldn't have the right to be pissed. It's not like he could've asked me to the event, but if we had agreed to see each other again, would he have taken Jeremiah Castleberry as his date?

What kind of name is Jeremiah Castleberry anyway? Probably a redneck from a hick state, and—I cut myself off from thinking derogatory things about someone because of their name. I, of all people, know names don't mean shit when it comes to social status.

It's possible I'm a wee bit jealous.

A little.

Okay, a lot.

Even if I have no right to be.

Maybe I wouldn't be so pissy if I'd at least heard from him since then, but I haven't. Not even a text. I'd contemplated sending him a message to wish him luck at spring training, but then I got in my head about Jeremiah seeing it and asking questions, which led to me imagining them in bed together and waking up to a stupid text about spring training and them laughing at how pathetic I am, and goddamn it. Is catastrophizing everything contagious? Is this what it's like to be in Kelley's head twenty-four seven?

It's no longer a mystery why he has issues.

It's not like I've seen any other photos of him with Jeremiah, but that doesn't mean anything. Jeremiah is on the NASCAR circuit, and Kelley's been at spring training. They probably haven't had the chance to see each other again.

Yet, I can't help picturing Jeremiah giving Kelley the same

Thad

sense of freedom that he had with me and Kelley forgetting all about our time together. Did I lower his walls for every man, or does he reserve that for me?

This revolving thought process has been on a loop for months, and when it all started to fade away and I've been super focused on work, my calendar this morning went and screwed it all up. Because there on my schedule is time set aside for a meeting today. With Kelley Afton.

It's the thing that has made all these thoughts come flooding back and how this whole cycle has started again. My heart flip-flops all over the place.

I want to see him. We agreed not to do that though. But what I wouldn't give to run my hand through his dark hair again. See him naked. Do things we promised we wouldn't. Things he probably can't do if he's dating someone.

I need off this hamster wheel.

When Brady arrives and dumps his backpack on his desk next to mine in the bullpen, I wheel my chair closer to his cubicle.

"Dude. Why am I in on this Kelley Afton meeting? Aren't you and Merek his co-agent or whatever you are?"

"You're sitting in on it?" Brady fires up his computer and logs in, receiving all his calendar events for the day. He has a lot more than I do. Sometimes I'm envious of him and how far he's already gotten as an intern, but I have to remember he's worked summers here every year since he was a freshman in college. Hell, he probably did some summers in high school too. It would be easy for people to look from the outside and say he's a nepo baby and is only as far into his career already because of who his uncle is or who his dads are, but I've seen the work he puts into this place, and I've seen how Damon treats him. Sure, they have this casual uncle/nephew banter and teasing that would in no way be appropriate for other employees to have with Damon, but I've also seen how hard Damon can be on Brady. Brady is his protégé, and he will take over this company at some point in his life. Brady needs to be perfect.

And fuck that kind of pressure.

Chapter 19

"Hmm. I bet Damon wants to teach you some sort of lesson."

I cock my head. "Lesson?" I'm suddenly worried that Brady heard me jump out that window all those months ago, that he has known the entire time Kelley and I hooked up, told Damon, and today will be my—

Wait, that doesn't make sense. Why would Damon string me along like that? The second he found out I screwed a client, I'd be out on my ass.

I'm beginning to think I really have caught overthinking from Kelley. The little voice inside my head saying it's more likely that I realize I don't want to screw up the good opportunity I have at King Sports and I actually want it—not just need it—is too rational to me.

"Maybe Kelley told him you were a dick to him for the first few days of the babysitting adventure, and he wants you to personally witness how the professionals do it."

"Kelley did tell him I gave him the tough-love treatment."

Brady snorts. "Man, did he tone that down for you, but I guess you must've done something right for him to refrain from telling Damon you basically called him an egotistical diva."

So yeah. I never told anyone about the bonus, and obviously, neither did Damon, and I can see why he'd keep it secret, but I don't know why I did. Other than it feeling a hell of a lot like prostitution.

"Just sit in the meeting, smile, nod, and look pretty. I'm assuming you're there to observe only," Brady instructs.

Observe. Like I'll be able to do anything else in Kelley's presence.

The thought alone of seeing him walk through those doors makes me jittery. No matter how many times I tell myself that nothing has changed between us, I left him with an open-ended invitation to message me if things got too much, and he hasn't.

So unless my cock really did cure him of mental illness—something I know can't be done—it means he chose not to come to me when he became panicky.

Thad

I need to deal with that. And fast. Because Kelley will be here any minute.

I'm too anxious to remain seated; my knee is bouncing all over the place.

"Why do you look nervous?" Brady asks. "Aww, is wittle Thad scared the big bad Kewwey is going to be a tattletale to Daddy Damon?" He screws up his face. "Eww. I can't believe I just called my uncle Daddy Damon. Excuse me while I go pour bleach in my mouth so I can never say it again."

I stand. "While you go take care of that, I'm going to make coffee." Okay, coffee and then thinking like an agent. Wait ... "Do I make one for everyone? So you, Damon, Merek, me, Kelley? Or will Damon not be there?"

Brady clicks his schedule to enlarge the full details again. "It doesn't say if he'll be in there or not, so make him one anyway. I'll take one for the team and double fist both coffees if I have to."

There's a joke in there about him being good at double fisting, but things have been quiet when it comes to Brady and those two guys. He never talks about his private life, and I get it. I do wish there was a way I could tell him I was cool with whatever that was and that he doesn't have to hide it from me.

Then again, it's not as if I'm confiding in him about Kelley. So that makes us even.

I make the coffees from the espresso machine in the break room. When I started, I barely knew how to make coffee using a coffeepot. Now, after almost a year of fetching coffees for senior agents, I'm a real barista.

Hey, maybe barista can be my backup plan to my backup plan. Sure, my parents will probably lose their house, and I'll be stuck with four roommates forever, even when I'm sixty when all my friends have their own houses and successes, leaving me with the only option but to be that creepy sixty-year-old who lives with college kids.

Okay, I'm spiraling again.

Shake it off, St. James. You can face him. You can be suave and cool and casual. You have not been thinking about him for months.

Chapter 19

You have not been obsessing over what he's up to, who he's with, and if they can fuck him the way I did.

Not. At. All.

As I finish up the coffees, the elevator to the floor dings, echoing in my ears, and even though it could be anyone, it's as if my body knows it's him. My gut swoops, and my hands shake as I wipe down the espresso machine.

Then, I do as I was taught by my many coaches and my dad over the years: shake off all the bullshit and get my head in the game.

I put the five coffees on a tray and head for the conference room, trailing Brady and Merek, who greeted Kelley at reception and ushered him in the right direction. Damon isn't with them, and because Kelley is kind of in between Brady and Merek, I can't see him properly.

I can see his smile as he turns his head to the side, that gorgeously tanned skin, and the single diamond stud in his ear. He throws his head back and laughs as Brady says something, and I could be reading into everything because fuck knows I've been doing that a lot lately, but he seems at ease. Relaxed.

He's a completely different guy than the one who was freaking out in the Catskills in the middle of the snow.

It's not until we're inside the conference room and they're all taking a seat that I get a good look at him. His hair has been shaved close to his skin on the sides with it longer on top. Not a lot. Not even enough to need styling product. His scruff is extra sexy, all dark and ... Ugh. Nope. Not going to check him out.

I have a job to do.

I place the tray of coffee on a sideboard and pick up Kelley's to give our guest the first cup. But as I walk toward him, it's like one of those slow-motion scenes in a movie. Not the ones where two long-lost lovers run toward each other, but more in the something is about to go terribly wrong and you know it's going to end in embarrassment kind of way. Because while I'm focused on Kelley and the way his face lights up as he sees me, I'm not so focused on my feet.

I have to say, for an ex-baseball player, I'm not as quick on the

Thad

reflexes as I once was. So when I trip over the leg of Brady's chair and crash to the ground, it's not only embarrassing for me but for the person I spilled hot coffee all over.

And yup, of course it had to be Kelley.

My future as an agent and possibly a barista has come to a crashing end.

Chapter 20
Kelley

For a quick moment, the world quiets. The room is frozen.

There's a sharp burning pain down my arm and some on my chest and stomach because as I'd turned to greet Thad—sex on legs and still so fucking hot—he fell and covered me in coffee. Coffee that I can only assume is illegal levels of temperature.

The sting only lasts a second longer than the shock before I'm out of my seat and trying to pull my button-down away from my body.

"Shit, fuck," Thad hisses. He comes at me again but is still holding the coffee cup. Which still has stuff in it.

I step back and glance at the mug, which he drops on the ground as soon as he realizes.

"I'm so sorry. That was an accident." The fear in his eyes makes me think he's telling the truth, and I want to believe him, but what the hell, man? "I swear."

Brady and Merek are now out of their seats too.

"I got this," I say to them. "I'm going to go to the bathroom to clean this up." I exit the conference room and head toward the public restrooms on this floor.

Okay, so I know I haven't exactly kept in touch over the last two months, but I didn't think my punishment from him would be third-degree burns.

Kelley

I reach the restroom and start unbuttoning my shirt. I have no hope of salvaging it, but I throw it in the sink and turn the cold water on anyway.

Maybe I should've messaged Thad, but I didn't know if he was only being nice when he said I could contact him or if he actually wanted me to. And considering he never picked up the phone to text or call me, I figured that was that.

We both stepped away. Like we said we would.

But I've wanted to get in contact with him. Especially after going on that date with Mr. Perfect.

Jeremiah Castleberry might be from the sticks, but he's a true Southern gentleman at heart. He comes from one of the richest families in Alabama, and considering his skin color, I can only assume his long line of inherited money came from his ancestors doing not-so-nice things to my ancestors. But that aside, he was raised right, he had manners, and we even had things in common, like wanting to compete in a sport that's inherently homophobic. We had a lot to bond over. And talk about. He was great. Wonderful, even.

So very wonderful.

Wonderfully boring.

There was no spark. He was polite.

Since when do I hate manners?

And the following day, when all those photos surfaced of me and my date, I had an eerie control over my anxiety. It turns out when I don't have the fear of losing something I really care about, I don't have the need to panic. I'm also getting better with the comments. I saw a few that were borderline ignorant and homophobic, but I was able to close down the article and forget about them. Mostly. I didn't dwell on them and obsess, at least. Hooray, progress.

Thad barges into the bathroom behind me. "Let me help you."

Ah. I think I've found the reason Mr. Perfect was perfect on paper but very dull everywhere else. Thad St. James.

Because the second he steps over that threshold and into my space, my body comes alive. Every inch of me.

Chapter 20

He has a wet cloth in his hand, but I drop my shirt in the trash can and try to avoid eye contact with him. If I look into his blue eyes, there's a very good chance I'll offer to get on my knees for him right here and now.

"I don't think my shirt's salvageable, no matter what we do. I don't suppose you have a spare lying around your office or anything?"

Thad looks so mouthwateringly hot in a bright blue suit that I'm sure would make his eyes pop if I had the guts to look at them. He has a dark button-up underneath, and I'm almost tempted to ask for it so I can see his hard muscles again.

As if reading my mind, Thad takes his jacket off and then starts undoing his buttons.

"I didn't mean the one you're wearing." I laugh.

"It's okay. I've got an undershirt too." He strips out of his black shirt and hands it to me, but I'm still staring at his sexy arms as he slips his jacket back on.

I force myself to look away and put my arms through the sleeves of his soft shirt that smells like his cologne. I have no idea what scent it is, but it's strong. Fresh. I might never take this shirt off again. "T-thank you."

"I really am sorry. My feet weren't cooperating, and—"

"It's certainly one way to get my attention. You know, if you wanted to get me alone so badly, you could've asked." The only reason I'm able to fake this confidence is because I still haven't looked at his face.

Thad lets out a loud breath. "I thought you were going to go ballistic on me. We don't see or speak to each other for months, and then the first thing I do when I see you is throw hot coffee all over you."

"You could've reached out to me," I point out as I focus all my attention on trying to do these buttons up.

"I didn't want to step on any NASCAR driver's toes."

I close my eyes and hate my brain once again for convincing me the reason I hadn't heard from Thad is because of me. "Are you telling me the reason you haven't messaged is because of Jeremiah?"

Kelley

I can no longer put it off. I have to look at him. I glance up in time to see his jaw tighten. His eyes are missing the sparkle I'm expecting, but maybe that's a good thing.

"How is good ol' Jeremy?"

I'd like to think he pronounced Jeremiah's name wrong because he's jealous, but I can't decipher his tone. It sounds genuine, but maybe ... "Last I spoke to him, he's doing well."

"Did he treat you nicely?" Thad's teeth are gritted now.

"Very."

"Good. You deserve to be treated with respect."

My heart melts. "Says the man who called me names and yelled at me for being addicted to social media."

Thad rubs his stubbly jaw. "Yes, well, if I recall, I more than made up for that once I knew your situation. I was quick to judge, so sue me."

"That would be a waste of a lawsuit."

"Oh, right. I don't have any money."

I turn serious for a second. "How has all that trouble been?"

"I thought that once Mom and Dad's cards were canceled, Wylder might come running back home, but he hasn't made an appearance yet. He hasn't had access to steal any more money, so things are good. I can't tell you how much I appreciate what you did for me—"

Thad's cut off by the bathroom door opening and Brady sticking his head in. "All good in here? Just wanted to make sure you didn't finish him off and are trying to dump the body."

"Where am I going to dump the body? In a toilet stall?" Thad asks. "Sorry, I forgot my bone saw today."

"Good to know," Brady says. "Damon's waiting." Then he disappears again.

Thad turns back to me. "Sorry. Again. About the coffee."

I smile. "It wasn't so bad." It allowed us to talk privately, so I'm not complaining.

Thad goes to leave the bathroom when I step closer.

"Can we, maybe, go somewhere after this? Get coffee and talk?"

Chapter 20

He hesitates. "You want to risk being around me and another cup of coffee?"

"Lunch, then."

He still looks unsure.

"Just as friends," I say.

"Sure. I could probably swing an early lunch. When do you have to head back to Philly?"

"Not until this afternoon. My first game of the season isn't until tomorrow."

"Lunch, then. After this meeting. Whatever it's about."

"It's about my upcoming season and schedule."

Thad frowns. "Then why was I brought in on it?"

"I don't know, but also, I'm not complaining."

"Even if it made you have a coffee shower?"

"What can I say? Third-degree burns might be worth scoring this shirt." I lift the collar to my nose and love the way Thad's eyes fill with heat. "It smells nice."

He's still staring, momentarily silent until he says, "I'm getting that shirt back, by the way. One day."

"I promise I will return your shirt." Maybe. Possibly. Okay, no, I won't. He doesn't need to know I'm crossing my fingers behind my back.

"Sorry about that," Thad says as we re-enter the conference room. "We're all good now."

I want to argue that my pants are still covered in coffee, but I don't because I don't want Thad to actually get in trouble for this.

"No use crying over spilled milk and whatnot. I do kind of wish I was able to drink my coffee instead of wear it though."

"Here." Thad moves to the tray of coffees. "You can have the one I made for me. It might be too sweet for you, though, as it's got sugar in it."

Kelley

Brady shoves out of his seat. "Why don't you sit, and I'll get Kelley his coffee."

Thad stops in his tracks. "Right. Probably best." He ducks his head and rounds the table so he's sitting opposite to where I was, and his skin is a nice shade of embarrassment pink.

Brady puts the coffee cup on the table in front of where I was sitting, and then he pulls out the chair for me. "I swapped over the seats before you came back in, so there's no coffee on this one."

"Thanks." I take my spot and sip the now only warm coffee. It is sweet compared to what I'm used to, but it's not too bad.

Wearing Thad's shirt, drinking his coffee, it really hasn't been a bad morning at all.

"Thank you for coming in," Damon says. "I thought it might be a good idea for all of us to meet up to discuss the upcoming season and what you might need from us going forward."

I glance at Thad out of the corner of my eye because he doesn't need to be here for that. Not that I want to kick him out, but I'm beginning to worry that Damon might be adding him to my team of agents, and I really don't want that. Not because I don't think he'll be good, but because we have had a personal relationship that shouldn't get mixed up with a professional one.

"And Thad," Damon continues, "you were wanting to see different styles of approach when it comes to clients, so I figured you were already familiar with Kelley, and you could observe how a soft hand can work in an agent's favor."

I let out a relieved breath. He's only sitting in. I can deal with that.

"Of course, maybe rule number one of using a soft hand would be to not throw coffee all over your client, but given you've handed over the literal shirt off your back, I'd say you handled that situation well."

I can't tell if Damon's giving him a serious talking-to or if he's joking. His face is stoic, and damn, Damon King is an intimidating man. But then Brady starts laughing, like he's been trying to contain it and can't.

Damon nudges him.

Chapter 20

"Sorry." Brady holds up his hand. "It's just, they all think you're being serious, and everyone looks scared."

"And this is what I get for working with relatives," Damon grumbles. "Complete undermining."

I relax enough to laugh now too.

"Now, how are you doing with the social media side of things?" Damon asks.

I don't mean to keep looking in Thad's direction, but he's really difficult to stop looking at with how damn attractive he is. Plus, because of him, I think I really do have a firmer grip on this social media problem. "The few weeks in the Catskills were really good for me. It was like a reset. Once I got out of the habitual motion of picking up my phone and navigating to my apps, it's become fairly easy to control what I see and what I don't see. And the stuff I do see, I'm getting better at letting it go."

"That's good to hear, but you let us know if anything changes on that front. We might not be able to lend you our interns all the time, but you could look into hiring a personal assistant."

As much as I'd love someone there to smack my hand every time I did something that might elevate my anxiety, I wouldn't think they'd have much else to do, and then I'd feel ridiculous having someone shadow me all day to make sure I don't touch my phone.

"We'll leave that as a last resort," I say. "I want to do this on my own, and while I'm under no delusion that my anxiety has gone forever, I am in a good headspace at the moment. Spring training was good. The team hasn't changed toward me at all since I came out—minus Cooper, who I've been avoiding since his online rant—and yeah, I'm looking forward to a great season."

And for the most part, I actually believe it.

Chapter 21
Thad

After the meeting with Damon and Merek, Kelley and Brady stay in the conference room to talk possible endorsement deals, charity events, and anything else they need to discuss while I get sent back to my cubicle.

When they're done, it's closer to lunchtime than this morning, so it won't be suspicious if I tell everyone I'm going for lunch. Only thing is, Kelley leaves the conference room and doesn't even look in my direction before heading for the elevators.

We did agree to lunch, didn't we?

Do I get up and follow him?

No sooner does he disappear into the elevator than I get a text.

> Meet me on the corner a block away?

I reply:

> OMW

I stand and pull my suit jacket off the back of my chair, where it's resting. I would've kept it on, considering I'm only in a plain black T-shirt, but it's a pain in the ass to type when the suit is so tight. It's a perfect fit for me while standing. It looks like a second

Chapter 21

skin. But when I have to sit or move, it doesn't work so well in my favor.

"Heading to lunch," I say as Brady gets back to his cubicle next to mine.

He's got his head too far in his tablet to do anything but say, "Have fun."

I get the impression I could have told him I was going to go sacrifice a virgin in the middle of Yankee Stadium and he would've said the same thing.

That weird, envious feeling mixed with dread courses through me again. Brady is so focused, so ... everything I'm not as an agent, and I know Damon says I need to go at my pace and do this the way that fits me, but whenever I see the overachiever that is Brady at work, it makes me feel like I'm not doing enough.

It's inspiring while also crippling.

I head into the elevator and down onto the street, where I find Kelley waiting outside one of the many cafes Midtown has to offer. "You want to go here?" I ask.

"We can go wherever you want," Kelley says. "I was thinking this might be too close to the office, and someone else might see us. It's also why I messaged you to come meet me instead of walking down with you."

I'm about to ask if he's embarrassed to be seen with me, but he catches on too quickly.

"I'm okay with here, but I wasn't sure you'd be. If someone in the office saw us, you might get in trouble or—"

"Here is fine," I say. "Everyone at the firm knows Brady and I babysat you—"

"I love that," he deadpans.

"Sorry, babysit isn't the right word."

"Eh, it kind of is though."

Kelley really is a lot more relaxed today than I've ever seen him, and I'm glad the time away did him good. Or maybe it was spring training that has put a calmness in him that I'm not used to seeing. Or it could be Jeremiah Castleberry's doing, and that thought pisses me off.

Thad

"What I mean is, if anyone from the office sees us, the most they'll suspect is that I'm trying to poach you from Brady, and you and I both know Damon would never allow that."

Kelley laughs. "Especially after you tried to burn me to death. Can't have my agent trying to kill me."

"Wow." I step back. "It's already escalating from spilled coffee to outright attempted murder. I'm worried where the story will go next."

"Well, if we are seen together, it might go from trying to kill me because you hate how I'm so much better at baseball than you to doing it in a jealous rage because you're obsessed with me, and if you can't have me, no one can."

"Ah. Being dramatic is fun." I hold my arm out for him to go in first. "After you."

He takes a step but pauses at the door. "If people see us, they might think that we're involved, and then you really could get in trouble."

"But we're not involved, and you have that boyfriend date person. You know, Jeremy."

"Jeremiah?"

"Yes. That's what I said." Am I so petty that I will forever mispronounce his name? You bet your ass I am.

"We should talk about him," Kelley says.

"Or, we could talk about a much more exciting topic. Like ... colonoscopies. Going to the DMV. Take your pick."

Kelley's smile is bright as he turns on his heel and heads to the counter to order. I grab a deli sandwich and a coffee that I never got the chance to have earlier while he goes for the burger, fries, and a Coke.

We find a table in the back corner, which is actually perfect because there are no windows back here, so if someone from the office were to walk by, they wouldn't be able to see us from the street.

Not that it would be a big deal if they did. I wasn't lying when I said to Kelley that it wouldn't be a problem if someone saw, but at the same time, any gossip is a pain in the ass. Of course, I could

Chapter 21

always say that I wanted to make it up to Kelley after destroying his shirt this morning.

"Are you allowed to eat all those trans fats the day before a game?" I ask.

"What can I say? I'm a rebel."

I chuckle. "You seem like the rebellious type."

"Don't hate me for my diet, but I can pretty much eat whatever I want. Spring training, we did all that healthy, high-protein, muscle-building shit, but I find it next to impossible to eat the amount of calories I burn off while playing."

"I can't help but resent you for that."

"What about you? You can't tell me you don't work out. Not when you look like ..."

My lips twitch. "Like what?"

"Like you have balloons for arm muscles. Steroids are bad for you, you know."

Now, I full-on belly laugh. "No steroid use here. Ever."

"Ah. So high-protein diets work for you, then. Unlike me, where I just get too skinny."

"Did you really ask me to lunch to talk about optimal diets for athletes? Want me to be your personal trainer and nutritionist? Because I gotta say, I'm not really qualified for that."

"N-no." Kelley's brown eyes seem unsure as his focus darts around the small space. "I just ..."

"Just ..." I prompt.

"I'm not dating Jeremiah Castleberry," he blurts.

It's annoying how much my chest swells at hearing that, but I can't help it. Even if it's not my business.

"I'm sorry to hear that." Yeah, right. So, so sorry. "But why did you feel the need to tell me that?"

That carefree Kelley out on the street is gone and is replaced with the unsure, stuttering mess I shared that cabin with. It's fascinating to me how quickly his whole demeanor can change.

"I thought ... well, I mean, no, I didn't think about you. I did, but I didn't need to."

Thad

My forehead creases as I try to work out what he's trying to say. "Are you even speaking English anymore?"

"Last time we spoke, we said we wouldn't see each other, but you gave me the courage to try to see if I could date publicly without freaking out about the media, and so I did that, and Jeremiah was great, but ..."

"But?" Come on, Kelley, you're killing me here.

"He didn't make me feel the way you did."

A sense of satisfaction and smugness fills me to the brim. "So, what I'm hearing is I've broken you for all other men. Got it. I wish I could say I'm sorry, but I'm not."

"Of course that's where you went with that."

"Sorry," I say, but I can't stop smiling.

"You already said you're not sorry."

Oh. Right. "Can you blame me though?"

"I guess not. You certainly set my expectations high."

Damn, if that isn't the biggest compliment I've ever been given by someone.

Of course, I wish it was coming from someone I could actually pursue, but it is what it is.

"So, that's why you invited me to lunch? To tell me how irresistible I am and how life-changing being with me those two times were?"

"Sort of. But, I also ,,, I guess I held back from contacting you sooner because I thought you didn't want to hear from me."

We're such idiots. "I thought you didn't want to hear from me."

"I did. I do. I want to keep in touch. Texts, maybe a cool beverage whenever you're visiting your parents and can meet me somewhere on the border of Jersey and Pennsylvania."

"What, no coffee?"

"No, I think you were right about that. I need to be careful around you."

Funny, I was just thinking the same thing about him but for an entirely different reason.

Chapter 22
Kelley

You know things are dire when you're two runs down, it's the bottom of the ninth, our bases are loaded, and the only available batter left is ... the pitcher.

All I can say is thank fuck I don't have to go out there. Hooray for designated hitters.

Not that I'm terrible at batting, but like most pitchers, when discovering my arm was my golden ticket, I focused mostly on honing that talent. I might not be able to hit a home run, but I could bunt the shit out of any pitch.

Considering we need all three runners to make it past home plate to win this game, a bunt isn't going to cut it. We need a miracle here.

I'm keeping my arm warm in case we manage to get two bodies across that plate and we head for extra innings, but I'm on the edge of my seat watching Zaka move to bat.

I have a baseball in my hand, gripping it tight and then releasing, spinning it in my hand, and doing every other fidgety thing I can think of.

It's the first game of the season, and I'm back in my safe place. Where the outside world doesn't matter, and the only thing important is the scoreboard. Whether we win or lose, baseball season is back.

I'm not going to lie though, walking into spring training was

Kelley

difficult. I didn't know how everyone would look at me, but the majority of my teammates acted like they always did around me. One said it wasn't a shock, considering who my agent was, and he never had a problem before, so he doesn't have a problem now.

Cooper basically ran from the room anytime I entered it, but he didn't say anything overtly to my face about his disapproval. The running away, I can deal with. Not wanting to punch my teammate for being a dick is more difficult.

As long as he stays out of my way, I'll stay out of his.

So no, it doesn't matter if we win or lose this game, but a win would be a nice way to start the season and maybe help us with team bonding. We have a few rookies on the team, and then veteran Frederik Zaka signed as a free agent after playing with Kansas for a couple of seasons. He's an amazing switch-hitter and will be good for the team.

I just hope he can do his thing out there right now.

I almost don't want to look. In fact, as he steps up to the plate, I close my eyes and can't make myself open them again to see it unfold.

There's a laugh beside me, coming from Hunter Berkley, our shortstop. "Worried?"

I smile and open my eyes but make sure I don't look onto the field. I look at him instead. "Terrified. I know in the big scheme of things, our first game doesn't matter, but it starts off the season on a good note, you know?"

"I get it. But you also gotta think that only fifty percent of teams get that first win, and first wins don't mean shit by the time the World Series comes around."

"I know. I just really want this for us." Because if we can win, I can show everyone that I'm doing it. I'm being an out and proud athlete and still succeeding. Sure, their four runs to our two could be put down to me not being able to strike them out, so it's actually my fault we're behind, but it's a team effort. Maybe if Forsling got to the ball quicker, we could've gotten an earlier out. If Hunter here called for the ball to be thrown to third instead of first, maybe that player

Chapter 22

wouldn't have made it across home plate. There's a whole lot of things that could stand in the way of us winning, and it's not entirely on me, but it is entirely on me to show that queer men in sports can win.

It's a lot of unnecessary pressure to put on me and my team, and to some, it's probably not rational because me being on a Major League Baseball team at all shows a level of success, but what I wouldn't have given to have this kind of representation in baseball when I was a scared queer child.

All the players back then who were gay didn't come out until after they had retired, so in my mind, that was what I would have to do. Sure, there have been out players since, but so far, the track record for how many seasons they've stayed after coming out stands at two. There are the "he wasn't good enough" excuses all over the internet, but I can't and couldn't help thinking as I was coming up through Little League that if I came out, I could give myself two seasons until I'd be pushed out.

I don't want that to happen, and I wouldn't have come out during the season break if I wasn't prepared for the reality of it possibly happening, but this win would make me feel better about it all.

As irrational as always, my brain doesn't see facts. It only sees worst-case scenarios. I hate that my anxiety is creeping into baseball in this way when this is supposed to be my safe place, but this has nothing to do with the actual game. It's about what happens outside of it.

The comments, the public opinion, team management's view of me. Is me being gay a liability for them?

This is why I struggle and have been struggling with it all. Brady was able to convince me to come out, and I'm happy that I can be here as my authentic self, but it feels like I've turned up the pressure on my career. Before, I only had to be good. Now, I need to be outstanding.

Irreplaceable.

And if Zaka can't get this done, they're not going to look to him for fault. They're going to look to me for the four runs New York has scored. Not that they'd point it out publicly or to the team, but I know they would be judging.

"You know if he strikes out, this loss wouldn't be your fault, don't you?" Hunter asks.

What, is he a mind reader now?

"Of course I know that. Baseball is a team sport."

He leans in closer. "Then why don't I believe you?"

I slump. "I know we're not going to win every single game we play. I'm not that delusional. But I thought ... that if I could, we could ..."

"Could what?"

"If we could win the first few, maybe the headlines would read Having a Gay Man on Your Team is Good for Your Game."

Hunter laughs until he sees I'm being serious. "Kelley ... that's—"

"Irrational? I know."

"No, it's ridiculous. You know the headline would read Anal Sex Helps Philly Win."

I snort so loud it almost sounds like I'm choking, and I'm met with glares all around. Right. Focus on the game.

I glance back to where Zaka is, poised at the plate, ready for the pitch.

The pitcher winds up, lifting his leg and leaning back, ready to fire this pitch right down the line.

Zaka doesn't swing, and the ball hits the catcher's mitt.

Not a strike. It wasn't over home plate.

God, this is torture.

Hunter bumps me with his shoulder. "In all seriousness though. If we lose, they're not going to blame you for who you sleep with."

As Zaka takes a strike on the next pitch, I have to hope Hunter's right about that, but I wish I had more faith in the media than he does.

Zaka and Skip signal for a bunt because they're trying to kill me. They want Zaka to sacrifice himself and maybe our runner on

Chapter 22

first base for a chance of tying this up? It's not going to be enough. He needs to swing and hit it as hard as he can.

And when he does just that, I can't help it when my hand flies out to catch Hunter's arm in shock. He was told to bunt. He took a risk.

Skip is going to be pissed if this doesn't pay off.

But as we watch the ball go further and further into the outfield, every single person in this dugout holds their breath. It's going, it's going. It has a good chance of getting over the fence. It's—

Caught by their right fielder.

He's out.

Even so, two of our guys have been able to cross the home plate to even the game, and now it's a race to get the ball back to home before our last runner can get there. That third runner being ... Cooper.

"Come on, Coop," I yell. Because I am a bigger person than he is.

The kicker of this whole stressful situation is that when Cooper slides into safe and we win the whole fucking game, I don't feel comfortable in joining the others out on the field and lifting Cooper up into the air.

I waited the whole game for this moment, and I can't even revel in it with the rest of my team. So, I stay behind and celebrate the victory alone. It's as empty as it is lonely.

I head into the locker room first while the others are still celebrating, and I get started on getting out of my gear and cooling down. As I'm standing at my cubby, shirt discarded, cleats and socks gone, my phone vibrates in my gear bag.

I pull it out and can't help smiling at the name that's in the little message preview.

> THAD:
>
> Congrats on your first win. You looked hot out there.

Having him reach out, knowing he was watching me, it takes away some of the sting of this moment where I'm separated from

Kelley

my team's celebrations because of one person's homophobic comments online. So, I reply.

ME:
It was hot out there. Whose idea was it to make the season start going into summer?

THAD:
Not what I meant, but it's good to be humble.

ME:
What makes you think I wasn't fishing for more compliments?

THAD:
Your ass looked amazing.

ME:
Just my ass?

THAD:
Geez, how greedy are you? I couldn't take my eyes off you, and every time the cameras panned elsewhere, I was yelling at my TV for them to go back to you.

Well, shit. That hits me in the feels.

ME:
Okay, now you've made things weird. Why are you so obsessed with me?

THAD:
I can't win with you.

ME:
Yeah, I wouldn't even try with me if I were you.

I hit Send before I can really think about what that might say over text. I mean it like don't try to win, not don't try with me at all. Do try. Please. I quickly type out another message.

Chapter 22

ME:
> I mean, don't try to win. I will always win. But you should try. Uh, with me. Like, messaging me.

THAD:

No, no, I might have to take your first answer. You don't want me to try with you.

ME:
> This isn't the Price is Right. You don't need to accept the first answer.

THAD:

Whatever happened to that game show?

ME:
> What happened to trying with me? Please?

THAD:

Win the next one, and maybe I'll text you again.

ME:
> And if I lose?

THAD:

Then I guess it will be your turn to reach out to me.

Now, that's a win-win situation.

Chapter 23
Thad

THE FOLLOWING WEEK, AS I SETTLE IN WITH ONE OF MY roommates and a beer to watch the next game where Kelley's pitching, I kinda hope Philly loses. It's not that I want Kelley to lose. I want him to be the one to reach out to me first. Even if it's only a quick text thread like we had last night. Even if it's only to say he's tired and is going to bed. I want him to make the first move, and I've given him the perfect opportunity to. You know, if they lose.

I'm a terrible human being.

The coverage opens with commentators spouting their usual bullshit before the game starts. They speculate who looks good this season and note those they think are going to have a tough time. I ignore them until they say Kelley's name.

"He's had a bit of a rocky start."

"Definitely looked shaky anytime he's played."

No, he fucking didn't. He looked good out there. Plus, he's played once. I don't see them picking on the team's other starting pitchers, like when Briar Warrick let in home run after home run yesterday.

The game Kelley has played was good. It wasn't outstanding, but he did really well. He was confident out there, and they won.

These know-it-all wannabes can go touch grass.

"Hey, isn't Kelley that guy your firm reps?" Josh asks.

Chapter 23

"Yep."

"The one you had to babysit?"

"Yep."

"What's he like?"

I turn to my roommate. "What's with the twenty questions?"

Josh shrugs. "It's cool, you know? Out baseball player and all that. Could've been us had we not been so shit."

"At least you still play baseball."

"Yeah, and look at what I have to do so I can."

Because Josh's baseball season is so short and pays next to nothing, he's been floating from part-time job to part-time job throughout the rest of the year. I understand why he does it in a way, because I would've done almost anything to keep the baseball dream alive for me, but it's not a possibility when I have debts and bills to pay.

Realistically, I have no idea how Josh will do with baseball, and if you look at statistics, his body will only hold out for, what, five years if he's lucky? Baseball might have been worth it for him, but it wasn't for me. I gave myself until I graduated college to be at the level I needed to be at, and I couldn't cut it.

Josh is more stubborn than me, I suppose.

"Where are you working these days?" I ask.

"Uh ... I'd rather not say." He looks away.

"Strip club. Got it."

He throws a couch cushion at me. "It's worse than that. It's dressing up as Batman for kids' birthday parties."

I suck my lips inward to try to stop the laugh from escaping.

"It's every bit as horrible as it sounds."

"Do you only do Batman? Or, you know, what if they wanted Spider-Man? Or Thor?"

"Once I can afford the costumes, I'll add to my repertoire." He says that like he has any chance of keeping this job for longer than a few weeks. I almost feel like once he has enough money to live off for a month, he quits whatever job he's doing and then repeats that step the following month.

He's going to run out of jobs soon.

Thad

Sean enters the apartment in a rush. "Did I miss first pitch?"

"Nope. Haven't even sung the national anthem yet," I say.

"Awesome." Sean throws himself on the couch in between Josh and me, and I regret not sitting in the solo armchair.

We're really close, but do we have to be physically close too?

Again, the commentators on the TV say something about Kelley Afton needing to up his game.

"Fuck off," I mumble at the TV. "Like he doesn't have enough pressure on him already. I'm going to text Onri and tell him to tell those fucksticks at his work to maybe not pick on the gay dude."

"He doesn't even work for that network," Josh says.

"Don't care. He can pass on the message." I pick up my phone and see a slew of notifications.

> KELLEY:
>
> I know we said I'd only text you if I lost, but I thought that was putting bad karma into the world.
>
> Oh fuck, what if me texting you has now forced fate's hand and will cause us to lose?
>
> I take it back.
>
> You saw nothing.

He messaged me first when he didn't have to, but now I'm doubly invested in this game, and instead of wishing him to lose, I really hope that he wins, or he may never message me again.

When I look up again, my roommates are staring at me. Josh looks confused, his brow furrowed, and Sean's mouth hangs open in shock.

"What?" I ask.

"We thought you hated Kelley Afton," Sean says.

"I do. I mean, I did. He's not so bad once I got to know him."

"When you say got to know him ..." Josh asks with all the subtlety of a drag queen in a church.

"I'd lose my job if I went there." Yet, I did it anyway. And would jump at the chance to do it again.

Chapter 23

I'm in trouble when it comes to Kelley. That one chain of slightly unhinged messages has me fucking giddy.

"Your mouth is saying words, but your face is saying something else," Sean says.

I turn to him. "Did you know Joshy is getting paid to dress up as Batman for kids' parties?"

Josh gives me the finger, but I've successfully diverted their attention away from me and Kelley.

That is until he takes to the pitcher's mound.

"Damn. No wonder you like his ... personality." Josh's mouth is begging to be punched.

"I'd do him," Sean says.

"Aww, Sean-y. I can get you his number if you want." I sip my beer to hide my amusement because Sean likes to act like he's all cool with Josh and me being gay by making jokes like that, but we know he's not serious.

"Pass."

Yup. Just as I thought.

"What about me?" Josh asks.

"Not on your life." Like hell I'd give any of my roommates Kelley's number for real.

They're both smug, as if I've shown my hand, but I don't care too much. I might not be able to date him, but Kelley's mine to quietly obsess over, thank you very much. As soon as they win, I head to my room and text him how great his ass looked again.

⚾

After having six home games, Philly has a six-day road trip. Kelley and I continue to text, even if I only get the chance to check a couple of scores instead of watching because I've been staying late in the office.

We remain flirty, but it hasn't gone into sexting territory. They're mostly congratulatory messages if his team wins or him wishing I didn't see how he was replaced with a reliever for fucking up one too many pitches on the game he pitched.

Thad

But that's the sport. Highs and lows, wins and losses. He has nothing to be embarrassed about.

As for me, I've been trying to come up with ideas that will help me build my client list. I'm not even sure if Damon will assign me to a client, considering I'm only an intern, but I figure if I can bring in new clients, Damon will let me oversee their accounts, kind of like Brady is doing with Kelley and the other guy on his roster.

I've been researching every up-and-comer that I can find, from high school players to college and everything in between. I've even been checking the Double-A and Triple-A leagues. They will have had agents when they signed their contracts, but in those types of cases, a lot of them pay an hourly rate instead of a percentage of their contract. That's what Josh did. If I could find someone who has the potential to go far, they could be my golden ticket.

I not only look at their baseball stats but also their online presence to see if they have bookmarked any pages on their public profile that could be problematic. I won't bother with anyone who blatantly has anti-LGBTQ views.

A lot of profiles appear to be locked down though, and I would assume if these players are looking for a contract, they'd have better sense than to spout bullshit on the internet. I do find some doozies though.

Instant nos.

When I come across a hopeful player from my own hometown who has the same coach I did in high school and has the potential to get drafted in his upcoming senior year, I don't hesitate to reach out to Coach Klein and see if I can come by the school for a visit. I don't need to tell him what I'm doing now or why I'm there. It'll be put down as a simple visit to my alma mater.

And while I'm at it, I might check Philly's schedule and see when they next play at home.

When Coach Klein tells me he's available this Friday and it just so happens Kelley's team is at home this weekend, I want to jump at the chance. But before I can look up tickets to Kelley's game, I have to clear it with Damon to take Friday afternoon away from the office.

Chapter 23

I'm nervous because this is stepping outside of what I've been told to do. It's true he has encouraged us to start scouting and trying to find the right client for ourselves, but scouting and approaching are two completely different things. Though, it's not like I'm going to pounce on this kid and force him to sign anything.

I make my way to Damon's office and knock with more hesitance than I'd like. I need to go in here confident.

He looks up from his desk, his more-gray-than-black hair shimmering in the overhead lights. The graying look suits him. Maybe too much. He's already intimidating enough as it is; the whole silver-fox vibe makes him more so.

When I was at Olmstead University, he gave the commencement speech for the graduating class the year before me. He went to Newport, but his husband—and I use that term loosely because they've never actually gotten legally married—is Olmstead alumni. I was watching some of my teammates graduate, and from the second he started speaking, I was entranced. He claimed that every silver hair he had was named after one of his clients but that he wouldn't change it for anything. He said things happen for a reason, and had he not blown out his shoulder and had to give up baseball, he wouldn't be where he was. He said he was happier than he ever could've imagined.

It might have been that moment that I started to realize I was never going to make it in baseball. His backup plan to become an agent suddenly became mine too. Because if Damon King could do it and go on to make an entire empire, then I could go on to find happiness too.

"What can I do for you?" Damon asks.

I enter his office, and he gestures for me to sit. I fidget with the edges of Rylan McAlister's file, which is hot in my hands. "So, I know you've said we should do our own research and scouting for clients, but you haven't explicitly said what we should do if we find one. This guy goes to my old high school, has the same coach as I did, and he looks like a promising draft pick next year."

Damon holds out his hand to take the file, and I almost don't want to hand it over in case he puts someone else on it.

Thad

So, as I pass it over, I add, "I've set up to go meet my old coach this Friday afternoon and watch the team's practice—"

Damon's head snaps up, and I find myself backpedaling.

"But I didn't tell him what I was going for or what I even do now. I just thought if I could see Rylan in person and introduce myself as a representative of the firm, then when the time comes, he might remember me."

Damon breaks into a small smile. "I'm loving the initiative, and I'll be happy to have you as a representative of the firm, but you're not in a position to be signing your own clients yet."

"I thought as much, but I was kind of hoping that if I did approach Rylan or anyone else I find that if they do end up coming to us and signing, that I could maybe shadow the agent on their case, like what Brady does?" Oh, no. I'm starting to ramble, and I can't stop. "I know it's different for him because he's been interning here every summer and has more experience, the family background and all that, but I'm not asking to be their agent. I want to be involved in their case. If he or anyone else signs, I mean."

Damon leans back in his seat, but his smile doesn't waver. "This is the kind of enthusiasm I've been waiting to see from you."

I hate that he's been able to tell I've been holding myself back, but I can't blame him. My face speaks my inside thoughts way too much. "I know it's taken a bit for me to embrace my role here, but I'm finally learning to let baseball go and have it in my life a new way."

"I understand that, probably more than anyone. Do you think you're ready to accept seeing clients getting the kind of contracts you wanted? Because I have to tell you, that first one is going to sting like a bitch. Ask me how I know." He has a point, and he understands more than anyone.

"I can't say for sure until it happens, but that's another reason why going to see Rylan could be good for me. Easing me in slowly."

"I like this direction for you." Now he leans forward, elbows on his desk. "I have to be honest, I was worried about you for a hot minute because I didn't think you'd be able to let go of your bitterness, but I'm very happy to see you taking these steps. I'll authorize

Chapter 23

the time away from the office to go see him, and make sure you email through how it goes and what you think of Rylan's potential."

"Will do."

"Good work."

I stand and leave his office feeling positive, and that's something I don't experience a lot.

When I get back to my desk, I lock in the day and time with Coach Klein and then go on one of those resale sites for a cheap last-minute ticket to Kelley's game. Because people generally watch baseball with others, finding a cheap single seat that's in a good spot is easy.

I want to text Kelley that I'm going to be at his game Friday night but refrain. I'd rather see his face when he finds me standing outside the players' exit.

I'm itching to leave by the time it hits noon on Friday. I've been antsy all day, and I can't be sure if it's because I'm going on my first unofficial scouting trip on my own or if it's because I'm going to see Kelley again.

Not that I'm expecting anything to happen because we've agreed to be friends, but if the opportunity arises, there's no way I'm going to say no.

It would be smarter to keep everything platonic, but that ship sailed the minute we got naked together.

Because ever since that happened, all I've been able to think about is hooking up with him again. Being inside him. Hell, if I had time the day he came into the office, I would've taken him back to my place and blown him in the entryway whether my roommates were home or not. My level of desperation to get him back into bed only grows with each day that passes. Each text.

I think it's safe to say it's Kelley that has my gut tied in knots.

When it's finally time for me to make my way home, I stand in such a rush that Brady flinches next to me.

Thad

"What the fuck, man?"

"I've gotta go."

"Oh, right. Good luck with that Rylan kid."

"Thanks." I take off for the elevator, but Brady calls after me.

"Don't throw coffee on him, and you'll already be ahead of your last meeting with a client."

The other interns snicker, because yes, that has been a nice piece of gossip going around the office. I decide to take the ever-professional route by flipping them off with both hands over my shoulders.

And just as I do that, Damon steps into the bullpen.

Of course.

"I wouldn't do that to a prospective client either," Damon says.

I cringe and go to apologize, but he laughs.

"You're all good. I would've done the same."

I seriously have the best boss ever.

The hour-long drive is a suckfest, turning into an almost two-hour drive, and I'm glad I left early because getting out of the city is a pain in the ass.

Pulling into my old high school, where I was prom king and captain of the baseball team, I can't help the nostalgic pang in my chest and the sense of failure looming over me.

Coach Klein would know I'm not playing pro ball. He follows that kind of thing with his old students. But going in there in a suit and passing him a business card is probably going to be a surprise.

I get out of the Jeep Wrangler the five of us roommates use between us. It's Sean's car. There's no real need for a car in New York, so Sean made us a deal. We all chip in for registration and insurance, and we get to share it. It mostly works. Onri was contemplating driving upstate to see his parents this weekend but relented when I said mine was for work. He doesn't need to know I have other plans on the agenda.

Walking these school grounds makes me miss the days I went here. To think, I couldn't wait to get out of here, and now I'm wishing I could go back. Not that I hate where I'm at, but like I told

Chapter 23

Damon, I'm finally adjusting my expectations for my life. There will be a part of me that will always be disappointed about baseball, but I'm going to turn it around and love the sport from the sidelines.

Starting now.

I turn the corner, and the baseball field comes into view. Coach Klein is there, talking to the team, who are all sitting on the grass of the infield. The kids spot me first, and then Coach Klein turns and waves me over.

"Everyone, this is Thad St. James, one of the best baseball players to ever graduate from Trenton Academy."

I shake his hand and address them. "Hi, everyone. I thought I'd stop by and see how my old team is playing and to say hi to my most favorite coach ever."

"Suck-up," Coach Klein says. "Okay, so why don't we get out there and show him what we've got?"

The players stand, and first up to bat is the reason I'm here: Rylan McAlister.

Some of the kids waiting in the very basic dugout send quick glances my and Coach's way before whispering amongst themselves.

"So, what's the real reason you're here?" Coach asks. He's not looking at me but watching the field. "For a second, I thought you were going to come asking for an assistant coach job, but with the way you're dressed, I get the sense you might not actually be here for me."

"Can't a man come and see his old coach for the sake of saying hi while he's in town?" I feign innocence, something I know he can see right through.

Rylan hits his first ball all the way to the back left field, an impressive hit for his warm-up bat.

"Considering you've been gone for, what, five years now and I haven't seen you once? No."

Fair. I should've made the effort to come back sooner. Coach Klein is one of the reasons I even got as far as I did in baseball. "Okay, so maybe I haven't exactly had time to come back and reminisce with you about how I've always been your favorite player, but there's a reason for that."

"So, what are you now? Talent scout for colleges? Manager? Agent?"

I must make a face on that last one.

"Ah. An agent. And let me guess, you're here to try to convince McAlister to sign with you and go out for the draft this upcoming year. What did I tell you when you were here?"

Rylan hits another one deep.

"That getting drafted right out of high school doesn't give enough time to hone your skills to make it in the majors."

"Exactly. McAlister has the potential to go far, but he won't if he doesn't go through a college program first."

"Is that what Rylan has to say about it? He might think differently. Especially with how he can hit."

"He's seventeen. Of course he thinks differently."

I love how protective he's being of his star player. "I want to reassure you that I'm not here to convince him of anything. I wanted to meet him, give him my name, and tell him if he's ever in the need of an agent, I work for an amazing firm who would love to meet him for a chat."

"Who do you work for?"

"I'm an intern at King Sports," I say proudly.

"They are a good firm. Reputable."

"I'm here because this is my alma mater, but even if I wanted to sign Rylan, I couldn't because I'm not even a full agent yet. I'm currently paying my dues and trying to recruit clients for the firm."

Coach studies me for a moment. "In that case, I want you to check out this pitcher too. He's only a sophomore, but I'm thinking of starting him this season because he has potential up the wazoo." He turns to the dugout. "Turner, get out there and strike McAlister out."

Turner jogs out to the mound to take over, but his first pitch is wide, and Rylan's smart enough not to swing.

I side-eye Coach.

"He's still green, obviously, but when he's good, he's fantastic."

Chapter 23

This Turner kid proves Coach right when his next three balls are strikes.

"Is Rylan not as good as everyone thinks he is, or is Turner a prodigy?"

"It might be a bit of both. They each have some growing to do, and if Rylan doesn't want to go to a four-year college, I'm going to try to convince him to go to a junior college so he won't have to wait until he's twenty-one to be drafted. He gets to grow stronger, sharpen his skills, and then maybe he'll have a shot at getting you fifteen percent of a multimillion-dollar contract."

That's the dream.

"Are you going to let me talk to either of them?" I ask.

"I'll introduce you and tell them who you work for, but that's all I can promise at this point."

"Hey, that's all I'm asking for."

Coach calls them over, and they both stare at me a little stunned when I say who I am and where I'm from, but when I tell them I want them to both work hard enough that I get to come see them again and wish them good luck, I swear one of them squeaks as I walk away.

The overall meeting went as to be expected, but it's a first step.

With work out of the way, now I get to go enjoy my night, which I'm hoping will end with orgasms, but if it can only finish with friendship, then I'm going to have to be okay with that.

I'm still going to hold out for the former though.

Chapter 24
Kelley

After the last few games where I've been switched out with a reliever and replaced in the early innings, I'm determined to make this game one of my best.

The plan is to not get booted this game, not even for our closer.

I have to up my stats, or all hell is going to break loose. Commentators from the best and worst networks are coming for me, each with their opinion on whether my inconsistent start to the season is because of coming out or not.

The thing is, I'm about as consistent as I was this time last year if I look at my previous season. But with the comments going around, I have to remind myself to look at the facts and ignore biased opinions. That, and remembering not to look at social media. I've been waffling on that the further the season goes on, even though I know it's in my best interest not to go searching.

Turns out getting rid of that impulse isn't as easy as getting laid by a man who tells me like it is. Either that or his magical dick powers have worn off.

If only I had time to go see Thad and get a recharge on that. Because that's how it works, right?

It's our last game against San Diego at home, and I need the W. Not the team as a whole—me. Because I'm the one letting everyone down out there.

This is the first time my anxiety has started affecting my game.

Chapter 24

Sure, I've been worried in the past, but before I was out, I was only concerned with playing well. Now that I'm an openly gay player, there are strings attached to playing badly, those connecting their ignorance to how well I'm doing. Which then feeds my insecurity about people judging me on who I am and not what I'm doing on the field.

In the last two games, I don't blame them for judging. I've been throwing nothing. Been giving walks. And at this professional level, I deserve to be raked over the coals. Just ... not in conjunction with my sexuality.

Tonight, I have to go out there and pull off a miracle. I'm the first line of defense when it comes to preventing the other team from crossing that home plate. It's not entirely up to me, but the majority of the weight sits on my shoulders.

I don't actually care whether we win this game or not. Well, I do, but my priority is letting as few runs in as possible. It's up to the batters to step up to the plate—literally.

My only focus is to strike every motherfucker out.

In my years of therapy, things like positive affirmations and positive thinking haven't really worked for me because that negative voice inside my head always disputes them in some way, but tonight as I take to the mound, all I can do is tell myself I can do it.

For the first few innings, it seems to be working, but when we get to inning five, six, seven, the positive thinking turns to bone-tired exhaustion, which is an absolute killer for confidence.

I've only let one person hit a damn home run, but there was another runner on base, so they've got two by the top of the ninth. We managed a killer fourth inning, where we pulled six out of our asses, along with a lucky three in the seventh inning on loaded bases and a successful bunt situation. The bunt only got the first across the line, but the second and third crossed home plate on the next hit.

Even though I'd like to think I can't fuck up big enough in the next inning to give seven runs, the more tired I get, the more negative I become about just getting to the end.

Kelley

I'm even beginning to look over at the dugout, wondering—hoping—they're pulling the closer out.

But I told myself I'm going to do this, and I'm going to fight until the end to do it.

Batter number one gets a home fucking run.

I strike batter number two out and send up a thank-you to whichever deity is watching over me. I needed that, or I was about to fall apart.

Batter number three gets a walk.

Batter number four hits deep into left field and is caught out, but batter three manages to round second, and we can't get the ball to third fast enough.

My worst fears are coming true, and I can't believe I have to agree with the commentators here, but my inconsistency is frustrating.

Two outs and two runs on only four batters is not bad. It's not great, but we're still ahead in this game, and I only need one more strikeout. One more strike and this game is actually over.

I don't get that strikeout.

The next batter misses the first pitch, refuses to hit the wide ball on the second, and teeters the line of a foul ball on the third, but it's fucking good, and then it's a scramble for the right fielder to get to the ball and stop this fucker from rounding second.

He does but then looks at the field and realizes he won't make it to third, so while Hemmings throws to third, the runner slides back into second to be safe.

Again, I find myself looking at the dugout, half praying they pull me out and half hoping they give me this chance.

One more out. Just one more. If I strike the next batter out, we win and don't even have to play the bottom of the ninth. This is my shot.

This is my *job*.

I take a deep breath and focus. I've pitched against Anderson before. He sucks at hitting a curveball but is also really good at judging when it's going to miss the plate. People joke all the time that he doesn't know how to run, which is how he pulls walks out of every pitcher he faces.

Chapter 24

I have a small chance—a window—to try to trick him here. Coach has been having me work on my curveball and putting that little bit of extra spin in it to make it look like it's not going over the plate, only for it to fully curve at the last second and register as a strike.

Am I always accurate? No. And if I miss, I'm risking another walk here. But this is the kind of pressure I thrive on when it comes to baseball. If I tune out the rest of the world and only focus on what I have to do here and now, I think I can do it.

My catcher, Jenko, gives me the signal for a change-up, but I shake my head. Anderson would see right through that and smash it out of the park. It's almost as if I can see the hesitance in Jenko's eyes before he signals for a curveball.

And when I nod, Jenko throws his head back. He's probably letting out a silent groan, too, that says this is a bad idea.

It probably is. My arm has been inconsistent, and if Anderson gets a hit, there will be two bases and runners to cover. But if he strikes out? I'll have finished a game on my own for the first time in *weeks*.

I take another deep breath before assuming my pitching position. I'm staring at Anderson, preparing for this pitch, when all of a sudden, out of the corner of my right eye, I see movement. Dixon on second base. He's trying to steal third.

From where I am, it's next to impossible to throw to third without being obvious, and then he'll simply run back to second. But ... if I can get him to think I'm throwing to third and throw to second instead—

Without overthinking it, I pitch, my elbow facing third and scaring Dixon enough to go running back to second, where, bam, it hits Rengel's glove, and Dixon gets tapped out.

Turns out I didn't need my curveball after all.

The accomplishment that washes over me as my teammates run out to the mound to congratulate me is overwhelming, but no way am I going to let that emotion show.

I might be inconsistent, but today was a good game for me. I hope for more games to come just like it.

Kelley

The high carries the team into our locker room, where I'm asked to cover media—which I generally hate, but not today—while the others all shower and change back into their game-day suits.

I do my interviews and jump right into the shower before even going to my cubby, so when I get back out there in only my towel and pull my phone out of my bag, I almost drop it—and my towel—when I see a message from Thad. Because it's not his usual message congratulating me. It's a photo. Of his view tonight. From the stands.

He came to watch my game?

He's here?

Stupidly, I instinctually look around the locker room, but no, of course he's not in here, but I'm so damn excited.

I type out:

> Please tell me you're still here? You have to come out and celebrate with me and the team.

His response is immediate:

> I'm waiting for you outside amongst all the kids who want autographs, but I'm starting to feel like I'm being stared at by all the parents thinking I'm here for the kids and not waiting on a player. Come save me.

I don't think I've ever gotten dressed faster in my life.

When I get outside, the kids have dispersed because my teammates have already left, and there's Thad St. James, looking so fucking gorgeous in that blue suit that drives me wild, hair slicked back, and his hands in the pockets of his insanely tight pants.

He smiles, and I almost melt on the spot. "You had an excellent game tonight. That ninth inning was impressive."

"It was inconsistent," I say.

"Hey, it worked on throwing everyone off. They didn't know what you were going to throw."

Chapter 24

I laugh. "I'm going to use that as a selling point for when Philly wants to trade me because of it.

"Nah, no way. If they trade you, it'll be the biggest mistake they've ever made."

I appreciate him saying that, but I don't have my head in the clouds. I know the realities of this game, and it's one of those things that I'm weirdly centered about, especially when it's my inconsistency that's the problem. My anxiety more revolves around being traded because of my skill but it being blamed on my sexuality in the media.

"Where are we headed?" he asks. "You said something about celebrating with the team?"

Shit. I did. But I really don't want to now. I want to take Thad back to my place and keep him there all weekend. Though, I have another game tomorrow. And the following day.

Baseball season is no joke.

People think hockey is the toughest sport, but when it comes to stamina, us ballers are incomparable. We play five to seven games a week, sometimes double headers, and we're on the road for a lot of it.

I should make an appearance with the team. It's not like we party hard because of our schedule, and I did win us that game. Even so, staring at Thad, his wide shoulders, that small peek of chest tattoo sticking out the top of his button-up, I don't want to waste any time while he's here.

He waves a hand in front of my face. "Did you space out on me?"

I shake it off. "Sorry. I did. I'm torn between taking you out with the team or taking you back to my place."

His lips curve up.

"To catch up, I mean. Not ... anything else. Unless you want something else. Then, you know I'm all for it, and—"

Thad steps into my space, his hand going to my hip.

I should be self-conscious about the small gesture of affection, but there could be a slew of media people out here, and it wouldn't be enough to get me to step back.

Kelley

"I want something else," he rasps.

I go to move, to grab his hand and drag him toward my car, but his grip tightens on my hip.

"But after that inning, you deserve to go out with your teammates. So, we'll do both."

"One drink. That's all we're staying for." If I can even last that long.

Chapter 25
Thad

Kelley says he'll leave his car at the stadium overnight, seeing as he can park in the players' lot, which I'm thankful for because parking is a rip-off. Though, I still have some of that Kelley bonus sitting in my account.

I'm trying not to touch it. After paying off Mom and Dad's Wylder debts, paying back my roommates what I owe them, catching up on rent, and paying the following month in advance, I have less than three thousand left. I intend to keep the rest in case I need it. Like, if Wylder comes back and takes more money from my parents or if one of their appliances breaks. It's there for emergencies, and it's going to stay that way.

Kelley directs me where to go, and even though I'm not exactly thrilled about having him in this beat-up old car that smells like dude and stale Doritos, I don't let it get to me too much. Kelley knows I have money issues. He can't expect me to own something as fancy as whatever he drives. Even if, technically, I don't own this car either, but that's not the point.

There's a parking lot nearby the upscale bar with private rooms —all things Kelley has rambled about on our way there—and as soon as we get out of the car, I have to fight the urge to take his hand in mine.

I deserve a damn medal for making Kelley come here instead of back to his place where we could be naked already, but this is

Thad

better. I don't want him to think the only reason I came to watch him play was to get into his pants.

I *do* want in his pants, especially after watching that game, but I can be patient.

Maybe.

I'd offer to blow him in a dark corner again like we did in the boat shed, but I don't want hard and fast this time. I want a repeat of our first time together. Exploring each other, trying different things, fucking him and then him fucking me. I want to go back to his place and stay up all night until the sun appears, and then we can sleep until Kelley needs to go back to the stadium for tomorrow night's game.

We enter the bar at an unmarked door, where a burly security guard opens up and waves us on through. There's no sign out here, nothing. I wouldn't have even thought it was a club.

"Are you sure this is a sports bar?"

"Yep. We get to use the side entrance so fans don't crowd us."

"Ah, so this is where the team goes to celebrate?"

"And commiserate. Not everyone comes because a lot of the guys have families, and we don't come out if we have a road trip the following day, but they treat us well here."

"I can see that." Lifestyles of the major leagues. I'm not jealous and bitter at all. Okay, I am. But not at Kelley. Never at Kelley again. He doesn't deserve it.

Kelley pushes open a frosted glass door in a corner of the hallway, and if I look to my right, it leads to where there's a nightclub area.

Inside the large private room are couches on one side and a long dinner table on the other.

Some of Kelley's teammates are already happily buzzed, and when they notice us, they throw their arms up and shout. I don't think it's words.

"The man of the hour," Frederik Zaka says and claps Kelley on the shoulder.

"And I did it without pissing Skip off too," Kelley says.

Chapter 25

"Hey, I thought that was the signal for swing, not bunt. At least, that's how it was when I played for Kansas."

I have no idea what they're talking about, but I don't buy Zaka's excuse for a second because his smile is too innocent to be real.

Kelley glances over at me. "How long do you think he'll be able to use the 'I'm new' excuse until he gets in trouble with his agent for not listening to team management?"

I pretend to think. "I guess it depends on the agent."

"It's Merek," Kelley says. "Zaka signed with King Sports before he got the free agent deal with Philly." Then he turns to Zaka. "This is Thad St. James. He's an intern at King Sports."

"Nice to meet you." Zaka holds out his hand for me to shake.

Actually shaking it is surreal to me. I've obviously met sports stars before, a lot more since starting at King Sports, but when one of your idols is standing in front of you, it's hard not to be starstruck.

"You too." My voice cracks. Damn it.

"So, what are your intentions with our dearest pitcher?" Zaka puts his arm around Kelley's shoulders, and I laugh.

It's tempting to tell Zaka exactly what I want to do to Kelley, but I don't. That will make things even more awkward with his teammates than Kelley has already said it is. That, and Zaka could tell Merek, his new agent. My superior.

"Kelley and I go way back. We were best friends from the moment we met."

Kelley playfully backhands my chest. "Lies. All lies." Kelley rubs his chin. "What was it you called me? An egocentric diva?"

Sounds about right. "I don't recall using those exact words, but yeah, close enough."

Zaka blinks in surprise. "And you didn't get fired? If Merek said that to me, I'd walk."

"Ah, see, but I'm not Kelley's agent, even though I was sent to babysit him for two weeks over the break."

"Baby ... sit?"

"Do you know he's addicted to social media?" I say, and I can feel the frustration rolling off Kelley's shoulders.

Thad

"I am not."

I ignore him. "He really is. He needed two interns to confiscate all his devices. There should really be a player program to help with this kind of thing like they do for drugs and alcohol."

"Now who's being dramatic?" Kelley asks.

I glance over at him, and for some reason, even though we're joking around and he's protesting everything I say, there's nothing but fire in his eyes staring back at me.

"That probably explains why he always runs to his phone as soon as we're off the field," Zaka says.

My heart skips a beat because ... could he be excited to see if I've messaged him?

"Zaka lies too. You're all a bunch of liars. I'm going to go get a drink."

"Get me one too," I call after him. He flips me off, but at least I know he heard me. He might even come back with a drink for me. Possibly one with spit in it, but hey, it's not like we haven't shared bodily fluids before.

Zaka inches closer to me. "Just a babysitter, huh?"

I break my gaze from Kelley's retreating ass to make eye contact with Zaka.

He's this huge, Norwegian-looking guy, and he even makes me feel small, but there's something in his eyes. Something I can't completely place. It could be judgment or suspicion, maybe, but he has signed with King Sports, and you don't do that if you're a homophobe. Because King Sports is known for repping the most queer athletes of any other—oh. *Oh.*

What I'm seeing in Zaka's expression isn't judgment. It's interest. But I can't tell if it's interest in me or in Kelley.

"Just his babysitter," I say. "At least, that's how we met. I'm here as a friend. My folks live in Trenton, so I figured it wasn't much farther to come see Kelley play." Why am I making excuses? And why can't I stop? "I also had to scout at my old high school for players, so you know, two birds, one stone. Type. Umm. Thing."

I don't think I've ever been this awkward in my life. That old

Chapter 25

saying, don't meet your heroes? It's not because they're assholes. It's because you'll make a fool of yourself.

It's hard not to think of possible reasons why Zaka hasn't come out, or maybe I'm reading this completely wrong, but his focus ping-pongs between us. It's possible he's only curious or maybe inexperienced, or maybe it's that before Kelley came out, there hasn't been an openly queer player in the league for a few years, and Zaka didn't want to be the one to do it.

Kelley did it.

And now ... now Zaka signed with Kelley's firm?

I'm starting to think I know which one of us he's interested in.

Jealousy and possessiveness try to make an appearance, but I have to squash them down. This is the first time in months I've been able to see Kelley. Zaka is with him every day. They would be a much more convenient couple.

Not that Kelley and I are a couple. Or even on the way to becoming anything that resembles one. This is ... sex. Friend sex.

"So, you're not together, but you're into each other," he says.

"Well, I work at King Sports, so I obviously can't date him or ... whatever."

His light eyebrows shoot up.

"I mean, I have no idea what you're talking about."

Zaka laughs. "Mmmhmm. Sure."

Kelley hands me over a drink with cute muttering about being disrespected in his own house.

"No idea what I'm talking about." Zaka raises his glass. "I'm going to need a refill." He downs the rest of his drink, even though he still has half of it left, and then heads to the bar.

"You two looked locked in a good conversation," Kelley says. At first, I get excited and think I hear a tone of jealousy in his voice, but then he keeps talking. "Were you trying to get him to choose you to be his assigned intern?"

"Damn it. That would've been smart. I actually spent most of the time trying to convince him we aren't hooking up. I don't think he bought it."

Thad

"If we want to get technical, we aren't hooking up." He steps closer to me. "Right this second."

"Let's make the rounds with your teammates and then get out of here," I growl.

Kelley's feet move quickly. He practically says, "Hi everyone, bye everyone," at each group of teammates and then runs for the exit.

Okay, running might be exaggerating, but he's really not being subtle.

I should be worried that maybe one of his teammates will say something to someone and it could get back to head office and Damon, but the only person Kelley introduced me to properly was Zaka, and I get the solid impression he's not going to tell a soul.

Chapter 26
Kelley

Things are awkward on the drive back to my place, and I don't know why. It's almost like ... I'm nervous for this to be happening, but it's not like we haven't slept together before. Actually, we haven't slept together. We've had sex. There's a difference.

My cock is hard just thinking about what's to come, but that familiar knot of anxiety sits in my gut. Which sucks. Once his hands are on me, I'm sure I'll be fine.

"You all good?" he asks from the driver's side. I directed him all the way to my house on autopilot, and now we're outside my over-the-top multimillion-dollar double-story house in Bryn Mawr that's all wood and stone and—

He's so going to judge me for it. He's struggling with money, and here I am, living in a house made for a family when it's only me here.

I screw up my face. "I know the house is ridiculous. And big. I bought it with the whole closeted 'make it look like I'm ready to start a family' thing, and now—"

Thad reaches over and grasps my hand. "Are you forgetting who I am?"

Yes. "No. You're ... Thad." An amazing man who has taken pity on me and is probably using me for sex, but I also don't care if that's all he's here for because the way he made me feel back in that

Kelley

cabin in the Catskills is the only time I've felt a true sense of freedom to be myself.

Ever.

And that's who he is.

"Tell me what I am for you," Thad says, and this time, I have a more articulate answer because with one touch of my hand, one soulful look, I'm reminded of it.

"You're my person." My eyes widen. "Uh, not like *my person*, but the person I can be me with."

Thad's lips curve on one side. "Seems your head is getting in the way of, well, getting head. Again. We'll work on it. Come on, show me this monstrosity of an amazing house."

Okay, easing me back into this. Amazing idea.

Only, as soon as we get through my front double doors that are twice the height of me, that familiar feeling of safety wraps around me like a blanket, and I'm no longer hesitant. I'm no longer worried about him judging me or shaming me for what I want. And what I want is him inside me.

My bedroom with supplies is upstairs, but I'm so desperate for him that when he asks, "How about a tour?" I point to the living room in front of us, the kitchen to the right of us, and the stairs to the left.

"Where I don't have the time to watch TV, where I rarely have the effort to make dinner, and where I want to drag you right now."

Thad smiles. "Seems we got over those nerves quickly."

Yep. And it's all because of him.

I grab his hand and pull him toward the staircase. He follows willingly.

"You know, I'm tempted to force you to give me a proper tour."

I look at him over my shoulder while I keep climbing the steps. "Would you rather see my bathroom fixtures or fuck me?"

Thad uses his free hand to push down his crotch. "You play dirty."

We reach the second-floor landing, and I pull him to me. "It's only going to get dirtier. When I saw your text that you were at my game, after I finished with all those stupid reporters, I had the

Chapter 26

showers to myself, and on the off chance you were still waiting for me …" I flick my gaze to his, almost shocked at the confidence I feel when I say, "I might have done some extra cleaning."

It seems he's done with being patient too. Thad surges forward, his mouth claiming mine, and suddenly, my bedroom is too far away.

My hands go under his jacket, peeling it off his wide shoulders, and he does the same for me. I reach for his belt while he undoes his shirt buttons. We have to stop kissing when I struggle with his belt and he takes his shirt off, but then we go straight back to being lip-locked, our tongues tangling.

I run my fingertips over his bare shoulders and down his chest and then blindly push him toward the hall leading to my room.

We run into the wall and laugh, but then Thad spins us so I'm pinned, and his big body covers mine. He's further along in the undressed process. I still have all my clothes except my jacket. Thad expertly undoes my tie with quick hands, so while he does that and then works my shirt buttons open, I continue with his pants. But instead of taking them off, I lower the fly and reach inside.

His hard cock is poking out through the hole in his boxers, and I give him a firm stroke.

He fumbles with my buttons. "Screw it." He breaks away from my mouth. "You're a pro baseball player, you can afford new buttons." As easy as tearing paper, the rest of my buttons are ripped open, one even flying off somewhere, but he's right. I can afford new buttons. Fuck the buttons. All of them.

My shirt's gone now, and Thad's mouth is back on mine.

We really should keep our hands and mouths off each other long enough to get to the bedroom, but it's a lot harder to execute than that. Because I can't get enough of him.

Slowly but surely, we make our way in the right direction, trying to take our pants off as we go, but by the time we cross the threshold, we have to pull apart to kick them off the rest of the way.

We're down to our underwear. Progress.

I take the opportunity where I'm not being consumed by his

touch, by his lips, to go to the nightstand and drop lube on the bed. There are condoms in there too, but considering we didn't use any in the Catskills, it might kill the mood if I brought them out now.

"Hesitating, are we?" He steps behind me, pressing his front to my back and laying a soft kiss on my shoulder. Then he sees what's in my drawer. "Oh. Wondering if I've been with anyone else since winter and need these?" He reaches for the box. "I haven't, but if you're more comfortable using—"

I take the box out of his hand. "I don't want to use one. I want to feel all of you, and I want your cum inside me."

His cock twitches against my ass cheek. "And how do you want that to happen?"

I pause. "W-what do you mean?"

Thad spins me and hauls me off my feet, lifting my legs to wrap around him. "Want me to fuck you like this? Shallow thrusts, face-to-face?" He winces, and I laugh.

"Considering you're struggling to hold me up as it is, I'm going to go with no on that one."

He lowers me to the ground and says in my ear, "Tell me what you want."

With anyone else, I'd clam up and say something generic. Missionary, please, because it's sooo... great. Not that there's anything wrong with that in the right moments, but what I want is primal. Raw.

"I want you to hold me down and fuck my hole, not letting me come until you fill me up."

Thad grips my ass in one of his large, firm hands. "Want it a bit rough?"

I nod.

His hand leaves me and then comes back down on my ass hard. My cock leaks.

"That okay?" he rasps.

"Yes." My voice is just as croaky.

"You need to take these off." He puts his fingers in the waistband of my underwear, pulling them down to my knees where they fall to the floor and I can step out of them.

Chapter 26

He stays behind me, hand trailing from my thigh up to my aching cock, where he takes me in his hold and strokes me teasingly. I lean back and turn my head so our mouths can come back together.

Considering I asked for it rough, he's being extra gentle.

Then the sting of his palm hitting my ass, bare skin this time, pulses along with the resounding crack that echoes around the room. I shiver as goose bumps break out over my skin.

"Get on the bed," he orders. "Ass up, legs spread, and let me take it from here."

My body hums with exciting anticipation. Long gone are the nerves I had in the car.

I get on the bed on my hands and knees but then lower my front to my forearms. With my ass in the air, my cock hanging between my legs, I feel exposed in a sinful way, and it gives me a thrill.

I turn my head to the side and watch as Thad takes off his underwear and picks up the lube. He begins covering himself, his hand sliding up and down his shaft.

My ass tightens and releases like it's trying to find Thad's cock. I need to be filled, and I need it right now, damn it.

When Thad finally moves and climbs on the bed behind me, I relax in relief because soon, all I'll be able to feel is him splitting me in two.

But of course, he doesn't get right to it. Instead of slippery fingers working my hole open, Thad buries his face between my cheeks and licks from my balls all the way up to my hole.

The breath leaves my lungs. "I want to come, not die. Fucking hell."

His warm breath lands on my hole as he chuckles. Then his tongue is on me, teasing me as he flicks it over my hole and then back to my balls and up again over and over. He grips me in his hand, jerking me, and it's so intense I can't hold back a tortured moan. With his mouth on my hole, his hand on my cock, I'm so close to blowing this. Literally.

Thad lifts his head, giving me enough of a break to remind me that I didn't want to come until I was full of *his cum*.

Kelley

And even though I should be self-conscious while he continues to turn me inside out, I'm not. All I can think about is how much I want more. Impatiently, I rock back on my knees right as he's about to tease some more. This time, he grips my ass cheeks and pulls them apart while he dives right in.

I've never, ever had someone do this before because I haven't been comfortable enough, but Thad—

"Fuck," I hiss and fist my comforter, balling it under my fingers. I can't come yet. I can't.

Thad doesn't make that easy on me though. He eats me out until I'm a trembling mess, subtly replacing his tongue with his fingers, where I enter a whole new level of pleasure because now he can reach my prostate.

I swear, if he ever gets to the point where his cock is inside me, it's going to take less than a minute for me to blow. I'm so on edge, I'm so ready for it.

And when I'm finally, finally put out of my misery and he eases inside me slowly, I have that buzzing sense of peace.

Right up until he somehow manages a tight grip on my really short hair and yanks my head back while he slams inside me.

A ripple floods my entire body.

Thad's going to ruin sex for me with anyone else because I have never, ever felt this kind of burning in my gut. My whole body is on fire, I'm already sweating, and my legs feel like they're running a marathon, but when Thad is inside me, I crave it all.

He picks up his pace, and I do everything I can to make sure I feel every inch of him. My hips meet his, I push back to make him go as deep as possible, and we move in sync.

Every peg of my prostate, every groan that falls from his lips, I get closer and closer.

"Fill me up," I whisper. "I need it. I need you to come."

He pushes me back further down on the bed so my legs are no longer bent, and he covers my back with his body. "That's my line. Let go."

He's heavy on top of me, and when he pushes back inside me,

Chapter 26

the friction beneath my cock on the comforter is what I need to get there.

Thad goes right back to getting me to the point of breaking, to the point I think I'm about to come but somehow keep hanging on.

"Kell," he grunts. "You're dangerously close to not getting what you want."

"Use me," I say. "Use my hole."

I find the thing my body has been holding out for. Thad stills right as my cock starts erupting. We come together, him slowly milking himself in my ass while I empty onto the bed.

Thad tries to move, but I reach behind me before he can slip out of me.

"In a minute," I say.

"I don't know how much longer I can keep all my weight off you."

I lift my head. "This isn't your full weight?"

"Nope."

"Eh, crush me. I don't care. I just want this to last a while longer."

He does as I say, and for the first time in my life, I'm beginning to understand the effect of a weighted blanket. My actual blanket might feel suffocating, but with Thad on top of me, I've never breathed easier in my life.

Chapter 27
Thad

Kelley has me pinned against the wall of his shower, his long, callused fingers wrapped around my cock while the spray from his rainfall shower covers us in warmth. "Are you sure I can't convince you to come to the game again tonight and go home tomorrow?"

Last night already feels like a fever dream, and I want nothing more than to repeat it, but after waking up, I realize I'm in real danger here.

My hands run down his sides and grip his phenomenal ass while I thrust inside his fist.

"You're not playing fair," I say.

And this is why it's so dangerous. I want to stay. Tonight, tomorrow, the next day. If I do that, though, I'll never want to leave, and then I'll have to quit my job in New York, move back in with Mom and Dad, and become a leech like my brother, all so I can be close to where Kelley is.

I can't think of a single reason why I wouldn't be able to stay tonight, and it's not like I can tell him I don't want to because I don't trust myself to be strong enough to leave tomorrow. I could use the car as an excuse, say a roommate needs it, but they don't. They know I have it.

Kelley continues to stroke me while my brain tries to hold on to a single rational thought. I pull him against me, pressing our bodies

Chapter 27

together so he can wrap his hand around both of us at the same time.

Kelley leans in and sucks on my neck while he jerks us both, getting faster and faster with every stroke.

I'm torn between agreeing to stay in the heat of the moment and knowing I shouldn't.

He's probably giving me a hickey, which I should care about, but I don't. My parents will ask who I'm seeing, my roommates will rib me about being at work and coming home with sex marks, but all I want is for Kelley to suck harder. Make it really purple and dark so every time I look at it, I'm reminded of this.

Of how Kelley let me be this guy for him again.

Going months in between having this is going to be next to impossible this time. There's nothing stopping me from coming to every game I can other than work, and who needs sleep? I could travel back and forth from Philly easily. Catch the train, get Kelley to pick me up ... because his schedule isn't hectic or anything.

I tell myself to focus on what he's doing to me instead of when I can make it happen again. And again and again and again.

Kelley's mouth becomes soft as he peppers small kisses down my neck and over my collarbone while his hand still moves frantically with only one goal in mind. He's going to make me come so hard I have no choice but to give in and stay another night.

Tomorrow, he's on the road again, and I have to get back to New York, so it's not like my fear of camping outside his house and becoming obsessed so much I quit my job and stalk the guy could really come true.

"So..." Kelley breathes hard. "You going to *come* to my game tonight?" The emphasis on the word *come* makes me want to do just that. Right now and tonight.

"You're playing even unfairer now." Is that actual English? I don't know. I don't care.

"Come, Thad. I want you to come."

Fuck, he wins.

I shudder and throw my head back until it hits the tile with a thud. The pain only makes me come harder, and the possibility of me having a concussion really must do it for Kelley because he joins me in spilling over.

He's still jerking us both, and even if my skin is becoming oversensitive, I don't want to stop him until he's finished riding that high. Until he's completely empty and all the evidence is washed down the drain.

Eventually, he slows, and his head lands on my cheek when he finally releases us.

We're both breathing heavily, both boneless, so I wrap my arms around his back and hold him tight, dipping my head into the crook of his shoulder until we recover enough to move again.

After a couple of minutes, when my head clears from orgasm brain and I'm thinking about it rationally, there's only one answer I can really give him about tonight. It's most likely the wrong answer, but considering I'm coming out of the sex fog and I'm still itching to stay, it's really my only option. I'll deal with the fallout of it later. While I'm wallowing in my cubicle at work, wishing I was with him instead of there. While my small infatuation will grow to full-on longing.

In the end, there was no way I was ever going to say no to begin with.

"I'll stay again tonight," I say.

Kelley pulls away from me, wide smile with a hint of smugness to it.

Now he knows not only can he get his way with me, but he knows exactly how to manipulate me into giving in. It's another one of those things I should care about, but I really fucking don't.

After dropping Kelley off at the stadium, I head home to Trenton to check in with my parents. I was going to on the way back to New York, but I have a few hours to kill before the stadium is open to the public.

Kelley scored me a ticket right above the team's dugout for

Chapter 27

tonight, and as much as I know staying an extra night could be detrimental to my heart, ego, and career in the near future, I'm excited for it anyway.

I pull up to Mom and Dad's house, assuming they'll be home because they don't have the disposable income to get out much. It kills me that they're in this financial situation at their age and that they should have their house paid off and be enjoying retirement by now. Or at least be close to it.

I will change that for them. One day.

Hopefully, we won't be waiting years for those high school kids to grow up to sign to the majors before I score a huge commission. Ideally, a superstar will fall into my lap.

I find Dad in the front garden, pulling weeds and swearing up a storm. Uh-oh.

"Hi, Dad," I say cautiously.

He lifts his head and smiles. "Theodore. What are you doing here?"

"I had to do some scouting for the firm, so I thought I'd drop by. What are you swearing at? Weeds getting out of control?"

"Your mother, more like it," he mumbles. "I came out here to get away from her excessive worrying."

My chest gives that twinge of guilt it always does. "Is it money?" I still have some of the Kelley bonus left. I should give it to them. I should—

"No, it's your brother."

"Wylder? You heard from Wylder?"

"No, and that's why she's worried. She's on the laptop, using the calculator to work herself into a worry about how his money would've run out by now, and we haven't heard from him—he changed his number, or his phone got disconnected, one or the other. She's convinced herself he's living on the street or is dead in a ditch somewhere."

That sounds like Mom.

"You're not worried?" I ask Dad.

"You know your brother. If he had run out of money, he'd be on

Thad

our doorstep apologizing until we gave him more, and then he'd disappear again."

I agree. I can't imagine Wylder running out of money and deciding to live on the street when he has parents who will give him a room rent-free, feed him, clothe him, dote on him—that's the type of parents they are. Wylder would've come back if he needed them. I'm sure of it.

"I'll go and try to talk her down."

"Thank you," Dad says. "Until then, I'm going to continue to pretend these weeds are too hard to pull out of the ground." He holds them up.

I'm guessing the key to a long marriage is … pretend gardening. I'll put that tip in my back pocket for when I get married. Or have a partner. Am dating someone properly. Anything, really.

The sucky part of all of that is I think I'm ready for a real relationship. Maybe not right away, but I want to start dating seriously. Up until now, it's been all fun, nothing too deep, because I've wanted to be established first. I'm still not there, but I'm on my way. And the one guy I could see myself possibly having more with is Kelley—the one man I can't date publicly for many reasons.

Yet, he's the one I want.

Oh, look, more self-sabotaging crap my mind likes to do.

I shake off those kinds of thoughts before I send myself into a spiral of overthinking and enter the house.

Mom's exactly where Dad said she'd be, hunched over their laptop at the dining table.

She doesn't look up at me as she says, "If you're hankering for lunch, you're on your own. I'm busy."

"Actually, I was wanting to know if I could take you to lunch."

She flinches like I've scared her and looks up at me. "I thought you were your father. But I can't go to lunch. I'm busy."

"So you said. What are you busy with?" I pull out the seat next to her and sit.

"How does Facebook work?"

I laugh. "You're trying to find Wylder on Facebook? Good luck. Even I'm not on that old thing."

Chapter 27

"Where should I be looking, then?"

If I know Wylder and he's trying to prove a point, he'll have all of us blocked across all social media.

"Give the laptop to me," I say, and yep, after a quick search on all my channels, Wylder's profile doesn't show up on any of them.

It's like he really did want to up and leave everyone and everything behind.

"Okay, give me ten minutes, and I'll find him. Go make us some coffee if you're not going to feed me."

"I'll make you lunch when you find your brother." She says that but gets up and starts puttering around the kitchen anyway.

This should be easy.

I set up a fake email address real quick, sign up to all social media platforms using it, then pull photos from stock sites of a random hot girl in a bikini with a guy, open it in editing software and add a bisexual flag love heart over the guy's face, post that to all my new accounts, and then add every Wylder St. James there is. There are a few that aren't him in the pic, a couple that don't have any identifying information, but I add them all because he could be using a fake photo just like I am. Most of the profiles are locked down, so it's easier to add them all to my friends list instead of going through them, trying to weed out the ones that might or might not be him.

That could be all I do and wait, but if he's being cautious of who he's adding, he'd be able to spot a fake account a mile away. So I find other fake accounts. They're usually easy to spot. Add some more of the stock pics of the same couple, not covering the guy's face this time. The only reason I did it on the profile pic is to entice my brother to look further. He loves women, but I also happen to know he can't resist a pretty man. I set the uncensored photos as available only to people who follow me.

It doesn't take long at all for the follows and friend responses to come in.

I realize that catfishing my brother isn't cool, but it's not like I'm going to talk to him as this chick. I only need proof of life.

Thad

And bam. Within ten minutes of posting my new profile, I find his.

"Got him," I say.

"Really?" Mom wipes her hands on a dish towel and comes to look over my shoulder.

"Yup. This was posted yesterday." I hit Play on a video I really should've looked at first.

It's my brother at a pool party, day drinking and making out with some woman. It's not too raunchy, but it pisses Mom right off.

She goes from worrying mother to raging dragon lady. "He's out there with our money, partying it up and not checking in to let us know he's okay. It's like he wants me to worry about him."

"Yeah, I'm assuming that's the reason he blocked us all on socials. Anything he does is because he wants attention."

Mom hangs her head. "We didn't raise him that way."

"I know," I say softly. "But even I understand why he does it. You and Dad put in so much time and effort with me and baseball—"

"We would have for him too, but he never wanted to do anything. It was all video games and friends."

"I know that too. And I'm not saying you did anything wrong. I'm just saying, I can see why he seeks attention."

Mom looks at the screen again. "So he's fine."

"More than fine by the look of it."

She slumps. "He's fine," she says again, like she's trying to convince herself.

I swear if I ever see my brother again, I'm gonna punch him in his big, stupid nose for making Mom upset. But by the look of it, he's living it up in LA and won't be coming home anytime soon.

Unlike me, who might make an appearance every weekend when there's a Philly home game.

Chapter 28
Kelley

Whether it's because I know Thad is right there behind the dugout or the team is having an off night, this game is not going well.

At all.

It's one of those times where nothing seems to stick. Usually, there'll be successful innings and bad innings, with always the hope of having the best yet to come. This game, though, it's terrible inning one after the other. It's not like the other team is doing amazingly either, but at least they're on the board.

The most annoying thing of it all is that I can't do anything to make it better because I'm not pitching tonight.

Zaka's up to bat, and after the whole "I thought that sign meant swing," he follows Skip's instructions to the letter. The last thing he wants is to go rogue when we're so far behind and still not get anywhere. But because he obeys our manager's signals, he strikes out.

It's not his fault. Not Skip's either. It's just a bad night.

Zaka throws himself down beside me on the bench. "That's embarrassing. Is your friend in the stands going to run home to Merek and tell them how shit I'm playing?"

"Friend?"

"Thad. I saw him in the stands, no?"

"Oh. Right. Yeah. He's there." I didn't realize anyone from last night would recognize him because who looks in the stands? I try to avoid all eye contact with the crowd as much as possible. Then I remember people who don't have crippling anxiety are able to do a lot of things I find daunting. "And don't worry. Everyone's choking tonight."

"Did they put something in the water in our locker room? Sucking pills?"

"I wish a childish prank was responsible because then we don't have to face the facts."

"We suck in general?"

"Yep."

He throws his head back. "I was hoping to impress Thad."

My heart thuds that tiny bit harder. "Oh?" Is he ... saying what I think he's saying?

Zaka's eyes meet mine, and they look like they're studying me. "You got dibs on him?"

"Dibs?" I have no claim to him at all, even if I might want one.

Then Zaka smiles, and I realize my wrong assumption.

"He's not even my agent," I say. "You're welcome to request him for your rep team, but he's only an intern. I don't think he has much of a say. Merek is great at contracts."

"I liked Thad's vibes last night."

Again, it sounds like he's asking about him in a social way, not in a professional manner, but I'm not asking him to clarify. You don't do that to someone.

"I have no doubt he'll make a great agent someday."

"But not your agent? Is there a reason for that?" Okay, now I definitely know what he's asking.

"There's nothing going on between us. It wouldn't be allowed."

Zaka licks his lip. "Okay, cool. Next time I have a meeting with Merek, I'll let him know I'm interested in Thad."

Does he realize at all how he sounds? I'm trying not to cringe because the thought of Thad with anyone else makes me antsy. Even if this is professional speak, I can't help hearing it differently.

We're pulled from the conversation by Hunter smashing one

Chapter 28

high and far. We stand, watching it as the ball flies toward the stadium wall. We collectively hold our breaths.

And when it disappears over the fence, we all start yelling.

Maybe we can turn this around after all.

We couldn't turn it around.

Like with any game we lose, I find myself asking what we could've done better, even if today's loss isn't on my head. I'm glad I wasn't out there, or I'd be a complete mess.

Losses happen, but maybe this one is hitting extra hard because I knew Thad was in the stands, and I might not have been on that mound tonight, but this is still my team.

I can barely look him in the eye when I find him again outside the player's exit, but he can either read my mind, or it's that he knows what it's like to lose a game, so he's there to welcome me with a warm yet sympathetic smile.

"Go ahead and say it. We sucked."

He lifts one shoulder. "It was an off night. They happen."

I step closer to him. "Let's get out of here before I give in to the urge to kiss you right here where anyone can see." Not only kiss, but I want to hold his hand on the way to my car, hug him for comfort over the loss, and never stop touching him.

We begin walking to his car, choosing to leave mine here again. The team is going on a road trip tomorrow, so it'll be here for the next week anyway. "Before we head back to your place, can I take you somewhere?"

"Like on a date?" I try not to sound too excited about that, but it's possible it shows all over my face because his easy smile drops.

"Uh, well, I was going to take you to eat, so I guess it could be considered a date? But, I mean ..."

"It's not like we're dating. I get it." Apparently, I can cover my disappointment better than my excitement because Thad's shoulders lose some tension.

Kelley

Once inside his Jeep, he turns on the ignition but doesn't put the car in drive. He turns to me. "You know, if it weren't for me being an intern at King Sports and having to pay my dues and we were allowed to date, I'd want to date you. Just want to put that out there in case you think I'm not in this for you or only want to get my rocks off."

While that makes my chest warm, it also makes me want to come up with a solution on how to rectify the situation.

"Can't you intern for a different firm?" I'm only half-joking.

"I was lucky to get this internship, if I'm honest. I think the only reason I got it was because Damon sympathized with me over the end of my baseball career."

I reach over and take his arm. "I was joking about changing jobs. I understand more than anyone about putting your personal life on hold for your career. But I wanted you to know if things were different, I'd want to date you too."

In the safety of his car, in this darkened and empty parking lot, Thad leans in and kisses me, his lips soft.

It's a sweet apology that only makes me more upset that our timing is crap.

I might not be completely ready to date out in the open for the public to ridicule my life, my choices in partner, and ultimately who I am as a person, but I'd take that step with Thad if I could.

It's most likely because this is still new. Sure, we first hooked up almost six months ago now, but in terms of seeing each other, these last couple of weeks are the only time we've actually spent together. We're still in the infatuated, sex portion of getting to know each other, so our thoughts on dating are probably wrapped up in that.

But there's no denying things are different with him. I can be myself. He accepts my wonky mental health … He has so much potential to be something more than anyone's ever had in the past.

I'm tempted to talk to Damon about it, ask if there's any possible way to make it happen, but I don't want Damon to lose respect for Thad or fire him for the mere suggestion of possibly dating a client. It's not like he's my agent though.

Chapter 28

But that does remind me...

I reluctantly pull away so I can fill Thad in. "So, Zaka and I had an interesting conversation during the game."

He laughs and shakes his head as he puts the car in drive and finally takes off. "I kiss you and you think of your teammate? If Zaka didn't scare the shit out of me, I might have to throw fists."

That image is sexier than it should be. Thad getting so jealous he wants to punch someone out for me. It's one of those things that's sexy in theory but not so attractive in real life when the fallout of that would be a media circus and charges filed, but the thought of it is hot.

"You might want to put those knuckles away, tough guy, because he's interested in you." I purposefully leave off the "being his agent" part just to see his reaction.

He frowns. "In me? I was sure he was interested in you last night at the bar."

That stops me because if he sensed the same thing I did, does that mean Zaka's queer? "Do you think he's ..."

"He bats for our team? I'm not sure. My gaydar has never been perfect."

"I don't think I even have gaydar. Or it's buried deep down inside me somewhere, and I refused to activate it in fear it would flash in neon above my head, giving me away."

"Last night, he ..." Thad bites his lip and weaves through traffic effortlessly as he talks. "He didn't say anything specifically, but he asked about us. I said that we were friends and weren't allowed to date because I worked for King Sports, which totally gave him the impression we want to, which is true, but I told him nothing has happened to cover our asses. Just the way he accepted it or, I don't know, had the realization that you might have been with me, it felt a lot like disappointment. Like he now thinks he had no chance with you. But again, I could've been reading into that."

"It sounds similar to how he was talking tonight but about you. Almost like he was testing the waters to see how I'd react if he said he was interested in you. But then he followed it up with he thinks you'd be a good agent on his team."

Kelley

The car swerves. "He thinks what?"

"Not expecting that?"

"Considering the only other client I've gotten close to has said he would never want me as his agent, I was beginning to think no one would want my kind of tough-love approach."

"Whoever that client is must have thin skin and a huge ego." I grin.

"Or an anxiety disorder and way too many intrusive thoughts running through his head."

"See, you can logically and rationally tell yourself why I'm not the right client for you, but that doesn't mean Zaka's not. I told him to talk to Damon about having you on his team under Merek. Like Brady is for me. I hope that's okay."

"It's ... yeah. It's surreal Frederik Zaka even knows my name. Even more surreal he wants me to rep him. Are you sure he meant me? We barely talked."

I shrug. "Maybe what you said to him spoke to him on a deeper level somehow."

"All I basically said was you and I can't date because of King Sports. I don't see how that would make him go, 'Ooh, I want him for an agent.' Especially when I get the impression he didn't believe me when I said nothing is going on between us."

"Are you saying you don't want to rep him?"

"Are you kidding? Repping someone like Zaka is a dream. The cut on his contracts alone ..." Thad whistles. "I'd be stable enough to stop worrying about my parents. But at the same time, I'm worried about getting clients the right way."

"Is there a wrong way to sign a client?" I look around where we are on the I-95. "And where are you taking me?"

"I'm kidnapping you, and that's my answer for both questions you just asked."

"Hey, I was promised food. You don't need to kidnap me. I'll go willingly. Who knew playing so badly burned a lot of calories?"

"You didn't play badly. You had an off night. That's all. Also, how did you not get kidnapped as a child if you can be lured away with the promise of food so easily?"

Chapter 28

I throw up my hands. "Right? Where were all the vans with free candy when I was a child? The way adults spoke about them, I expected there to be more."

Thad pulls off the interstate and heads toward the Delaware River, where he turns into a parking lot for an old Irish pub.

"This is where you wanted to take me for dinner?" I ask. It's the opposite of romantic. It might be on the water, but it's a dive bar. At least by the look of the outside.

"This place holds a special place in my heart and means a lot to me, and you take that tone?" He mock gasps.

"Sorry. Not judging. Just ... thought this was going to be a date. The first and last of ours, seeing as we're technically not allowed to go on dates together."

"Luckily, we're not allowed to date because if you think this is bad, this is still above my dating budget."

I want to ask where he takes his other dates, but at the same time, I don't want to hear about those.

We climb out of the car and make our way to the entrance. It smells like I thought it would, of fried food and stale beer.

We're seated at an old wooden table. The place is loud, the crowd is ... an interesting and eclectic bunch, but I guess it does have this old-time charm to it.

We're handed menus and given two empty glasses with a pitcher of water, and when our server walks off, I lean in and ask, "So, why is this place so special to you?"

"When my friends and I used to go into Philly to party with fake IDs, we'd come here first and fill up on the cheap beer so we didn't have to spend as much in the city."

I flop back, no longer leaning toward him, and hold my heart. "So, it's the most special place of all your special places."

He looks over his menu and doesn't make eye contact as he says, "Play your cards right and I might show you my mostest special place later."

I'm sure he's talking about his dick, and I am one hundred percent okay with that.

But I can't lie. I'm also enjoying this. Just being with him. I want to do more of it, even if it runs the risk of getting in too deep.

Kelley

It's weird that I can be anxious about dating, too scared to put myself out there, but with Thad, I'm doing that despite knowing I shouldn't.

If I had a dollar for every time I wanted to make sense of my brain, I wouldn't have to play pro ball. I'd be the richest man on the planet.

Chapter 29
Thad

With us being in the dive bar this is, no one notices us in our own corner of the restaurant. Kelley's animated and happy, and it does things to my insides to see him so uninhibited.

His suggestion—joke or not—to change firms, while practically impossible, held real temptation. I could look at changing jobs. I could leave King Sports and chase being an agent with a less reputable brand, but doing that just for a chance to date Kelley? It's extreme, even for self-sabotaging me.

Plus, with this chance to work with Zaka and the possibility of the two baseball kids who seemed in awe of me when they're the ones with the bright futures ... King Sports is where I need to be.

Even if I can barely restrain myself as I look over at Kelley smiling, his dark eyes holding a spark I've only seen a couple of times on him.

He's downed a plate of fries and battered fish, and now he's eyeing off mine.

I push my basket—because this place is classy and food comes in a basket—toward him, and he starts eating my fries so casually, like we've been here a thousand times and he's stolen my food a thousand more. It has a sense of familiarity to it that makes me crave more of these small moments with him. Moments we shouldn't have.

Thad

"So did you go see your parents today?" His question is as casual as his posture, and even that feels familiar.

"Yep."

"How are they?" Kelley throws another one of my fries in his mouth.

"Getting on each other's nerves, but good."

"And your brother?" He eyes me now, as if bracing himself for bad news.

"Mom's worried, but Dad and I aren't. I set up a social media account to catfish him so we can keep an eye on him, seeing as he blocked us all. You know, just your average day in the St. James house."

"So he is okay?"

"According to his socials, he's partying it up. He's no doubt run out of the money he stole from Mom and Dad, but he's obviously got someone paying his way."

"Or maybe he got himself a job and is supporting himself?"

"You clearly don't know my brother."

"Everyone has to grow up sometime."

I press my lips together because he's right. But I don't see my baby brother ever doing that. "I hope he's growing up out there. There comes a time in everyone's life where they have to take a hard look at themselves and do what's best for them."

"Like me deciding to come out."

"Exactly. Or me realizing I didn't have what it takes to make it in baseball."

"I'm sure he's out there learning big lessons."

I hope Kelley's right. For Wylder's sake.

Kelley shoves my basket of food back in my direction. "Unlike me, who knows I should've stopped eating about twenty fries ago."

"I guess that means you don't have any room for dessert?"

"If we're talking ice cream, no. If we're talking something else ..." Kelley cocks an eyebrow at me.

"Oh, look at that, it's time to go."

My only regret is driving him all the way out here because we're so far away from his place now.

I can't wait to have him in my mouth again. Last night, it was

Chapter 29

all about his ass. Tonight, I'm going to suck his cock until he comes so hard that all he'll be able to think about until the next time I see him is all the phenomenal things I can do with my mouth.

I'm already thinking about when I'll be able to come to Philly for another weekend. It'll have to be when he has a home game again, and I could borrow the car from my roommates. Though, I could also catch the train if I had to.

I'm so busy thinking about the next time that I forget to stop and ask if there will even be a next time. We've both said we want to date each other while acknowledging it's not a possibility.

We could keep doing what we're doing, see each other whenever we can, and have a secret fuck buddy relationship going on behind the public "friendship," but it's only a matter of time before this friendship gets back to Damon. And when that happens, I don't exactly want to lie to him, but telling him I'm sleeping with the client who gifted me ten thousand dollars for "being there for him" screams of an inappropriate use of power on Kelley's behalf.

The more we mess around, the worse it's going to be if it gets out. Which means we're only boxing ourselves into a corner.

Yet, I don't want to stop.

I try to concentrate on driving, but all I can think about is the man in the passenger seat next to me. His warmth, the way his hand is creeping up my thigh with every mile that passes.

By the time I pull the car into his round driveway, I'm tempted to get the job done here.

Screw going inside, getting undressed, and being comfortable. I'm craving quick and messy, where the transmission gets in our way, with the steering wheel poking me in the back, and all-around awkwardness that somehow makes everything even hotter.

I'm too impatient for anything else.

Kelley opens his car door, but I pull him back before he can make a move to get out.

"I'm so not going to make it inside." I lean over the center console and slam my mouth down on his, groaning against his lips. "I'm so fucking desperate for you."

He moans but breaks away, so I kiss down his neck instead.

Thad

"I'm desperate for you too, but you can't even make it inside the house?"

I chuckle against his skin. "You're the one who's been practically jerking me off through my pants all the way home. I need you in my mouth now."

Kelley grips the back of my head and guides my lips back to his.

I should've specified I want his cock in my mouth, but his tongue is just as welcome. That is until he sneakily pulls free of me and is out the car door before I can stop him.

"Looks like you'll have to come in the house after all."

"Is that a coming pun or an accident?" I call after him as he's walking to his front door.

If he thinks giving me a breather is in any way going to calm me down, he's wrong. He better run if he wants to make it to the bedroom.

He's already inside the house by the time I get out of the car, but he doesn't make it far because my stride is wide, and he really must think that pulling away from me would settle the need I have for him.

That need is more impatient than I am, and I'm like a toddler when it comes to having to wait for the things I want.

At least Kelley has the decency to be shirtless when I'm closing the front door behind me, but he doesn't get to his pants. He literally has no time because I pounce on him.

He laughs when I spin him to face me, and our teeth clang together as I try to kiss him, but then he sinks into it. That is until we stumble over the stairs and both fall.

He grunts. "Should've let you do this in the car."

"Yes. You should have. Because now I'm going to have to blow you on these stairs, and that's going to be more uncomfortable than in a car." Not that I'm really upset about that, because this is still what I wanted.

Fast.

Messy.

Mild discomfort from the stairs digging into my back.

Chapter 29

It's fucking perfect.

Sort of.

Okay, I have no idea how this is going to work, but I'm going to try. I roll on top of Kelley and kiss him while I work open his pants with one hand. My other is resting beside Kelley's head, elbow on one step while my hand grips the edge of the stair above.

My muscles strain to keep the majority of my weight off him, and the tightness in my body only makes the ache in my balls more intense.

When I get his pants undone, Kelley helps me pull them down to his knees. His amazing cock springs free, making my mouth water.

It has to be uncomfortable with how he's positioned on his back, so I do what I do best. I slink down and engulf his whole shaft, taking his cock to the back of my throat.

Kelley's hand flies into my hair as he lets out a string of curses, and an urge to slow down tries to take over. I could suck his cock all night. But I won't be mean. He has to get up early for some road games, and I have to drop him off. We might have all night together, but we don't have all night to fuck around.

I'm going to make him come his brains out and then take him to bed where I'm going to let myself hold him until morning.

I hum around his cock and suck harder. It's my goal to get him to blow as fast as possible, so I bring my A game, and when I sense him getting close, I reach between his legs and play with his balls.

They draw up tight, and in the next second, his release floods my mouth. I swallow him down, every last drop, but even when I suck him dry, I want more.

Kelley has to tap my shoulder to get me to pull back when he's had enough. I force myself to my feet so I don't crush him, and staring down at him with his pants still around his ankles, his naked body on display, and that CA tattoo that makes me mad every time I see it, I know how I want to get off.

"Can I at least return the favor in a bed?" he asks, still breathless. "You know, when my limbs aren't spaghetti?"

Thad

"I have a better idea." There's a growl in my voice as I undo my pants. "Turn on your side."

"Oh, sure, because that's not going to be even more uncomfortable."

I do it for him. I grip his shoulder and twist his body so that tattoo of his is on full display. "I'm going to come all over this tattoo." I hold him in place with one hand while I lower my pants and underwear to my thighs.

To me, CA is a faceless guy from Kelley's past, and when I mark it all up with my cum, I'll be the one he thinks about every time he looks in a mirror and sees these initials. That thought gets me so close to the edge my cock leaks all over my hand.

I use my precum as lube, spreading it all over my tight skin. "I'm close. I'm so fucking close."

"Come on me," he whispers, and it's all over.

I've been so focused on his tattoo, but when I come, I make eye contact with him.

His gaze moves from my cock where it's spilling all over his skin to my face and back again. His tongue darts out to wet his lip.

"You want a taste?" I ask and release where I'm holding his shoulder.

He nods and, as if that was what he was waiting for, sits up and closes his mouth over my tip, licking every bead of cum that remains.

I shudder, my knees weak, but I manage to stay upright. Somehow.

When I'm completely done, I pull out of Kelley's mouth, and he smiles up at me.

"Are you able to walk upstairs now?" He's smug, snarky, and instead of responding with something similar, I lean over and kiss him.

It's soft, far less urgent than before we got off. It leaves me feeling content. Happy. Kelley sighs into my mouth, and I get the same sense from him.

I pull back and stand again, fixing up my pants, and then I hold out my hand for him to take. "Come on. I'm going to take you up to bed."

Chapter 29

He kicks off his pants when he gets to his feet, so he's completely naked. "Oh, so now you want a bed. Just when I want a shower." He gestures to the cum all over his rib cage.

"You're keeping that until at least the morning. I don't care if it will stain your sheets and scent your bedroom to smell like me."

We're not in a hurry as we climb the rest of the stairs and turn down the hallway to his room.

"What's with the tattoo thing anyway?" Kelley asks.

"What do you mean?"

Again, he gestures to his side. "Why?"

"Why do you think? Whoever CA is, he's an idiot for ever letting you get away. Though maybe not as big of an idiot as you are for getting someone's initials permanently on your skin."

Kelley stops walking. He blinks at me. Once, twice. Then he lets out the loudest laugh that's so unexpected I don't know what to make of it.

He takes a while to catch his breath enough to talk. "The only idiot here is you."

"Aww, you say such sweet things to me."

Kelley shakes his head. "I almost want to let you continue to think the initials belong to another man because the possessiveness is kinda hot. Especially when you went full-on alpha by marking your territory."

"When you put it that way, it makes me sound like an asshole."

"Nope. You're adorable."

"That's too far the other way. Coming all over your skin is not supposed to be adorable."

His lips land on mine, but it somehow feels as condescending as calling me adorable. His eyes are still shiny with amusement as he pulls back and says, "CA is the Charlotte Arrows. You know, who I played for in college?"

As his words sink in and I take in his tattoo again, the arrow that holds the letters together, I realize I really am an idiot. "Yeah, well, they can't have you either."

Kelley smiles. "Everyone got one. Do you want to track down all the guys I went to college with and come all over theirs too?"

Thad

"And I'm back to hating the tattoo. You have a matching tattoo with like twenty other guys?"

"I do. But if you really hate it that much, I'll let you mark it up every time we see each other."

"Look forward to it."

But that really only begs the question: when will we see each other again?

Chapter 30
Kelley

THESE ROAD GAMES HAVE BEEN BRUTAL, AND WHERE I WAS having some shitty games before mixed in with some wins, it's only gone downhill after Thad's visit.

I can't get a pitch over the plate if my life depended on it, and I'm starting to worry it does. Not that I think my teammates will kill me, but when your coaches send you to the team physiotherapist to "balance you out," you have to worry. That's when you know they think it's more than a slump. They're worried for your health and physical ability to get the job done. They think you're injured.

And this is probably the worst thing about it all: I'm convinced if I hadn't come out, if I didn't have all this extra pressure on me, this slump of mine wouldn't be seen as anything more.

I'm just about convinced that the reason the average career for a queer man after coming out is two years is because they crumble under the notion that they have to be perfect now. They need to prove themselves more than anyone else. They need to win a pennant to show their worth, while everyone else only needs to do their job.

It's exhausting. I'm worried I'm already approaching burnout, and it's still the beginning of the season.

I need to not let it get to me the way it is, but as usual, telling

Kelley

myself to be logical and actually being able to do it are two separate things.

One good thing about this road trip coming to an end is I have a day off tomorrow, and it's Saturday night, so I was hoping to get in my car and head to New York once we arrive back in Philly.

I haven't mentioned it to Thad because I wasn't sure how I'd feel after ten road games, but I'm wired. I'm exhausted and feel insecure about my season, but I know if I go home, all I'm going to do is dwell on how badly I'm doing.

The thought of driving to New York, seeing Thad, maybe getting us a hotel room for the night ... it's giving me that safe feeling I used to get from baseball.

I type out a message, purposefully making it sound like a booty call because it kinda is, but I also know he'll get a kick out of it.

It's three simple letters:

> WYD

I bite my thumb as I wait for him to answer, but I don't have to wait long.

THAD:
Someone's home from their road trip, I'm guessing?

ME:
Yup. And I have a day off tomorrow.

THAD:
I saw that on your schedule. Got any plans?

ME:
Are you checking my schedule?

THAD:
I do work for your agent. Maybe it was part of my job.

ME:
Was it?

Chapter 30

I can't help smiling. Especially when he replies with:

Nope.

ME:

I was thinking I could drive to New York tonight.

THAD:

Yes. Do it. When will you get here

ME:

Plane should be landing in thirty, and then it's just a matter of getting my car.

THAD:

Perfect. Hopefully by then, my roommates' party will have died down, and I can sneak you in without them seeing.

ME:

Party?

THAD:

There's a birthday thing. I'd offer to come to you, but I'm a wee bit tipsy.

ME:

Tipsy or drunk?

THAD:

Not drunk. But had too much to drive anywhere. You should come take advantage of me.

ME:

Sounds fun, but I don't want to drag you away from your friends. I was thinking of getting a hotel room for us, but you're at a party. You should celebrate with your friends.

As disappointing as it is, it's not fair for me to take him away from his real life for a night of sex. Amazing, hot, freeing sex. I've just about given up on the idea when another text comes through.

Kelley

> THAD:
>
> Please come. I want to see you. And the party really should be winding down in a couple of hours.

I bite my lip. I really want to see him too, but I don't want to impose.

> ME:
>
> I'll come pick you up. Send me your address.

He replies with the address and an eggplant emoji. Tonight is going to be fun.

Tonight fucking sucks.

It's pissing down rain, there was an accident on the interstate, it takes four fucking hours to get into the city, and now that I'm here, Thad isn't answering his phone.

He's probably asleep, though last time I checked in with him to say I was stuck in traffic, he gave me a passive-aggressive thumbs-up emoji. He's younger than me. He should know how rude that is. Only old people do the thumbs-up as an affirmative. I almost want to reply with middle fingers, especially now that I'm outside his place, but I refrain.

I try one more time before I let myself give up, but this time, it goes right to voicemail.

Okay, so his phone either died, or he's made me drive all this way, changed his mind, and now I'm out on the street. I should go to the hotel. Any hotel. But I was really excited to see Thad, and I'm already here. I found a parking spot, and sure, it's actually nowhere near his place, but it's a spot. In New York. That's a miracle in itself. I have an umbrella in my car somewhere. I could go see if he's awake or still interested in coming to a hotel with me. I'll be up there and back super quickly.

Maybe I wasted a trip, or maybe he lost his phone and has no idea that I was still coming.

Chapter 30

Ugh. I'm getting into overthinking mood again, and I need to put a stop to that.

So I search in the back seat, find my umbrella, get out of my car, and then make my approach to the building. Before I can chicken out, I hit the buzzer for the apartment number he gave me.

The door clicks open, so someone is obviously still awake up there, and I let myself in. I have no idea which floor apartment 19 is on, but I get in the elevator anyway, and luckily, the numbers are next to the floors, so I hit level 3, and then I'm on my way.

I knock, but then I remember Thad and I need to sneak around. Kind of difficult to hide from four roommates.

That's if the guy who answers the door is even a roommate. Maybe he's a random guest of their party. Which seems to still be in full swing.

Though, why a random guest would be shirtless is beyond me. With a baseball cap on sideways and bloodshot eyes, he has a look of bewilderment on his face. "You're Kelley Afton."

A loud crash comes from inside the apartment, and when I try to stick my head around him to see the commotion, Thad stumbles, literally, out of nowhere and falls at my feet. He's also shirtless. I get the feeling I'm intruding on something I have no right to be upset about but irrationally am anyway because it took for-fucking-ever to get here, and it looks like he forgot I was even going to show up.

"You're here." His eyes are glassy, and I'm guessing that his little bit tipsy status changed to blackout drunk a while ago.

"Dude," the other guy says. "You got Kelley Afton to come to your birthday? I thought you said he was a dick?"

Thad gets to his feet and shoves his friend, but it's not the dick part I get stuck on. I know he used to think that about me. It's the birthday part.

"It's *your* birthday?" I ask Thad. I really am a dick. "You should've told me. I would've let you have your party, and—"

Thad's on me a second later. His arm goes around my back while he cups my face with his other hand. "I wanted you here. I *do* want you here."

Kelley

I want to give in to his touch, sink into his arms and start this over, but his friend is still staring at us.

I step back, out of his hold.

"Ooh," the friend says. "He's not a dick. You want his dick. Got it."

"Fuck off, Joshy." Thad's arm goes back around my waist and tries to tug me inside. "You should come meet my other roommates."

"Is that okay?" I ask softly. "They're not going to tell anyone I was here, right?"

"Nah, Josh is queer too, so he understands sometimes needing to be on the DL. The other two are straight, but they've never once done anything assholish when it comes to this stuff."

Josh. Other two. The math ain't mathing.

"Don't you have four roommates?"

"Who am I forgetting? Joshy"—he starts counting on his fingers—"Onri, Gus ..."

Josh raises his hand like he's in elementary school. "Sean."

"Yes! Seany." He pouts before yelling, "I'm so sorry, Seany. I'm the worst roommate ever."

"What the fuck did you do?" someone yells back, but the voice is muted as if yelling through a door.

"Question," Josh says. "Why are you two on the DL? You're both hot, and you'd be doubly hot together. Can I watch? Oh shit, that was out loud, wasn't it? Eh, fuck it. Can I?"

My anxiety spikes thinking about it. I'm self-conscious enough when it comes to sex. Having someone watch as I—I shudder. No, thank you.

"No," Thad snaps at Josh. "But you can fuck off."

Josh shrugs. "There's no harm in asking."

"Except for making it awkward." Thad shoves him.

Josh puts up his hand and backs away.

"Okay, let's go to that hotel." Thad tries to take my hand, but I step out of his hold again.

"Maybe this was a mistake. You should party with your friends. I don't want to drag you away from that."

Chapter 30

"There's only my roommates left. Oh, and some chick and her boyfriend, who disappeared into Onri's bedroom with him, but I think they're doing something kinky. They said they were going to smoke weed, but that was, like, an hour ago. So really, it's just Josh, me, Sean, and Gus. Ooh, you should meet Gus. He will love you."

"You want me ... to meet your friends?"

His face falls. "Is that, like, too relationshippy for what we are?"

I smile. "I'm good with it if you are, but I don't want to make you uncomfortable."

"I'm too drunk to be uncomfortable. The guys fed me shots."

"Uh-huh. I'm sure they force-fed them to you as well."

"Sure. Let's go with that and not that I was excited to see you so I might have kept drinking to pass the time, and then I lost count, and then one of my roommates stole my phone because I was checking it too often to see where you were at." Thad sways, and I have to admit he's kinda cute when he's drunk.

I wrap my arm around his waist this time. "Come on. Introduce me to your friends."

"Yes. You'll love them all. We all played baseball, so they all know who you are, but unlike you, we all only had mediocre talent, so we never got anywhere. Unlike you, who's super talented. And hot. You're really hot."

I snort. "Thanks."

Josh jumps out of nowhere. "I play in a high-A league, so some of us made it, fuck Thad very much."

"High-A? Aren't you a little old for that?" I ask.

Thad lets out a laugh. "Ooh, burn."

"I might be the oldest one on my team, but I still have potential. I could make it to Double-A. Maybe. Then Triple-A. Then this fuck here will be begging to rep me, and I'll be all 'Nah, bro. Thanks though.'"

Thad pats Josh's shoulder. "Sure that'll all happen, buddy."

Inside the apartment, the place is as messy as Josh and Thad. There are two guys on the couch playing video games, but there are empty cups, chips, and other party snacks all over the floor, a

Kelley

birthday cake that looks like people have grabbed chunks of it with their bare hands, and there are sex noises coming from somewhere.

While I might have been regretful before that I couldn't get here sooner, I'm glad I get to be here for this. It's giving me a glimpse into Thad's life outside of King Sports, outside of baseball, and outside of us.

It might be chaotic, but I think I like it. Chaos and I don't get along usually, but I think there's solace in knowing everyone else isn't perfect.

Perfection is overrated.

Chapter 31
Thad

I have a belly full of cake, liquor, and maybe a teeny tiny bit of regret. If I hadn't gotten so drunk at the hands of my roommates, I could've been balls-deep inside of Kelley.

Instead, he's here. In my apartment. Looking as delectable as my birthday cake. I'm not usually big on celebrating my birthday, and for this one, I wanted to pretend it didn't exist, but only because at twenty-four, I told myself I'd be so much more successful than where I'm at right now. It's depressing, so I didn't want to acknowledge it. And okay, twenty-four is ridiculously young, I get that too, but at the same time, my goal was to be a high-paid baseball star by now. My expectations on age and success are skewed because of that.

My parents and roommates weren't okay with forgetting about becoming another year older.

Mom drove into the city while Dad was working an overtime shift and took me to lunch to give me their present, which was a scarf Mom's friend made. She wouldn't have spent a lot on it because it's not that great a scarf, and her friend only knits as a hobby, but I don't care what it looks like or how much it was. I'd rather her keep her money.

When I got home from lunch, my roommates had a "surprise party" waiting, but I think they all forgot it was my birthday, too, because it was a haphazardly thrown-together gathering with

Thad

people I haven't seen or spoken to since college, who all had a couple of drinks, some food, and then left.

Anyone else might have been disappointed by the turnout, but this here is what I wanted for my birthday. My roommates doing their thing and Kelley by my side. Or, technically, on my lap. Because there was only room on the armchair, so oh no, it's the only seat available. Sorry not sorry.

I never in a million years thought he'd come in and leave my roommates in shock and awe, but he's here. And he came all this way.

My brain starts thinking all the thinky thoughts it probably shouldn't, but it seems that's the norm whenever I'm near Kelley now.

Josh brings Kelley a drink, while my other roommates ask Kelley question after question about playing in the majors. They ask what the team plane is like, if a professional locker room smells as bad as the ones at Olmstead University, and a million other things that Kelley takes in stride and answers easily.

"Sorry about them," I say.

"Don't worry about it. I'm used to the questions. I'm just glad they're easy ones to answer."

"So, how long have you and Thad been fucking?" Gus asks.

I groan. "You were saying?"

Kelley laughs. "It started last winter."

Gus and Sean, who have been playing video games this whole time, even while talking, both put down their controllers.

"I'm sorry, what?" Gus asks.

"Uh," Kelley stammers. "I mean … since he came to see me two weekends ago?"

I facepalm.

"Oooh," Sean taunts. "Someone's been keeping secrets."

"You said you had to work, and that's why you needed the car," Gus says. "Onri complained all weekend about you taking it for three whole days."

I sigh.

"Oh, shit," Kelley says. He stares down at me over his shoulder.

Chapter 31

"I figured ... you didn't tell me they didn't know. I assumed they did if you were comfortable enough to invite me in here and then pulled me into your lap."

"I said they wouldn't say anything to anyone. Not that they knew everything." Am I actually annoyed? Nope. I don't care. But I will have to apologize to Onri.

"Sorry," Kelley squeaks.

I slap his ass. "You will be. Let's go to my bedroom."

Sean and Gus look at each other, and as if having a silent conversation, they turn their game back on. Loudly.

It's bad enough hearing the noises coming from Onri's room—noises I can't help thinking of the dynamics considering there are three people in there. Are they all together? Is Onri watching? Is—

Then I realize I don't want to imagine my friend in either of those situations and have to shut those thoughts down. It's easy to do when I have the sexiest baseball player in the world in my room.

I close the door behind us and push him toward my bed. My hands are on his hips, and he runs his fingertips up my arms and over my chest, where they settle on my pecs.

"It's cute you think this is going to lead to anything other than cuddling."

"What? Why?" My whine is loud.

"Because you're drunk."

"I'm not that drunk."

"You gave me a thumbs-up emoji. At first, I thought you were rude, but now I'm guessing you were too drunk to string two words together."

"It was probably one of my roommates. They stole my phone ... Fuck, they still have my phone."

"You can get it in the morning. I'm exhausted from all the travel and then the long-ass drive. You're still drunk. And even though it's not the night I planned, it's the perfect way to end your birthday."

I make a sound like a buzzer for an incorrect answer on a game show. "The perfect way to end my birthday would be with a bang. A literal one. From my dick."

Thad

Kelley laughs, but I don't see why the truth is so funny. "Maybe after a few hours' sleep, when you're sober, we can work something out."

He guides me to the bed and pulls back my covers for me. Once I'm tucked in, he moves to the other side and slides in next to me.

"Mm. Sober." My eyes suddenly feel like lead. "Sober sex is also fun." Any sex with Kelley would be fun. I want more of it.

More chances to have it. More visits.

I wish he lived closer than Philly.

Kelley says something about wanting that too, but that doesn't make sense unless he's a mind reader.

"Or if you're talking in your sleep."

"Oh. Inside thoughts are being said out loud." Good to know.

Kelley kisses the tip of my nose. "Please say your inside thoughts out loud. I like them."

I try to think of something funny to say, but all that comes out is "Pineapple nipples" and then I fall into the darkness of sleep.

I awake with a killer hangover but an optimistic outlook on Kelley's and my future possible ... situationship. Because if last night showed me anything, it's that I am undeniably, one hundred percent invested in Kelley, and I want more. Instead of getting pissed at me for being drunk and stupid last night, he stayed. The only thing he was upset over was that I didn't tell him it was my birthday.

I was drunk enough to have fuzzy memories of last night, but I wasn't blackout drunk or anything. I remember the words he murmured to me in bed while I was falling asleep. That he wanted more from me too.

Or maybe I dreamed that part.

Either way, that's not going to stop me from putting it all out there today. I'm not sure how it could work other than me coming

Chapter 31

to stay with him every weekend he plays home games, but I'm willing to do it. The only real question hanging over our heads is if Damon found out, would he allow it, or would I have to choose between my career or Kelley? With Zaka being interested in me as an agent, it doesn't feel as daunting going with another firm as it originally did. If Damon didn't allow it, I could still have both. It would be the more difficult route, but the more time I spend with Kelley, the more I realize some of the best things in life are the things you have to fight for.

I've spent my whole life wanting to be the middle of the pack. I've wanted to be good enough but not one of the greats because I've always thought the higher you are, the harder the fall. But with Kelley, I might be ready to fall.

I roll over, still half-asleep and brain fried, but where I'm expecting to find Kelley, I find nothing but a cold, empty bed.

I swear I woke up multiple times last night with him wrapped around me. Or me wrapped around him. It was as hot as a damn furnace in here, but it was amazing.

I sit up and rub my head. Did I imagine the whole thing? Did last night really happen, or did I pass out drunk after all, miss my party, and dream the most amazing dream about a man driving half the night to come and see me?

My room is quiet, but the TV must be on out in the living room because there are muted voices that I can't make out.

"Get him some water," I hear clearly. The voice is getting closer.

Josh appears a second later in my doorway, wearing only his boxers.

"Aww, you talking about me? I need some water for this hangover." I throw my legs over the side of my bed, preparing to stand.

"Get your own fucking water, but you need to come out here. Now."

I have no idea what's going on, but for Josh to sound this worried, it has to be bad.

"What happened?" I ask.

When I round the bed, I notice Kelley's clothes on the floor.

Thad

Okay, I definitely didn't imagine him being here, but now I'm freaking out that something is wrong with him.

My suspicions are confirmed when Josh says, "I heard yelling, and it woke us all up, but when we got out to the living room, Kelley was on the floor."

I can't get to him faster. While I like that my room is down a hall while three of the four other rooms are right off the living room because it means my room gets less noise than theirs, I'm pissed it takes more than ten extra seconds to get to Kelley.

He's on the floor, like Josh said, and Gus stands above him, holding out a glass of water, which Kelley refuses to take.

He won't even look at it.

I don't think he can see it.

His knees are tucked up to his chest, and he has his arms wrapped around them like he's hugging himself and trying to make himself as small as possible.

He's in full-blown panic mode, and I'm not sure anything can bring him back.

I fall to my knees in front of him. "Kell?"

I get some movement, a flickering of his eyes as he moves his gaze to mine, but it's like no one's home. His dark brown stare almost looks like he's in a trance, a hypnotic state.

I grab the water from Gus, and Kelley takes it from me. He needs both shaking hands to lift it to his lips, but he downs the whole thing.

"Just breathe," I say.

I want to ask him what happened, but he's in too high of an elevated state. Making him talk about it right now will only make things worse. His phone is beside him, and seeing as none of my roommates would've been yelling at him or vice versa—they don't have reason to—I can only assume he was on the phone.

"Did any of you hear anything that was being said?" I ask my roommates while I pick up Kelley's phone.

He doesn't try to stop me. Not even when I use his face to unlock his screen.

Chapter 31

I go to his call log, and my heart sinks. "Where's my phone?" I demand.

"What is it?" Josh asks.

"You fuckers took my phone last night. Go get it."

Gus disappears and then hands over my phone, which, weirdly, has full charge. Knowing Gus, he probably confiscated it and then charged it for me. He has a weird sense of punishment.

I'm terrified my suspicions have been confirmed when I have three missed calls from the office. On a Sunday.

I go to my voicemail, and the first one is Brady telling me to answer my goddamn phone. The next is just a frustrated rumble of random noises and swears, and I think it was Brady again but can't be too sure. It's the third one that gets my heart pumping.

"Hey, Thad, it's Damon. I know you're not technically Kelley's agent, but we had to give him some tough news this morning, and now, Brady, Merek, and I can't get a hold of him. We were hoping you could try. One of us might need to go to his place to make sure he's okay if we can't speak to him. Anyway, let us know as soon as you can."

There'd be no point in them trying to go see him in Philly when he's literally only a couple of blocks from the office.

"Kelley," I say again. "Damon and everyone at King Sports are worried about you. What happened?"

In my head, I'm silently chanting, *Do not be a trade. Do not be a trade.*

"I-I ..." He sucks in a sharp breath. "I've been traded to LA."

Motherfucking son of a whore.

It couldn't have been the two teams in New York or even the one in Boston. It had to be as far away from me as possible.

It might be selfish to have that as my first thought, but considering five minutes ago, I decided I want to be with this man in any capacity I could be ... I can't help thinking this trade was fate's way of reminding me I can't have what I want.

I couldn't have baseball, I can't have Kelley, and I can't have happiness.

Is this my karmic justice for getting all of Mom and Dad's

Thad

attention growing up? Did my brother put a hex out on me to be miserable forever? Alone? Bitter?

"I knew it," Kelley says.

I rub his leg. "Knew what?"

"That coming out would be bad for my career. I'm in a slump, and instead of having faith I'll come out of it, they're shoving me out. Making me someone else's problem."

"I know it might seem that way, but I'm sure there are other reasons for the trade." I'm not, actually, but hey, look at me, learning how to use supportive words instead of non-dismissive or tough-love words finally.

Kelley's finally coming out of the fog, catching his breath slowly, and when he manages to calm down and looks at me, it's with ire and confidence. "Whatever the bullshit reason, I'm going to prove them wrong and make them regret the day they ever let me go."

I force a smile. I genuinely am proud of him for pulling himself out of a panic attack, but I can't smile for real when my heart is hollow.

Chapter 32
Kelley

I'm pissed. No, I'm more than pissed.

I've been worried about this moment happening. About being traded or made to feel like I'm not good enough.

I had an amazing season last year with Philly, and now, because of a string of unfortunate games and a slump, they're kicking me out. Really? Trades happen all the time, and from the outside, this move might seem warranted, but the first chance they get, and bam, I'm out of there.

"I need to call Damon back," Thad says. He's staring at me with concern in his eyes, and I don't blame him.

I went full meltdown mode on him. *Real attractive, Kelley.*

Not that it really matters because now, with me moving to LA and Thad living in New York, whatever I thought we were building or could possibly build has been cut off at the knees.

Which is another thing I'm mad as hell at.

I'm so mad I could cry, but I'm not going to let that happen. I stare up at Thad. "Call Damon and tell him I'm going into the office."

Thad hits Call on his phone. It's not until he says, "He's here with me," that it registers it's a Sunday, and Thad and I have no logical reason to be together on a Sunday morning. "Yeah, I'll bring him in. We'll be there in twenty." He ends the call and turns to me.

Kelley

"I need to shower, get in some fresh clothes, and try to get rid of this lingering alcohol and sweat smell."

"I can wear what I wore home yesterday, I guess."

Thad shakes his head. "Joshy, go grab one of your suits for Kelley to borrow." He holds his hand out for me to help me stand. "I'd give you one of mine, but you'd be swimming in it."

He's being so nice, so ... boyfriendy, and not at all like the Thad I first met, and now he's put everything on the line for me.

"What did Damon say?" I ask. "When he found out I was with you?"

Thad doesn't seem rattled. "Surprised, but nothing happened last night. You came to my birthday party because we're friends. That's all it was."

Even if that's the truth of what happened, we both know there was more to it than that. Maybe he was too drunk to remember, but last night, he said he wished we could see each other more often. We were on the same page.

I was even thinking about talking to him about asking Damon if we could date without it affecting either of our positions with King Sports. It wouldn't have been the best time to come forward publicly with a relationship with how bad I've been playing, but I was seriously contemplating it.

And now ... now everything is falling to pieces, and I'm not sure I'm going to recover from this setback. Every time I head toward that pitcher's mound now, all I'm going to think of is that I was traded. That I only have another year and a half left on my career.

Because that's all I get.

Two years after coming out. I wanted to be the outlier, not the rule, but it's looking like I won't get that.

I dress while Thad showers, and it only takes us ten minutes to head out the door and another ten to walk to the King Sports office.

We're silent most of the way, only asking important questions like "Do you know where you're going?"

To which Thad replies, "Yeah, I think I know my own way to the job I work at five days a week. Unless you're talking about a

Chapter 32

philosophical life kind of way. In which case, no. I have no fucking idea."

Fair enough. It was a stupid question to ask, but he's been leading me down side alleys and across streets. I don't know New York well, and it feels like we've gone in circles somehow.

I'm not sure if it's the hangover or if Thad's as mad as I am that I've been traded. I want to ask, but I also don't want to seem full of myself. It's not my ego wanting to ask him how he feels about it; it's my heart.

Because aside from coming out and playing badly and the all-around dickness of the team's management for deciding this, one of the things that is most upsetting is I don't get to see how Thad and I turn out.

Sure, we're only getting started, but the potential ... it's such a wasted opportunity.

Thad lets us into the building and uses his staff ID to get us up to the right floor.

Damon, Merek, and Brady are waiting for us. Brady has two large cups of coffee—the cafe-bought kind, not the office kind—and he hands me one and Thad the other.

Thad frowns but accepts it, and then they lead us to the infamous conference room where Thad spilled his coffee all over me.

Ah, the good old days.

I want to make a joke about keeping Thad away from me with the weapon Brady just gave him, but I don't have it in me.

As we all take a seat and Thad sits next to me, Damon, Merek, and Brady have documents in front of them.

"We're sorry Merek had to call you like that," Damon says. "Especially seeing as the team hadn't informed you beforehand."

Getting trade notice from your agent can be common, but it's another big fuck-you from Philly. They couldn't even call me themselves. And Merek is great with contracts but not so great with delivery. He assumed I already knew, which made getting the news ten times worse.

"Los Angeles has taken over the remainder of the three-year contract you signed with Philly, and now it's a matter of working with your new team to get you on a flight tonight for tomorrow's game. Don't worry about packing up your house and all that. We can organize that for you."

Brady's frantically jotting down notes.

I slump. "I hadn't even thought about my house. I bought it using my signing bonus as a down payment. Now, it's what, just going to sit there empty? And if I sell it, am I going to get anywhere near the same amount I paid for it only a year and a half ago? Why did I buy a house when I knew this was a possibility? What is wrong with me?"

"Nothing," Brady and Thad say at the same time.

Damon, who's usually ready to step in after one of my anxiety-filled tangents, remains sitting there, watching me almost have a second meltdown of the day.

"It's going to all work out," Brady says. "Yes, this is unfortunate, but trades happen, and we're used to handling these things. We can do it all. Pack you up, move your stuff, sell your house. You don't have to worry about anything except dusting yourself off and holding your head up high when you walk into that locker room tomorrow and greet your new team."

My stomach is in knots, and I want to vomit.

New team.

I'm leaving Philly.

I naïvely thought I'd stay there for most of my career.

I naïvely thought I could keep my anxiety and baseball separate forever.

I don't regret my choices over coming out when I did, but I am heartbroken that the world of sports can still be ass-backward when it comes to gay athletes. I can also acknowledge that if I hadn't played as badly as I have been, they wouldn't have done this to me. They would have no cause.

"At this point," Damon says, "is there anything else you need from us?"

I'm guessing asking to send Thad with me to hold my hand isn't on the table, even if I want it to be.

Thad must be able to sense I'm holding back, too scared to ask,

Chapter 32

because he leans forward. "Whatever it is, you can ask. If one of us can't handle it, we'll find someone who can. We're here to make your life easier."

That's just it. I can't ask for this. I can't ask for *him*.

"Would it make you more comfortable if I flew out to LA with you?" Brady asks.

Damon huffs. "So you can go see your boyfriends? No."

Thad and I glance at each other. Brady has boyfriends? We knew because of the Catskills, but it's all official now?

"Excuse me," Brady says. "I'm actually offering my services here. Going beyond for the client. The fact Kit is with Prescott in California at the moment has nothing to do with it. Except maybe the convenience of seeing them next weekend. On my days off."

"Thad, what's your schedule like?" Damon asks. "Can you take a few days to represent Kelley and the firm while he settles in with the new team?"

Thad hesitates, which hurts, but I also understand it.

His hesitation also brings Damon to pause. Damon's gaze narrows, his lips purse, and is it just me, or did the thermostat short-circuit and turn up the heat a few degrees? I'm sweating in Thad's roommate's cheap suit.

Damon leans forward and puts his forearms on the table while he fiddles with a pen between his fingers. "Merek, Brady, you two can get started on working on Kelley's trade and organizing anything that will make his life easier. I'm going to talk logistics with Thad and Kelley."

"Am I looking for one or two seats on the plane?" Brady asks.

Another pause from Damon. More pursed lips. "Two."

I try to tell myself that everything is okay. That him asking for two seats is a good sign. If he suspected Thad and I were together in any romantic capacity, he would ask for one.

Then again, this morning, Thad didn't hesitate to call his boss and admit we were together when this all went down. I can tell Damon is suspicious, and with everything going on, with there being no future between Thad and me, the urge to protect him outweighs all the stress, all the worry I have over this move to LA.

Kelley

As soon as the door is closed after Brady and Merek leave, Damon says, "So ..."

And it's so intimidating that I blurt out, "It was Thad's birthday yesterday."

Damon's brows shoot up. "It was? Happy birthday."

"Thanks," Thad mumbles. "It wasn't a big deal. My roommates threw a party, and Kelley was there."

"Uh-huh." Damon leans back. "And why are you telling me this exactly?"

Oh. Fuck. He only got one word out before I answered a question that wasn't asked. If that doesn't scream guilt, I don't know what does.

"I thought you were going to ask why we were together when you called this morning. The answer is I went to his birthday party, crashed at his place, and so yeah. I was in the city already. We've become friends since our time in the Catskills."

"Friends," Damon repeats. It's not really a question, but it sounds like one.

"I went to his game while I was in town a few weeks ago. Went out with the team afterward."

"When you went to scout those high school players," Damon says.

"Yep."

"And is that why Frederik Zaka is calling about you?" Damon turns to me. "Are you thinking of asking to move from Brady's client list to Thad now you're 'friends'?"

"The air quotes hurt, boss," Thad says lightly. "But no. I'm still not the right fit for Kelley as an agent, but I could be good for Zaka."

"He'd be great for Zaka," I say.

Damon sighs. "I'm struggling a bit here. I'm trying to wrap my head around the timeline of this ... *friendship* and decide whether or not I feel like something inappropriate has happened. Especially seeing as there was money that exchanged hands. If it was just the bonus, that would be one thing. But you've kept seeing each other

Chapter 32

since then, staying over at each other's houses ..." He lets that linger there.

I swallow so hard the sound echoes in my ears. There's no point in telling Damon the truth. I'm leaving and moving across the country. This trade has put the last nail in the coffin that was our ... fling.

"Thad hasn't done anything inappropriate," I say. "He's not trying to poach me as a client, and he didn't approach Zaka either. That was all me. I introduced them, and then Zaka asked about Thad, and seeing as we are friends, I recommended him. Though I did warn him about his tough-love style of management. All he's been doing is using the network you gave him to his advantage. He's passionate about being a good agent, and he's trying and learning, and other than baseball, being an agent is basically all he talks about."

Damon glances at Thad. Then back at me. He leans back in his seat, his brow scrunched as he tries to process what I'm saying.

Then, his gaze lands on Thad once again. "I'm going to come out and ask point-blank. You've slept with Kelley, haven't you?"

I'm apparently not as good at covering as I hoped I would be.

Thad hangs his head and sounds so defeated when he says, "How much trouble am I in?"

Chapter 33
Thad

Happy birthday to Thad. For your twenty-fourth birthday, you get to go to the unemployment office. Have fun!

I know I'm in trouble, but I'm hoping I can find a way to hold on to my job here.

Damon takes out his phone and hits a number. "Can you come take Kelley into my office and then book what flights he needs, go home to Philly with him and help him pack some things, and then go with him to California?"

Brady's excitement can be heard where I'm sitting two seats away from Damon. I shouldn't have hesitated when Damon asked if I was willing to go with Kelley to LA, but minus when we were in the Catskills, I haven't been with Kelley on Damon's dime.

I understand that with me being a representative of King Sports, a friendship with a client might be crossing lines. I didn't set out to do that, but just because there was no intention behind it, that doesn't mean lines weren't blurred.

Kelley stands and leaves the room when Brady pops his head inside the door. I want to tell him I'll message or call him later, but I don't want to make this worse than it already is.

"Okay," Damon says and opens his big black folder slash notebook on the table. "From the top. I need to know when, how many times, if you're in a serious relationship, and if anything can blow back on the company when this all gets out."

Chapter 33

"Umm ..."

Damon's green eyes meet mine, and it's easy to see how Kelley is intimidated by him. He has this commanding presence that forces you into admitting things you're not willing to just so you can get his approval. He's got this whole Daddy vibe that I'm usually not into but for some reason is extremely attractive on him.

"The first time was in the Catskills," I say. "It was the only time we were together while I was technically representing King Sports."

"Don't you understand that you're always representing King Sports? You are part of this brand, which means you are King Sports. Always."

"Sorry, yes. I understand that. I mean, it was the only time I was, I guess, being paid by you to be in the same vicinity as Kelley. All the other times, either he or I made the effort to see the other, knowing full well it shouldn't happen, could look bad, and would put my career on the line."

Damon runs his hand over his silver hair. "My main concern is the money. This bonus. It could be seen as payment for sex—"

"God, no. It was nothing like that." If I want to keep my job, I'm going to have to be completely honest. "I'm in no way complaining about the job you assigned me in the Catskills, but you have no idea how boring it was up there. It was cold and we couldn't go anywhere and we didn't have technology because Kelley couldn't be around social media, so all we really had time to do was talk. And after I got over my bitterness that Kelley had everything I ever wanted, we ... bonded." I wince at the word "bonded" because could it sound any more like *bondage*?

"Where was Brady? No, wait, knowing him ... you had a threesome, didn't you? He—"

"No. He, uh, he might've invited his boyfriends to stay in a nearby cabin, so Kelley and I had a lot of alone time." Sorry, Brady, for throwing you under the bus.

Damon doesn't even flinch. "Of course he did. Okay, so the Catskills. How many times?"

"Do I really have to answer that?"

Thad

"I'm preparing myself for a deposition if one should arise."

"There won't be. Kelley and I really have become friends. This isn't a relationship. It's been a ..."

"Situationship?" Damon asks.

"Yeah. I guess. I would've loved to have seen if it could go further, but considering the distance between New York and Philly and now LA, it's not exactly possible."

"What was the bonus for?" he asks again.

I put my hands up. "I didn't know he was going to do that, and if I was in the position to turn it down, I would have because I knew it was unethical."

"Then why didn't you?"

"I, uh, might not have told you the whole story about my parents. I have a younger brother, and he stole their mortgage money from them and disappeared. They're both still working full-time, they're nowhere near set up for retirement anytime soon, and if they keep going the way they are, they'll still be working when they're eighty. Then Wylder goes and steals from them, putting them further in debt, and I wanted to help them out. Kelley overheard a phone call with my mother while we were trapped inside a tiny cabin for two weeks. I in no way tried to get money from him or trick him or anything. I wasn't expecting the money, and I'd be happy to pay it back if it's an issue. I mean, it will probably have to come out of my paycheck, a little each month, but that's assuming I still have a paycheck, which now saying that out loud and considering you were talking about depositions, I'm not sure I'm going to have a job at all anymore."

Damon taps his pen on his notepad. "I haven't decided yet. I don't like this whole situation. The money, the secrets, the sleeping with a client—"

"I don't want to pull you up on a technicality, but he's not *my* client."

Damon seems unimpressed by that. As he should be.

"I knew you wouldn't like it, and because we didn't think it was going to go anywhere, we didn't think it would ever need to get out. I know that sounds like an excuse or a way to dismiss how serious

Chapter 33

doing something like this is, but there was never any bad intent behind it. We thought no one would find out, and even though we'd been talking about disclosing it all so we could properly date, with the LA move, it's all moot now."

"If you didn't want it to get out, calling me and telling me you're with our client when there was absolutely no reason for you to be with him isn't the smartest thing to do," Damon points out.

"I know. In the moment, I wasn't even thinking about me. My only concern was Kelley and his panic attack. His trade. I was in agent mode."

Damon smiles. "Not to throw your technicalities back at you, but you're not his agent."

"I'm not. And I still don't want to be. I just ... I want to be there for him. Any way I can."

"Because you're friends," Damon says.

"Exactly." Sort of. Not really. "Okay, so there's a chance I could have serious feelings for the guy, but again, moot point, unless you're firing me. In which case, I won't be able to afford rent, I'll get kicked out, and hey, maybe I can follow Kelley to LA, and he can be my sugar daddy with all that baseball money." I forget who I'm talking to for a single moment, and that comes out. "That was a joke, by the way."

He cocks his head. "Was it though? Or is it one of those jokes that holds fifty percent truth?"

"Joke. That maybe holds twenty percent truth. But my focus really does need to be on my career. Not following some guy I've slept with a handful of times. And with how Kelley's season is going, he really needs to focus on baseball."

"So, this is over, then," Damon says. "Nothing more is going to happen between you two?"

My chest aches, and it's hard to breathe as I say, "It's over."

"Okay, you've saved your job, at least, but if anything else happens between you two, you need to tell me."

I'm relieved but also cautious. Like, would kissing Kelley goodbye be included in that? What if we had time for a goodbye fuck?

Thad

As if Damon can read my mind, he adds, "After you say goodbye to him, that is." He nods toward the door. "You better go get it over with before he and Brady have to head to Philly."

I stand, but on my way out, he stops me.

"Happy birthday. Again."

Yeah, such a happy birthday.

I might get to keep my job, but at what cost? I'm still losing Kelley, and I'm fairly certain I've lost whatever respect Damon had for me.

The only question left lingering is was it worth it?

As I leave the conference room and head for Damon's office, where I can see Kelley sitting on Damon's couch, his head buried in his phone, and the stress lines in his forehead ... I have a resounding answer.

If I took away those stress lines for him at all over the time we were together, then yes, it was worth it. Anything is worth seeing him escape his demons and look happy.

Chapter 34
Kelley

"He's getting fired because of me," I say.

Brady doesn't even take his eyes off the computer screen to tell me I'm overreacting. "He won't get fired. Uncle Damon has put up with a lot from some of his agents, and they haven't been fired yet. Sleeping with a client is probably right up there with sleeping with another agent or having a public throuple relationship."

"H-how long have you known? About me and Thad?"

He grins and looks over at me. "I didn't until just now, but I assumed. You were at his place on a Sunday morning. It wasn't a stretch to get there. Plus, also, I suspected something in the Catskills with that whole bear bullshit, but I couldn't decide if you were fucking or fighting."

Thad appears in the doorway, lazy smile on his face as he leans against the doorjamb. "To be fair, it could've been both."

"I always knew your hatred for Kelley was too emphatic," Brady says and gets back to work.

I stand from where I'm sitting on the small couch in Damon's office. "What happened? Are you okay?"

"I'm not fired if that's what you mean, but, uh, we do need to talk."

I gulp.

We need to talk is never good news.

Brady continues to type away on the computer. "You have

about fifteen minutes until we have to leave if we're going to have enough time to get you back to Philly to pack a bag and go. Use your time wisely." He smiles. "Oh, and whatever you do, don't use the stairwell to hook up. You think that is private, and it's not. I can recommend the bathrooms though. No security cameras in there."

Damon breezes in while his nephew is talking, and instead of getting angry, all he does is say, "I'm going to pretend I didn't hear any of that." He holds his hand out for me to shake. "Kelley. It's always a pleasure to represent you. I guess I won't be seeing you around these parts as much anymore, but we'll keep in touch."

He sounds professional, but part of me wonders if he'll be happy that I can't jump in my car and come talk to him when I have a concern about my contract or Merek or my whole brand.

"Thank you. I know I'm a lot to deal with."

Brady snorts. "You think you're a lot? You haven't met my brother, have you?"

The famous NFL quarterback? Nope.

"Peyton's only a lot because he's your brother," Damon says to Brady.

While they bicker back and forth, Thad takes my hand and drags me to the elevator.

"Where are we going?"

"For a walk. I was hoping we'd have time to go back to that cafe to have coffee, but if you have to go, you have to go."

Even though it would be socially acceptable for him to drop my hand when we reach the elevator, he doesn't. If anything, he holds it tighter.

"I wish you were coming with me instead of Brady."

Thad wears a sad smile. "Me too, but Brady's the right choice. He's your agent. Well, your intern."

"Yeah, but you're my ..." He's my, what?

"I'm just the guy you were catching up with every now and then and sleeping with occasionally. And once you're in LA, I'm still going to be your friend."

He has been so much more to me than that, but I'm relieved he still wants to be friends. "So, we're going to keep in touch?"

Chapter 34

The elevator doors open in the lobby, but before we step off, he turns to me. "I want you to know you can call me anytime you want. If you need something—reassurance, advice, anything—I'll be there for you. I promise. I'm only a phone call away."

Or a shortish flight, I want to say, but I don't. Because there's something about the way he's acting, something in his tone that has me questioning his sincerity.

I follow Thad out onto the street, and without a direction in mind, we wander. "What really happened with Damon?" I ask.

"At first, he kind of implied that I was your whore."

I stop dead in my tracks. "He what?"

Thad laughs and keeps pulling me along. "I set him straight, but I'm on thin ice with him at the moment."

"This is all my fault. I shouldn't have given you that money."

"I shouldn't have crossed that professional line and suggested we sleep together."

"Okay, yeah, that too. Though ... I have no regrets." I bite my lip and let that linger in the air.

"Neither do I," he says softly.

"None at all?"

This time, it's his turn to stop. He turns to me and pulls my body flush against his. "There might be one."

Before I can panic about what it is, Thad moves in closer, his lips nearly touching mine. "I regret not having time to give you a proper goodbye."

I touch my forehead to his and breathe him in. "You mean you don't want to come to Philly to help me pack? I'm offended."

"No." His voice is full of sadness. "I'm saying I can't. Damon said I get to say goodbye, but that's it."

Ah. "So this is all we get?"

"Almost. There's just one more thing I want to do." And then his mouth is on mine, right here in the middle of the street in New York City. For maybe the first time in my whole life, I don't care who judges me. Because if this is all we can have, I'm taking it.

If this is our last kiss, I'm only going to pay attention to him, to the way his tongue tangles with mine, and to the sound of his soft moan that reaches my soul.

He might be kissing me to set me free, but all it's doing is locking up my heart and throwing away the key.

I'm not free at all.

I completely and wholeheartedly belong to him.

I've stopped looking at whatever I'm throwing in my suitcase by this point. We have to leave for the airport in five minutes, and I have no idea how a boy who grew up straddling the poverty line accumulated so much crap in a year and a bit, but I have.

"Want me to Marie Kondo this place while you're gone?" Brady asks, holding up a Hawaiian shirt I got from fuck knows where or why.

"Marie Kondo?" I ask, emptying a whole drawer of underwear on top of the pile of clothes already overflowing out of my suitcase.

"Yeah, you know. Go through everything and ask if it gives you joy. If the answer is no, you throw it out. Or donate it. Like this." He holds up the Hawaiian shirt that's covered in baseballs and palm trees. Because those things often go together, of course. "I'm offended on behalf of my Hawaiian boyfriend."

I laugh. "Go for it."

"I'll put this in the donation pile. The donation pile I'm going to send Prescott to piss him off."

I stop dumping stuff and get to my knees to try to squash everything into a space or at least get it in some kind of chaotic order. "You said Prescott and Kit are in LA?"

"Uh, yeah. I didn't want to make a huge deal of it—having two boyfriends—because I thought it might affect my clients, but Damon assures me it's not a huge deal."

"How do you make it work? New York to LA?"

"With a lot of frustration and sexting. I'm lucky in the sense Kit is in between jobs so he can flit from one city to the other, so I

Chapter 34

have one of them with me a lot, but it's been forever since I've seen Pres. I just can't wait to be transferred to the LA office after my internship. It'll be handy for you too, seeing as Damon's talking about letting me take over your account completely once I'm a junior agent."

"You're moving to LA too?"

"Eventually. I'm learning everything I can from Uncle Damon until he says I'm ready to transfer over."

I want to ask if that's an option for Thad too, but distance isn't the only thing that is in our way. Damon has told Thad we can't be together, so even if he was in LA, we couldn't go back to how it was.

"Long distance is hard but doable," Brady says. "Might even be easier for, say, a baseball player who gets sent all over the country for nine months of the year. You know, could meet up in nearby cities after games ..."

"Might be possible for others, but not for me. Not with Thad, at least."

"Bummer. He not into it, or—"

"Damon said it can't continue."

"Huh. Want me to beat him up for you? I can. He might be our boss, but he's my uncle first."

I laugh. "Thanks for the offer, but no. I don't want Thad to get into any more trouble than he's already in. Maybe things would have been different if we told Damon as soon as something happened between us, but because we didn't, there's not a lot of trust there."

"Okay, fair enough. I won't hurt him, then. I'll just threaten to." Brady's alarm goes off on his phone before I can tell him not to threaten Thad's boss on his behalf. "Ope, we need to head to the airport. You ready to go?"

I stare down at my suitcase, which is still in disarray. "Uh, maybe? Help me get this closed."

It's difficult, but once Brady sits on top of it, we're able to zip it up.

"Ready." I stand.

Kelley

"Are you sure?"

This is a big deal. It's huge.

Tomorrow, I'm meeting a new team, settling in somewhere new, and probably living out of a hotel for a few weeks before I can find something more permanent. All the while, playing baseball a billion days in a row and trying to move on from the brief but amazing tryst I had with Thad.

"Kelley?"

I snap out of my melancholy. "Am I physically? Yes. Emotionally? Maybe ask me again in a few months."

I hope it doesn't take that long to settle in to my new city, but as we drive to the airport and check in through security, it's all too overwhelming.

Saying goodbye to Philadelphia is like saying goodbye to a part of me, but it's nowhere near as hard as saying goodbye to Thad.

I give myself the six-hour flight to wallow over what could have been, and then after that, I'm just going to have to let him go.

My conscience scoffs at myself: Sure. Because letting go is something I'm so well-known for.

I hate that the loudest voice of doubt is my own.

Chapter 35
Thad

With Kelley gone and my position at King Sports rocky, I don't really have anything else to do but throw everything I have into proving to Damon that I can do this job.

Sure, I was lazy in the beginning, bitter toward clients, and I wasn't much of a go-getter. I didn't want to stand out because I was sure every single flaw would be ridiculed, but if Kelley has taught me anything, and if I've learned the one most important quality I need to have to be an agent, it's that I can't half-ass it and hope I coast by.

I need to stand out if I want to be the type of agent who signs clients and keeps them. I need to push. I need to woo. And I need to show that I'm as passionate about my clients' careers as I would be if I was in their position.

Which is why I'm in the office every day before anyone else. I proof senior agents' contracts, get them coffee, do whatever errand they want me to during office hours, and then after hours, I stay behind and do whatever I can to show Damon that I'm not just showing up, I'm putting in the work.

Bonus to this is I make myself so busy I don't think about Kelley. I don't have the time to.

Brady has been staying behind a lot too, but he and Damon get up to super-secret business in the conference room.

I leave before they do though, and while I want to be nosy and

Thad

stick my head in to see what they're doing, if it's some freaky-ass uncle-and-nephew incest porn, I don't want to know. Not that it would be actual incest, as Damon's only Brady's honorary uncle or whatever, but still. No, thank you.

Damn it, now I'm picturing it. I don't need to see that. Though the imagery is hot.

For fuck's sake. Maybe I need to get laid. I'm so focused on work, and being here for such long hours, all I have the energy for is to go home and go to sleep. I barely have time to even jerk off, and when I do, all I can think about is Kelley Afton and the sounds and noises he makes while we're having sex. Which then makes me feel sad after I come. And no one wants that. No one wants to have to wipe up tears as well as cum.

Tonight, I'm not the first to pike out of here. Brady runs from the conference room, yelling, "Kit is coming home." Then he sees me in the bullpen and stops, shrugs, and then keeps on running all the way to the elevator.

"If you didn't catch that, one of his boyfriends is visiting from LA," Damon says, and it makes me jump.

Ever since our talk about Kelley, about his warning, and knowing he's not exactly impressed with me, I'm jumpier around him than Kelley ever was. I've caught the intimidation.

Damon smiles at me though. "You're here late."

"Yep," I say oh so articulately.

Damon pulls over Brady's chair and sits next to me. "What are you working on?"

"At the moment, I'm working on ideas on how to better protect athletes from public scrutiny after coming out and looking at contractual law to see if there's any other protections that are possible to be implemented."

Damon blinks at me. And then again. "Did someone ask you to do this?"

"Oh, no. Not at all. This is on my time, but the resources in the office are a lot better than I can find on my internet at home. I've been here late every night, researching."

"I've also noticed in the system that a lot of the agents' proof-

Chapter 35

reading has been completed by you. More than you were doing before."

"I almost don't want to admit to you that I've been coasting, but I have. I've been doing the bare minimum because—and please don't hold this against me—when I first got this job, I was bitter because it wasn't my first choice. This was my backup plan, so I didn't have a lot of passion for it. Now that I've put that behind me, I'm ready. I know I need to prove myself and put myself out there."

"Not going to lie, I'm happy to see this change in you, but what happened to turn it around for you?"

I bite my lip.

"Ah. Kelley Afton happened."

I nod. "Yep. But not in the way you might be thinking."

"Then explain it to me."

So I do. I tell Damon all about why I was bitter at Kelley—not only saying he had what I wanted but going into the resentment I held toward him, not understanding that it was his poor mental health that was making him seem ungrateful.

"Shouldn't you have known all that from his file?"

"I should have. But I didn't. "

Damon tries to cover an inappropriate smile. He's either entertained by my dumbassery or my ability to get away with not doing a lot of work for him in the first six months of my employment.

"What I learned from my time with Kelley is that I have to look deeper than my preconceived notions. I need to get to know a client and tailor my approach to their case to fit them. I know we talked about this briefly after the Catskills trip, but that's what I mean when I say Kelley changed my outlook. It had nothing to do with us hooking up. In simpler terms, he made me pull my head out of my ass and realize not everything is about what I want or what I'd do in any situation. Because of him, I want to be a better agent, and I want to give it my all. So I've been doing that. First with the prospects from Trenton, then Zaka, and now this." I wave to my computer screen, which has some case law on discrimination in the workplace. I'm trying to figure out if there's a way to prevent trades from happening, like

Thad

it did with Kelley. Not only for him but for Zaka as well. If he ever feels the need or want to open that closet door. It's still just a hunch, but even if he isn't queer, this firm represents a hell of a lot of clients who are.

"And what have you found so far?" Damon asks, quickly skimming my screen.

"Not a whole lot. The issue about bringing in LGBTQIA contract ruling is that if we do that for them, we have to for heterosexual players too, so unless the leagues put a bylaw in place with a baseline stat athletes have to maintain to protect them from being traded, it's a no go."

"I'm impressed," Damon says, and it makes me preen. "And while it's admirable that you want to do this for your clients, I can't help thinking that's not who you're doing this for."

"I'm not doing it for Kelley if that's what you're getting at. His trade is done, he's in LA, and there's no going back from that. But there could be something in the future to protect other players."

"Okay, I have a question for you. Do you think Philly traded Kelley because of his sexuality?"

That's a hard question to answer because it's not that simple. "If I take my personal feelings out of it and look at the stats, then no. They had every right to trade him."

His lips quirk.

"But," I continue, "to me, they gave up on him way too quickly, and there might have been a reason for that. It was almost as if they were looking for the excuse to get rid of him. And after that horrible drama around Cooper saying an angry slur online, it wouldn't surprise me if Philly thought it would be easier to get rid of the one they saw as the problem. It couldn't have been the homophobic dickweed."

"Cooper has the most runs out of anyone on that team this season."

"I know. That was a bad example because the stats are on the team's side, and I'm not saying they did anything wrong by trading Kelley. I just ... I want to try to make it better for future athletes going forward."

Chapter 35

This time, Damon's smile is wide. "I love it when I'm right about people."

"Uh ... right?"

"I knew when I hired you that you were going through a lot. I knew there could be some teething problems with you settling in because I saw a lot of my bitterness from when I played inside of you. But I also knew that if you could grow past that, that you would make a great agent one day, and I really think you will."

Weight from all of my insecurities, all my downfalls, my fear of failing ... it's all lifted when Damon says he has faith in me.

"Have you spoken to Kelley lately?" Damon randomly asks, and I'm worried it's a test. It won't matter if it is, though, because I can tell the truth without feeling any shred of guilt.

"There's been a few texts, but not really. He told me when he was all settled into his new place. I congratulated him on a few of his wins. Things like that."

They've been friendly but more toward the side of cordial.

"Oh, other than one that said he was burning my roommate's itchy suit and sending Josh a replacement for the one he borrowed from him." When the Armani suit showed up, Josh wondered if he could sell it and buy a cheaper one so he could put the rest of the money toward this month's rent. His job as a party clown did not last very long. Sorry, *party Batman*. Not clown. He is a bit touchy about that. Something about clowns being scary. Either way, I gave him the money for rent from my Kelley fund, and he kept the suit.

"All itchy suits should be burned," Damon says and stands. "Okay, I'm going to leave you to it. Don't stay here too late. You're an intern. You have the rest of your life to work. If you don't find the right work-to-home-life ratio from the jump, it's a struggle. Take my word on that."

"Thanks, but other than going home to an apartment with four ex-baseball-playing roommates where the whole place still somehow smells like locker room, I don't really have much going on in my life other than work."

"How are your parents doing?" he asks.

At least I can smile about that. "Really good."

"And your brother?"

Thad

"Haven't heard from him, but Mom can keep an eye on him on social media, thanks to a catfishing account I set up for her. To Wylder, Mom is a twenty-year-old college student who loves spring break."

Damon shudders. "I really hope he's not sending your mom all the kinds of pictures my nephews send people they're interested in."

"Fuck. I didn't think of that. Maybe I should log in and do a sweep of the DM folders."

Damon laughs. "There you go. Something else to put your energy toward. Go home. Get some rest and maybe some therapy for whatever you see on that account, and I'll see you in the morning."

Now that he mentions it, I'm really tired, but I have this urge to keep going until I can find something that will protect our queer players better.

It's going to be a long road though, so I should listen to my boss and come back tomorrow refreshed.

Chapter 36
Kelley

As opposed to this trade as I was, I have to admit, it's been good for me.

LA is daunting, mainly because it's another area I'm not used to—like New York—and its traffic is enough to give me a headache, but without sounding elitist, the facilities here are better, so far the team hasn't shown any homophobic tendencies, and I mean, it's California. The weather is great, and there are Pride rainbows on every corner.

Okay, exaggerating that part, but it feels a lot more openly accepting than Pennsylvania.

The transition has been smoother than I imagined, but that doesn't mean much because I imagined a fiery hellscape in which my game, my mental health, and my all-around will to live took a massive dip.

I'm happy to say that maybe Philly did me a favor. Even if it hurts to admit that when I'm single, alone, and missing Thad, even though we rarely got to see each other as it was.

Or maybe it's that he's the only person I've ever felt more than sexual attraction to, so it's harder to move on from that emotional connection.

A few of my new teammates have offered to go to gay bars with me so they can play wingman, but I haven't taken them up on the offer. Mainly because I think they're only doing it to assure me they're cool with the gay thing. Because every single member of the team telling me that on my first day wasn't enough.

It's a stark contrast to when I came out to Philly, and I can only think it's because with them, they felt like I had deceived them for a year by keeping it a secret. This new team have known from the second I became one of them, and they've gone out of their way to make me feel welcomed. Sure, it's made me feel more awkward, but they're trying. That's much better than ignoring me and dropping slurs on social media.

I've gone to text Thad a billion times since I've been out here, but I don't have much to say. My game could still be considered in a slump, but I've had a few breakout games where my body and my head have been in sync. He's sent me congratulatory texts after those games, so I know he's still watching me, but other than "Thank you," I don't reply. Part of me is worried if we get to talking again, go back to those flirty messages, I might not be able to keep biting my tongue.

I might not be able to hold back all the feelings that have only intensified since I left. The ones that make me fantasize about going on a road trip playing against New York, and Thad turns up to watch with a huge sign that says, "I'm here for you, baby," and then, because it's a fantasy, we have sex on the pitcher's mound in front of everyone, and we don't even get dirty from it.

Yes, I definitely do not want to scare Thad off with those kinds of thoughts when our interaction has been reduced to polite but short texts.

As if knowing I'm thinking about him and his texts though, my phone vibrates, and I get the notification that I have a message from him.

Another thing I'm not going to let him know is how embarrassingly fast I reach for my phone every time that alert goes off.

THAD:

How are you feeling about the next three games?

Ugh. He had to ask that, didn't he? Tonight, I'm facing Philly for the first time since being traded. At least it will be a home game for me, so I don't have to go back to the city that once held my

Chapter 36

heart, but at the same time, I've been trying to avoid the knot in my stomach.

When I was traded, I vowed to show them the mistake they made. I'm certainly not doing that with my game lately.

It's not that I'm having a totally poor showing, but come on. Why is it impossible to just say you want to be the best, and then it happens? What is this actually having to work for it crap?

I hit Reply but don't know whether to be completely honest or stick to what I have been doing and not putting any emotion into my texts.

ME.

> I feel like if Cooper is up to bat, I might lose all of my natural talent in my arm and give him a dead ass with my curve ball.

THAD:

> I would pay to see that. You know, if I had any money.

ME:

> Oh no! Wylder trouble again?

THAD:

> Nah. Just poor intern still. Though, being promoted to junior agent is coming up fast. I kind of can't wait, while also silently shitting myself.

He's either extra chatty today, or he's trying to make me feel better about my upcoming game. I hate that my pitching day has landed on the first game against Philly.

I have no doubt Thad's messaging for my benefit, and that makes me miss him even more. This is why we can't have texts. Because with only three, he has me fawning all over him again.

I reread his text and feel appalled at myself. He's talking about shitting himself, and I'm all aww, look at the love hearts in my eyes.

Pathetic.

Kelley

> **ME:**
> Are you worried you won't get the job or worried you will and will be bad at it? Because I can tell you now, if it's the latter, you're going to do great. I dare say after the last time we saw each other, you might have even been able to be my agent after all. You handled my meltdown like a professional.

THAD:
Nah. I handled that unprofessionally.

> **ME:**
> Is that what Damon thinks?

THAD:
No, it's what I think. Had I been your agent, I probably would've told the Philly execs to go fuck themselves. That would be highly unprofessional. Warranted, but unprofessional. How's the new team treating you?

I don't want to boast about how amazing it is here because while I do love it, there is one tiny bit of resentment that lingers from it. I resent that it ended our chance. So I go vague. It's the truth, but it's vague.

> **ME:**
> They're great. Very accepting.

THAD:
Maybe the trade was a blessing in disguise then?

Even though I've been saying that, it doesn't make the sting of it coming from him any less. It takes a while for me to respond to that because I have to refrain from telling him I wish he missed me as much as I missed him. Luckily, I'm in a good headspace and can manage to pretend to be an emotionally stable human being. I've been pretending most of my life, so this should be a walk in the park. Then again, it's not like I've been pretending very well. People like Brady and Damon could see right through me from the beginning. Thad took a while, but even he could read me like a book by the end.

Chapter 36

> ME:
> Maybe.

Okay, so I didn't quite hit the mark, but instead of dragging out the conversation any longer, he replies with a simple:

> Good luck tonight. I'll be rooting for you.

That makes one of us.

Actually, no. I am rooting for myself, but that doesn't seem to matter when I'm out there on that mound, facing loaded bases with a power hitter at the plate. When it gets to that, I always think of Thad watching me, and then I do my best to make him proud.

Sometimes it works, and sometimes it really doesn't.

By some miracle, tonight, it's fucking working. It's working so well that I'm scared to change anything up in case it all begins to go downhill.

Whether I'm thriving under the pressure or my petty bitterness over being traded has superpowers, I don't know, but by the bottom of the seventh, when the only base Philly has gotten was by a walk, I'm trying to keep all my teammates' mouths shut when it comes to saying the thing that starts with N and H. I won't even let myself think it.

My nervous energy has moved from failing in front of my old team to kicking their asses so hard they walk away embarrassed.

I have two more innings to go, and I can't stand still. With us now up to bat, I head to the locker room and shove hand warmers up the sleeve of my jacket and keep a hold of one to make sure my arm stays warm.

Pacing helps calm my mind, but I'm a jittery mess. I can't say I hate it when it's from anticipation instead of anxiety.

This isn't a brand-new feeling for me, but it is rare, and it's like a drug. I want more of it.

Kelley

I hear some yelling come from the dugout, some cheering, so I'm guessing one of our guys crossed home plate or had a good hit. Whatever it was, I internally cheer, "Woo! Go us," and then get back to focusing.

Is it bad that I want us to strike out so I can get back out there and finish them? All this waiting around has the ability to make me begin to doubt myself.

While I'm pacing, our assistant manager pokes his head in from the dugout.

"Afton. Skip wants to talk to you."

Oh, fuck. No, no, no. Don't do this to me, Skip.

I head back to the dugout, where our manager is still watching the game play out. His arms are folded, he has a full-on seventies porn mustache, and he looks like an older Freddie Mercury. Minus the giant teeth. Skip doesn't have that.

"How's your arm feeling?" he asks.

"Good. Better than good. You can't pull me out."

He doesn't take his eyes off the play. "With the amount you've thrown tonight, there's no shame if you want to hand it off to Barstow."

"I know. I just really want to finish out this game. If I can't continue with my streak, then bring out the closer."

"I know you think you have something to prove to us and to them, but you don't."

"Oh, this has gone so far past that now. Because you know why."

"Don't want to jinx it, huh?"

"The minute there's a hit, take me out, and I'll be sure to rest up completely tomorrow."

"Deal. Now, go make sure you're warmed up properly because we're two strikes down, and Fresno hasn't been able to hit anything all night."

I swear the next few minutes move in a blur, along with the next inning, but when my streak continues into the ninth, the jitters are gone, and it's replaced with an eerie calm. They try to come back while it's our turn to bat, but there's something that

Chapter 36

settles in my gut. Something I can't describe because I don't think I've ever felt it before. Not on this level.

Is it confidence? Faith? Whatever it is, it's never been this strong. I've also never been so close to a Nmm hmm-mm before. I'm still refusing to say it.

When I'm eventually called back out to that pitcher's mound, I have only one thought in my head. I only need to focus on getting these fuckers out one person at a time.

Just one at a time.

The first to come up against me is Hunter, my old friend. The first two strikes are easy. The third isn't so much. He has a keen eye when it comes to judging if the ball will be over the plate or not, and even when it's super close, he doesn't swing. And then, on a perfect pitch, he swings. It makes contact. My heart sinks. Right up to the point they call the foul ball.

Thank fuck.

I might be running out of steam, but I can't let it get to me. I can't let the pressure of having the best goddamn game of my life make me crumble, even if I'm on the edge of it.

That confidence I had fifteen minutes ago? It's on shaky ground.

That's when my arm decides to cooperate.

Hunter goes down on my next pitch, and then Zaka heads to the plate.

He takes his practice swings, switching to lefty after having batted right-handed all night. It's probably to throw me off or try something different, seeing as I've already struck him out tonight. A few times.

First pitch: ball.

Second pitch: strike.

Third pitch: he almost gives me a heart attack with a hit deep left field. Just when I think my streak is over, that my confidence is going to shatter into a million pieces and my lifelong dream doesn't come through, Natsen gets under it, and it lands in the safety of his glove.

Kelley

My heart thunders in my ears while I try to get my mind wrapped around only needing one more out.

One more, and I could claim that my career is complete. Not that I'd want to retire after only my second season, but I never thought in a million years I could do this. Not yet. Not now. And not against Philly. I should still be playing for them, damn it.

Skip calls a time-out, and he and the assistant manager come out to the mound.

"Don't get in your head now," Skip says.

I shake out my arm. "Kind of hard not to."

"You've come this far," Walling says. "Whether you get the out or not, all I can say is I'm thankful you're playing for us now."

He's right. I've played my damn heart out, and it doesn't matter if I get this next out or not. It doesn't. Do I want it more than anything I've ever wanted in my life? Yes.

Though, I'd argue I would contemplate giving it up for a fighting chance at following my heart with Thad.

The bottom line is this is important. So fucking important. But if I don't get it? I'm still the hero of this game.

Time runs out on the break, and my managers head back for the dugout.

And then? I face the one guy who has the power to make me falter. The one who made my coming out less than ideal and the one whose face is so punchable I'm tempted to give him a base just to throw this ball right at his nose.

Maybe I should go for the leg and give him a walk so I don't have to face someone who makes me anxious. But at the same time, the thought of striking Cooper out in this moment feels like the right petty revenge for his bullshit.

He moves to the plate, and I take a deep breath.

I try to focus on only the strike, but thoughts of Thad watching, the thought of succeeding, it all races through my mind on a runaway train.

I take my stance, close my eyes, and even though I'm having flashbacks of Little League, where my coaches gave me step-by-step instruction on how to pitch, it's like I forget how to throw a ball at all.

Chapter 36

The first pitch almost does hit Cooper, and he has to jump back. Okay, ball one down.

I kick at the mound, dig my cleats in real deep, and try again. I so badly want these next three pitches to be perfect I'm almost tempted to throw fastballs and hope that he's too slow for any of them. When my catcher calls for my curveball, I consider it an option too. Cooper has more misses than hits on them, but when he connects with one? That thing is going over the fence.

I shake my head, and Alverez signals for a fastball, and I nod.

At the pitch, the second I release the ball, I close my eyes. Not smart, but I can't look.

"Strike."

Yes.

One down, two to go.

Of course, because that worked, this time, I close my eyes again. And when that "Strike" hits my ears again, I almost freak the fuck out.

If it weren't for having to wait for Cooper to be ready, I'd probably have the next pitch flying through the air already to get it done before I can overthink it.

I tell myself to watch this time. This is the pitch. The pitch of a lifetime.

Yet, when that ball leaves my fingers, darkness covers my face.

And then I hear it.

All my dreams coming true.

"*Strike.*"

I fall to my knees while the rest of my team runs toward me and picks me back up. My cheeks feel wet, and everyone is screaming in my face, and when I glance over at the visitors' dugout, Zaka and Hunter haven't disappeared inside with the rest of their team. They're on the top step, applauding and cheering for me. I'm overcome by their sportsmanship and their true friendship.

I give them an up-nod, and they return it with wide smiles that match my own.

"Fuck yeah," Natsen says. "Way to show Philly they never should've let you go."

Kelley

My teammates hoist me on their shoulders.

This is the highlight of my career and something I've only ever dreamed about.

I've pitched my first-ever no-hitter, and life doesn't get much better than that.

And although I'm surrounded by countless people, my only wish is that I had one special person to share this moment with.

I wish I had Thad.

Chapter 37
Thad

"Yes!" I stand so fast my desk chair topples over behind me, and I'm thankful the office is empty at this time of night. But that performance deserves a standing ovation.

Damon and Brady appear from the conference room where they've been doing their nightly brainstorming to try to find ways to better and expand in this business—something I've actually been invited to join in on since Damon realized I was basically doing something similar. But tonight, I wanted to watch Kelley and analyze every pitch, like doing that could tell me how he was doing emotionally. If his game had anything to say about his emotion, he is doing so amazing that I have to question if he misses me at all.

A no-hitter is a pitcher's dream, and he not only crushed it, he did it against the team who traded him.

"What happened? What's going on?" Damon asks. "I heard yelling and then a loud crash."

Oops. "Sorry, but it's probably a good thing you're here. You might want to sit by the phone for incoming endorsement deals, interviews, the works." I hit Settings on my phone to turn off Bluetooth from my AirPods and turn the sportscast on my phone toward them. "Kelley pitched his first no-hitter as a second-year rookie."

Brady's eyes widen, and he grabs my phone off me. "No way."

"I told myself I was only going to check in on the first couple of innings, but I couldn't take my eyes off him. He was magic out there."

"You should've gotten us sooner to come watch," Brady says.

Damon gasps and slaps his nephew over the back of his head. "You should know better."

"You don't jinx a pitcher in a possible no-hitter game. Hit him again from me."

Brady holds up his hand while still watching the feed on my phone in his other one. "Okay, sorry, jeez. And they say hockey players are superstitious." He hands it back to me and takes out his own phone. "I'm going to text him and congratulate him."

I should do that too. I want to, but at the same time, I'd rather call him later and hear his voice. Even better, video call him later. Maybe while I can play dirty and be shirtless.

There's something about seeing him so confident, something about seeing him take something that he was anxious over and turning it into success, that is such a turn-on.

I've missed him as a friend, but in this moment, I miss him as a lover. If I was in LA, there is no way I wouldn't be outside that players' door waiting for him. I guess it's a good thing I'm grounded from Daddy Damon and not allowed to chase after Kelley. But also, damn him.

"Ooh, Prescott's calling." Brady leaves to answer his phone, leaving me with Damon.

Just like he did a few weeks ago, he pulls over Brady's chair to sit next to me. If I could sit back down. Which I can't because my chair is upside down.

I'm quick to fix that and settle beside him.

"You're following Kelley's games?" he asks.

"I'm also following Zaka's. And New York. And Boston."

"East Coast boy through and through?"

"Of course."

"That's a shame."

I frown. "Huh? Why?"

"The reason I've been giving Brady this crash course in being an agent is because as soon as he graduates law school, he's going to

Chapter 37

become a junior agent in the LA office. He wants to be there so he can be with his boyfriends. And I was thinking that if you maybe wanted to transfer to the LA office for, let's say, *reasons*, then I can look into that and see what I can do."

"Umm ..." This for sure has to be a test. I haven't yelled out, "Yes, immediately. Transfer me right now," so that should win me some kind of an award in self-restraint, because moving to LA? Keeping my job and getting to be in the same city as Kelley? Sign me the fuck up. But Damon offering this to me after explicitly telling me Kelley and I can't have a relationship? Test, test, test. "Thank you for thinking of me, but I'm happy where I am."

"You are?"

"I feel like I have purpose here now."

"That doesn't mean that you're happy," he points out. "And if there's something or someone out there who could make you happy, don't you think you should go for it?"

If this really is a test, it's a mean one. "Being in the same city as that someone would be hell for me if I wasn't allowed to be with him."

Damon's lips twist. "Did I say you weren't allowed?"

"Yes. Right after you basically accused me of being a whore."

Brady's voice comes from behind me. "Uh, I'm going to back away and let you two talk."

"You can stay," Damon says. "I'm talking to Thad about possibly moving to the LA office with you when you go."

"What, like my babysitter? Is that the real reason you sent him to the Catskills too?"

"Contrary to what anyone with your last name believes, not everything is about you. Thad's been putting in long hours, coming up with some great ideas and leads to follow on how to better protect our athletes, and I think hard work should be rewarded."

"So to get this straight," I say. "You're saying you're giving me the opportunity to move to LA to pursue something with Kelley, and I won't be fired if we're together?"

"HR forms would need to be signed, stating you're both entering into a relationship of your own free will, blah, blah, blah.

Thad

You wouldn't be allowed to have any input on Kelley's career in any official capacity, and if it all goes to shit and you break up, I can't guarantee a job will be waiting for you back in New York, but if you want it, the offer is there."

The only things holding me back from jumping right in are leaving my roommates high and dry and moving to the other side of the country, away from my parents. But fuck, I really want this. Even if it doesn't work out, I can't say I didn't try.

Kelley is the only man I've ever contemplated getting serious with. Or trying to get serious with. He's the only man I've ever felt like I could fall for. We might have started out thinking we were completely different, but the truth is we're more alike than I ever could've thought.

My fear of failure was holding me back from shining bright.

Kelley's anxiety over not being accepted affected his light.

We're two sides of the same coin, and I want us to be together.

"You can think about it," Damon says, and I realize I haven't said anything in a really long time.

"I really only have one question," I say. "One for you and then one for Kelley."

"What's your question?"

"Why now? Like, why didn't you offer this back when Kelley first got traded?"

"Good question. When I first hired you, I didn't know if you were going to stick it out. And even when Kelley was traded, you were still coasting—those were your words. But since he left, you have proved to me that you're an asset to this firm. And if I don't go out of my way to make my employees happy, then I may as well invite other firms to poach you." He leans forward. "I want you to understand that I was never against you dating Kelley. If you had been assigned as his intern agent instead of Brady, then yes, there would be a big issue, but not one that couldn't be fixed by simply pulling him off your client list. The problem I had was that you weren't up-front about it, you kept it from me, and money exchanged hands in a way I wasn't comfortable with and probably shouldn't have allowed to happen in the first place. But I can see it.

Chapter 37

How you feel about him. Tonight, when I came out here and you looked so damn happy to see him succeed, I knew it wasn't purely a physical thing. As I've watched you research for ways to protect future athletes from discrimination and put all your spare time and effort into doing so, I knew your feelings were real. I've been contemplating giving you this offer for a few weeks now, but I needed to be sure before I did."

I know it might be about ten years too late, but is this what it feels like to accomplish something? To excel? Instead of being middle of the pack, I'm making my boss take notice. The fact it's paying off is just a bonus.

Damon stands. "Brady and I will leave you and let you ask Kelley what he wants to do."

Well, shit. Can I really do this over the phone?

"He's probably doing press conferences and everything at the moment. I can call him later."

"There's no rush. It will take a week or two for the transfers to come through and to set you up with an LA office ID, get you moved. So even if you say yes, it won't be an instant thing."

In that case, do I really want to ask Kelley? What if I get his hopes up and then something with the paperwork falls through, or I tell him I'm moving in two weeks and then get delayed?

I'm already itching to see him, and hearing I'll have to wait a week or two makes me impatient. I don't want to put that on him.

"I might head home and give him a call, then."

"We'll see you back here in the morning."

"See you then."

The walk back home is short, but the anticipation of speaking to Kelley makes it feel like an eternity. The amount of times I almost hit Call on his number is ridiculous.

As soon as I open my apartment door, I'm hitting that button.

It rings and rings, and okay, the short distance between the office and here obviously wasn't enough for him to finish his interviews, shower, and change, but as I'm about to give up and hit End, he answers, and his smooth and sexy voice fills my ear.

Thad

"Did you watch?" The background noise is intense, like he's in a huge crowd.

"I did. Are you out celebrating?"

"Not yet." He's practically yelling into his phone. "The team is about to head out though."

"Go out and have fun. You deserve it."

"Thank you."

"You looked amazing out there. I'm so proud of you."

He doesn't answer, but I can't be sure if it's because he didn't hear me or if it's because he doesn't know how to take compliments well. Actually, I know the second thing is true about him, but I was hoping that maybe, coming from me, he'd be able to.

I almost chicken out asking him what I need to because I don't want to bring down his good mood by serious talk. But I have to know.

"I have a hypothetical for you if you have a second to talk?"

The noise dies down behind him. "I just snuck into an empty room at the stadium. What's your hypothetical?"

"Hypothetically, if you hadn't been traded, do you think we could've found a way to date and make it work?"

His answer is quick and confident. "There's no doubt in my mind."

"That's all I needed to know. Go celebrate with your teammates. I wish I could be there with you."

He sighs wistfully. "I wish you could be here too."

Your wish is my command.

We end the call, and I text Damon immediately.

Put me in for the transfer.

Chapter 38
Kelley

Other than that random phone call a couple of weeks ago to congratulate me on my game and give me a crushing sense of hope, I haven't heard from Thad. Technically, I have, but it's been the same old random text here and there without any substance.

I've been on the road again, so maybe that's why he hasn't called, but I'm itching for the day we play in New York so I can hopefully see him. Even if we played in Philly or Boston, I'd hire a car and drive the rest of the way while I'm expected to be in a hotel bed sleeping. Desperate? Don't know her.

The farthest east we made it this time was Atlanta, so I didn't even get near anywhere close enough.

Thad calling me at my highest of highs really meant something to me, and I know I could easily dial his number too, but I don't want him to give me an inch and I take a mile. I'm going to save that for in-person meet-ups. Wear my tightest suit, flash him a smile. Do anything I can to make him weak in the knees.

The fantasy of it all is nice, but the bottom line is there's still an entire country between us, and being with me puts his job on the line. I'm holding out for the day he becomes a full agent, maybe changes firms. Preferably in a city with a baseball team. Though, that's extreme. Moving for a guy I'd barely started seeing? On the outside, it seems absurd, but when I think about Thad, about our connection, it's really not.

Kelley

I kind of hate that I love it here in LA though because if I'm offered a new contract at the end of next season, I want to take it. Sure, I haven't been here long, and anything could happen—my first year with Philly was good—but there's something about LA that feels like home already.

Oh no. I've become a West Coaster. I'm never admitting that out loud. And never to Thad, New Jersey boy born and raised.

We have a home game tonight, but I'm not pitching. I've been playing well since my no-hitter, and I think it was the confidence boost I needed to get out of my slump. If I could do that every time I got into a funk, I'd have my choice of team and contract anywhere I wanted. Unfortunately, while I have hope I'll be able to get another no-hitter in my career at some point—maybe one day, I could even have a perfect game—I can acknowledge the timing of this one wasn't a coincidence.

It was a combination of the anger of being traded, knowing Thad was watching, and the most powerful source there is known to man: pettiness.

I no longer hold resentment over the trade, my beef with Philly is done, and even though I don't like how management handled everything, having Zaka and Hunter come out to the mound to celebrate with me took away the tarnished edges of my time in Philly.

I'm one of the last of the team to arrive at the stadium because I don't need to warm up, and walking into the locker room puts me at ease. I get dressed and am putting on my cleats when my phone goes off with a text alert.

At first, I'm confused by the picture that sits in my inbox. Because Thad is at a baseball game. My brain doesn't make the connection that he could be here because my initial reaction is he's at a stadium on the East Coast. Where he lives.

It's not until I zoom in and see the huge LA team logo that it clicks. I'm up and running out onto the field in a second, even though my laces aren't tied and there's a real chance of falling flat on my face in front of thousands of people.

Chapter 38

I don't care though. Because somewhere in this crowd is the only man I've ever considered as someone I could truly be with.

I can be myself with him. He accepts me, flaws and all. He's supportive, surprisingly, seeing how he was when we met, but that's the beauty that is Thad St. James. He can admit when he's wrong. He's loyal, even if it's to his own detriment. And he's there for me.

He's here.

I don't care why he's here, whether it's to see me or for work and I'm a side perk, it doesn't matter. All that matters is it's been months since that day on a New York street where he kissed me goodbye, and if it's only friendship he can give me, I'll take it. If it's a single one-night, secret hookup, I'm okay with that. I've just missed him so fucking much.

I can't see him anywhere because the stadium is huge. No shock there. I glance down at my phone again to try to work out what angle his point of view is from when I get another text.

Turn around.

I do a 180, and there he is. With Brady. Standing in the seating area of left field, right by the fenced-off area.

He's almost the farthest away he could possibly get, and my shoes are still untied, so instead of running all that way and risk tripping over in front of the stands, which are filling up rapidly as it gets closer to game time, I kick off my cleats and run to them in my socks.

I don't care that everyone can see me.

I don't care that this might make the news later with everyone asking, "What is Kelley Afton doing?"

The second I reach them, I'm already halfway through my sentence. "What are you doing—"

Thad leans over the barrier, cups the back of my head, and presses his lips to mine.

I'm not expecting it, but I sure as fuck welcome it. Even if my cap hits him in the forehead and gets pushed halfway off my head.

The millions of concerns I would normally have over this situation are blurry, melting puddles of goo, burning up from the heat in his kiss.

With the warmth of his tongue, the desperation in the firmness of his mouth, his job and public perception of kissing a man in front of media and thousands of spectators is the last thing on my mind.

That is until Brady's voice and then the screaming of fans breaks through the spell.

"This is cute and all, but as your almost-sole agent, I want to advise you that all of the screaming is for you. You're welcome to keep going, but you've always wanted to keep a low profile."

I pull back and look into Thad's blue eyes, and the way they shine under the stadium lights, his gaze holds more than lust. It holds a promise. Something deeper. Thad's lips turn upward into a bright smile, and my insides flip.

"Screw low profile." Before I go back to kissing him, which is the only thing I want to do, I take my hat off and throw it aside.

We come back together with full, open-mouthed kisses, tongues tangling, and I never want it to end.

When it ends, I'm sure he's going to say he's only in town for the night or that getting fired over this would be worth it. If he hadn't kissed me first, I never would've taken that leap. Not only because I wouldn't want to risk his job, but also because I would be too self-conscious to go for it.

But Thad taking that step first? It gives me the courage to keep this going. No matter what anyone says outside of us two, it's irrelevant. This is about him and me and how much I've missed him in my life.

"Okay, now it's getting kind of porny," Brady says, and I can't help laughing, which makes us break apart once again.

I'm standing still in shock, unsure that Thad is really here and with my agent, and—wait. My gaze ping-pongs between them.

"Damon knows you're here?" I ask.

They smile at each other and then at me.

"He sent me here, actually," Thad says.

"Here... like the stadium?"

Chapter 38

Thad leans further on the railing. "As in LA. It turns out there was a position available as a junior agent at the LA King Sports office."

It's too much to process at once. Too many questions. He's moving here? Damon sent him? But what about the rules and the crossing lines and the—

"Kell," he says and locks eyes with me once more. "Breathe."

I suck in air.

"Everything is okay because I'm here now. Permanently."

I might not understand how, but I do understand that everything I've wanted for the last few months has landed right in my lap, and I'm going to do anything I can not to screw this up.

"Permanently…" I repeat.

"Yup. And I'm here to ask you on a date."

"Is that allowed? What about—"

"Damon has a list of rules for us, but he's not going to stand in our way."

My heart is so full I'm scared my eyes might tear up. "So you're here to date me?"

"I'm here to do more than that. I'm here to make you fall in love with me."

Little does he know I'm pretty sure I'm already there.

Chapter 39
Thad

Kelley grunts as he moves inside me. "I still can't believe you're here."

He hovers above me, and with me holding my knees up near my head, his cock pushes against my prostate over and over again. Kelley looks so hot like this, glistening with sweat, eyes hooded, and all of his lust and attention focused on me while he fucks me.

"Is that why you felt the need to fuck me again? To make sure it's real?"

As soon as the longest baseball game in history ended last night, Kelley took me home to his place, and we haven't left the bedroom since. I haven't even been given the tour of his new fancy LA home yet, but there'll be plenty of time for that. This, reconnecting, is more important.

And I can't think of a better way to reconnect.

Kelley lets out a long moan. "I'm going to do whatever it takes for me to finally believe you moved here to be with me. That you asked your boss for it. For me."

I let one of my knees go so I can cup Kelley's face. He leans into it and closes his eyes.

I swallow hard. "I didn't want to give up on us without giving us a real chance. I want you more than I've ever wanted anyone or anything in my life."

Kelley's eyes fly open. "Even baseball?"

Chapter 39

That might have been a hard question to answer not that long ago, but there's one massive difference between my love of baseball and my feelings for Kelley. "Even baseball. I didn't love it enough to fight for it. All I've wanted to do since those two weeks in the Catskills is fight for you."

My unspoken words linger in the air. I didn't love baseball enough, but I do love him. I love him more than I can even say. More than I'm willing to admit because, technically, we haven't gone on that first date yet. I'm scared putting it out there will put way too much pressure on us. We don't need that when we've had so much working against us already.

Kelley's head falls forward, and he grunts again. "I need you to come. I really need it."

I drop my hand from his face and reach between us, jerking myself to get me there faster. My whole body tightens as I get closer and closer. "I'm gonna come," I warn him.

"Thank fuck." He speeds up, pegging my prostate harder.

I spill over, and a second later, he follows.

We barely have time to catch our breaths before my alarm goes off. Kelley's still inside me, and if it weren't for me needing to show up to my first day of work, I'd want to keep him there a while longer.

He pulls out of me and flops onto his back.

"Damn it." I reach for my phone to turn off the incessant sound.

"Perfect timing if you ask me," Kelley says. He sounds sleepy, and I can't blame him, considering we spent most of the night making each other come.

I sit up and throw my legs over the side of the bed. "Some cuddle time would've been nice."

Kelley leans up on one elbow and kisses my shoulder. "We'll have a lot of time to do that tonight."

I smile, mainly because I doubt that's true. "Until one or both of us get hard again."

"It's not my fault you're irresistible."

Thad

"I could say the same about you." I stand. "I have to shower and head into the office to meet my new bosses."

"Bosses, plural? You'll have two Damons to work for?"

"Yep. Camden is managing partner, and his boyfriend, Xavier, is the PR managing partner. I've met Camden in passing but haven't met Xavier before. Though to snag someone as hot as Camden, he'd have to be drop-dead gorgeous."

An adorable growl comes from Kelley. "I already hate them."

Aww. "No matter how good-looking they are, I'm not fucking this up." I wave a finger between him and me. "I didn't move all this way for them or the job opportunity."

"So you moved here to find your brother?" he teases.

"Oh, for sure. Only for him."

He nudges me, and I laugh.

"Mom does want me to find him though. When I told them I'm moving here for a boy, they got way too excited, so I expect them to come see me the first chance either of them can take off work to check you out. Warning you now."

Kelley falls backward, head hitting the pillow, arms stretched out. "And I thought making the public love me was anxiety-inducing. I wouldn't even know how to impress parents."

I put one knee back on the bed and lean over him. "Luckily for you, they rarely get time off, so there's nothing to worry about."

"Yet."

I give him a quick kiss and stand again, grabbing my clothes off the floor. My suitcase is back in my hotel room, where I'm staying until I can find a rental, so the suit I wore to the game last night will have to do. The good thing is it's my favorite bright blue suit. The bad news is it's wrinkled. Way to make a great first impression.

But as I leave to shower and glance back over my shoulder at a satisfied and happy Kelley, I know it'll be worth it. I don't care if my new bosses think I'm a slob.

Okay, maybe I do care.

Chapter 39

Not because Xavier is even hotter than Camden, but because both of them are so put together, and they're already looking at me with judgment as they take in my appearance. The only saving grace is I was on time. Brady, on the other hand, is late.

Camden and Xavier look at each other and then back at me. We're in a conference room that has a very similar vibe to the New York office. It's welcoming but still spacious.

"We probably shouldn't wait any longer for Brady to get this started. Xav, do you want to bring in Holloway and Fox?" Camden asks.

"At the same time?" Xavier smirks and heads down the hall toward the offices we passed on the way into the conference room.

Camden turns to me. "Xavier and I finished training our associate agents this past month, so now it's their turn to be mentors. They're both great guys, and I'll assign you and Brady to whoever feels like the best fit for you and the firm, but if there's any issues, come to either me or Xav."

While he talks, Brady shows up, running into the room, rapidly apologizing for being late.

Camden grins. "You moved here to be with your boyfriends, who you've been doing long-distance with, didn't you?"

"Uh, yes." Brady cocks his head, as if wondering why Camden's asking.

"Then I understand why you're late."

Brady takes the seat next to mine. "I was actually late because I miscalculated how long it would take me to get from Marina Del Rey to here." He points to me. "This one moved here to be with his boyfriend, who also happens to be my client, and that's why he's wearing a wrinkly suit."

"Ah, yes. The Kelley Afton viral moment from the game last night. We're familiar and have been filled in by Damon."

Suddenly, I'm starting to think they weren't judging me for my suit but for the kerfuffle they've probably been dealing with all morning, seeing as Kelley's case is moving to LA with Brady.

Xavier returns with the two agents Brady and I are going to be learning from.

Thad

Where Camden and Xavier are in their thirties, these two look maybe mid-to-late twenties—not much older than Brady and me at all.

"Brady, good to see you decided to show up," Xavier says. "Thad, Brady, this is Archer Holloway and Lincoln Fox." He gestures to the guys as he says their names so we know which is which.

I'm immediately drawn to Archer purely because he's not wearing a jacket, and his shirtsleeves are rolled up, revealing amazing forearm tattoos. His hair is bleached, his eyes are bright, and on appearances alone, I totally vibe.

Lincoln looks like he's gritting his teeth and wants to be anywhere but here.

Xavier sits next to Camden again while Archer and Lincoln sit across from us.

"I want to go over each of your profiles before I make my decision on who to place where," Camden says. "Working together cohesively is important."

Lincoln scoffs but then covers it with a cough.

Archer laughs, and Lincoln's scowl deepens.

"Obviously, Brady, you don't need much of an introduction—"

Brady interrupts. "I know I'm seen as some kind of nepo baby and I'm the name partner's nephew, but I'd rather be treated like any other while I'm here."

Camden smiles. "Good. Because all I was going to say is that you got your undergrad from Franklin U, law degree from NYLS, and you're bringing over three clients you were working with in New York."

"Oh. Umm. Yep, that's me in a nutshell."

Archer cuts in. "You have your brother Peyton Miller, Kelley Afton, and ...?"

"Torey Nelson."

"Who's that?" Archer asks, and even though he's still my preference to be my mentor, there's a mini red flag waving at me with his dismissive tone.

"He's a quarterback and was on Chicago's practice squad for

Chapter 39

two seasons before being picked up by San Francisco as their backup," Lincoln says. It's the first words he's said, and his voice is surprisingly smooth for someone who's scowling.

"Good to see one of you have done your homework," Camden says.

And with the way Archer's now gritting his teeth, it's all but confirmed Lincoln and Archer have beef.

"And Thad here has an undergrad from Olmstead."

Wow, way to make me feel inferior. I'm quick to put my best foot forward because I want to make a good impression. "Becoming an agent was a backup plan of sorts, so I'm not as experienced as Brady, who has been aiming toward this goal his entire schooling."

"Backup plan?" Lincoln asks. It's with genuine curiosity, and I soften toward him a little.

"I was an MLB hopeful, but I didn't make it. I had to let that bitterness go before I could move on, and now here I am, ready to jump in. In New York, I was in talks with Frederik Zaka for him to sign with me once I became a full-fledged agent, but I haven't had a chance to follow that up yet."

"I heard about that," Camden says. "Poor Merek is stressing over what he's doing wrong to have all these hotshot interns steal his clients."

"Respect," Archer says with all the cockiness of a total fuckboy.

I swear Lincoln is trying to hold back an eye roll.

I feel judged. "I didn't set out to sign Zaka. We met at a social thing and clicked. The plan was for him to stay on Merek's roster and I'd be assisting with him on his case, but the last-minute move to LA threw a wrench in the works."

"Fair enough," Camden says, but I notice Xavier write something down on a notepad and shove it over to Camden. Camden reads it, smiles, and then passes it back. "Okay, here's what we're going to do. For the moment, I think Brady and Archer will be paired up, and then Thad and Lincoln."

I swallow the small pang of disappointment. Archer seems less uptight and more like me in terms of style, but I'm sure there's a business-related answer why I've been paired with Lincoln.

Thad

Brady and I are instructed to shadow our mentors while they show us around the office. Lincoln is professional, and I think I'll be comfortable enough to ask him any questions if I get stuck. He might come across as more serious than Archer, but he's friendly and down-to-earth.

It's around lunchtime when we sit down in his office. He emails me some contracts to read over to give me an overview of the kind of cases and workload he has, but I don't get far into the first one when he randomly asks, "Can I ask about Zaka?"

I glance up at him from my laptop. "What did you want to know?"

"I tried to sign him when I was fresh out of college, and he said I was too young. He signed with OnTrack Sports, and then I know he recently transferred over to Merek in New York. So, yeah, I was curious how you met him socially."

"Ah." I rub the back of my neck. Zaka is a big fish, and I still ask myself why our one conversation drew him to me, but I'm not complaining. "If you followed any of the big sporting news this morning, you'll know Kelley Afton and I are together. We'd been friends for a while, and I went to one of his games while visiting my parents near Philly. We went out with the team afterward, and yeah ... I guess Zaka and I vibed."

"What kind of vibed?" So not hard to pick up on the accusation there.

I hold up my hand. "Honestly, I was as shocked as Damon when Zaka asked for me. I didn't set out to sign him. We had one conversation, and none of it was about work."

Lincoln rubs his chin. "Maybe that's why he liked you. Because you didn't have an agenda."

"Possibly?"

"So long as you don't have an agenda to steal clients from me, we'll get along fine. I do feel for Merek though. First Kelley and now Zaka."

I wince. "You sound like you're talking from experience."

"You could say that. It's almost like Archer gets a kick out of stealing clients from me."

Chapter 39

"Ah. So that was the dynamic I was picking up on."

Lincoln's face falls. "Sorry, it's unprofessional to bitch about a colleague."

"Please do. I was in all the headlines this morning because I kissed my boyfriend last night. Any other drama is welcome."

"Yeah, well, you did that in front of a stadium full of twenty thousand people and countless sports reporters. What did you expect?" Lincoln snickers.

"Fair point, but give me some gossip that doesn't involve me."

He waves me off. "There really is no gossip. I'm just bitter Archer is a sniper and beats me to signing the people I wanted and or brought in to the firm."

"Okay, note to self: keep him away from Zaka."

"I really am overexaggerating. Besides, he's probably not interested in Zaka. He's probably plotting how he could use Brady to get to the top while also sleeping with his dads."

"Please tell me that's more hyperbole."

"Little bit. Archer is obsessed with being the best. If that means fucking over the people in his way, he won't hesitate. It's how he had the highest commission check out of any agent last year—something he won't let anyone forget. He's annoyingly arrogant but has the goods to back it up. It sucks."

Maybe Lincoln's bitterness comes from awe as well as jealousy.

At least with him knowing I'm not here to steal any of his clients, he's more relaxed and not as intimidating.

I'm happy with my mentor, even if it wasn't the one I originally wanted.

Chapter 40
Kelley

Considering we thought Thad moving to LA would mean we'd see more of each other, we really underestimated the demand of Major League Baseball and being a junior agent needing to prove your worth.

Still, during the times I have home games, Thad is there in the stands, cheering me on. He has a studio apartment he stays in while I'm away, even though I told him he's welcome to stay at my house, but he says he's happy to pay for an entire apartment to himself, considering it costs the same as his tiny bedroom in the shared loft back in New York. He got a pay raise with the promotion, and he used the very logical reasoning that he didn't want to move in with me so soon.

Even if I'd love to have him there every time I got home. The vision of it makes me giddy.

Stupid logic and needing to be patient. Who needs a stable, healthy relationship when you can have suffocating and codependent?

Okay, yeah, that's probably a good thing with the way my mental health can be.

I can't say everything with my anxiety is going smoothly, but it's a thousand times better than what it was this time last year. I have my setbacks, my breakthroughs, and Thad is by my side for all of them. So is Brady. I'm so happy I chose him to be my agent

Chapter 40

because Brady knows how to take care of what I need from an emotional point of view.

He and Thad have grown close too, and I finally have the perfect team in place that feels more like family than professional, which is something Damon sold me on when I contemplated signing with King Sports.

Even though Thad has been here for a few weeks already, today's the first day I'm going into the offices where he works. I would've done it sooner, but Thad didn't want his new colleagues and bosses to think he was using me and our relationship to get ahead.

Today, though, isn't about me.

It's about Zaka.

And as if the mere thought of him summons him, my doorbell chimes.

I open the front door to my new mansion near Elysian Park, which I've been smart enough to rent instead of buy after learning my lesson back in Philly, and there, my old teammate stands with a wide smile on his face. He's growing a beard, which is more reddish tinged than the blond that sits on his head, and it's been a while since I last saw him. It was my no-hitter, actually.

It was only a couple of months ago, but it feels like a lifetime has passed since then.

"Seriously?" is the first thing he says. "I sign with Philly to be on the same team as you, and then you leave me?"

I laugh because I sometimes still don't know how to take Zaka. He said something similar that night on the mound, but I thought it was referring to the no-hitter I'd just pitched. Now, I'm not so sure.

"Did introducing you to your new agent make up for abandoning you when I had absolutely no choice in the matter?"

Zaka pretends to think about it and shrugs. "I guess it'll have to do. Show me your new place."

I let him in and give him the tour. It's an amazing house, with its modern, boxy shape and the stark range of colors between blinding white, mute gray, and black. And yes, that is sarcasm with a capital S. There are only those three colors. But whether it's only because I'm renting it or because the house back in Philly was my first big purchase with more money than I ever could've dreamed of having access to, the new place doesn't hold any particular sentiment to me.

Yet. I'm hoping I can change that the longer I'm here and the sooner I can convince Thad to move in with me. Though, I should probably start by telling him that I'm irrevocably in love with him.

We've said things. Heavily implied the L word or at least hinted at heading in that direction. But we haven't had that moment yet. It's probably because we started as friends, were sleeping together for a bit, but then were cut off from chasing more. So it feels like we've been together longer than only the few weeks he's been here.

Whichever one of us says those three little words in succession first ... oh, who am I kidding? It has to be him. Anytime I've come close, I've chickened out because what if it's too soon? He says it's too soon to move in together, so maybe he's waiting to be head over heels for that.

Then again, just because he isn't willing to live together this soon, that doesn't mean that he didn't make the first giant step for us, moving across the damn country for me. So maybe it is my place to say it first.

"How are you liking LA?" Zaka asks while he stares into my perfectly landscaped backyard to detract from the very average-looking neighborhood beyond the fence.

"Ever since Thad got here, I've been a hell of a lot less bitter about it, but even before then, I have to admit I've been less stressed."

"Good to hear." He hesitates before turning to me. "Can I ask you something?"

"Of course."

"Do you think the team traded you because you're gay?"

My initial response is to say yes, but considering I suspect Zaka is struggling with his own identity, and if he really did sign with Philly this season because of me—perhaps to not feel so alone—I don't want to scare him into not speaking his truth.

Chapter 40

"Do I think they would have traded me had I not come out and brought a lot of attention on myself? No. But at the same time, I was in a terrible slump. I don't think the franchise itself is homophobic. But it wouldn't surprise me if they decided that having the gay guy struggling with poor mental health and his game was a liability to their season."

"Good to know. You ready to take me to your man's office so I can sign these papers?"

I'm more than excited to. Not only for Thad to sign his first big client but because I get to see where Thad works. And more importantly, meet the agents mentoring both him and Brady. From the stories Thad has told me already, I want to put faces to their names. I swear, sometimes when he comes home, the things he tells me are like listening to a telenovela drama.

It takes us way too long to get to downtown LA, and that's one thing I absolutely can't stand about LA, but I'll endure it for everything good here.

When we finally arrive at the office, it's around lunchtime, so when Thad meets us at reception, he suggests we go do a business lunch first before signing the papers. Brady's by his side, enthusiastically nodding, and before we know it, both he and Thad usher us back onto the elevator.

They both slump in relief when the doors shut.

Zaka leans in close to me. "Is it just me, or are they acting weird?"

They're for sure acting weird, but I don't know why. "Soooo, how is work?" I ask.

"If I didn't have important documents to sign this afternoon, I'd be drinking," Thad says.

"Ditto," Brady adds.

"Anything we should be concerned about as your clients?"

Brady turns to me with pleading in his eyes. "Promise me you won't jump ship. Or, if you do, go to someone like Thad, because Jesus H. Christ, if I have to deal with any more of Archer's shit—"

"Or Lincoln's," Thad cuts in.

"I'm quitting. I will move both my partners to New York and

go crawling back to Damon, asking him to give me a padded office with no door where I only have to deal with clients on the phone and no other agents."

"More competitive drama?" I ask.

"It's exhausting," Thad says. "I wondered why Camden and Xavier assigned us to them. I've come to the conclusion this has to be a hazing ritual."

"I feel a lot better about switching representation from New York to LA," Zaka deadpans.

Thad claps Zaka's shoulder. "Don't worry. If you ever need me, just call. I will jump on a plane and head for New York. It's closer for you and so much more convenient."

"Convenient you get away from Archer and Linc," Brady grumbles.

"I'm starting to feel remarkably better about the dramas in baseball," I say.

The elevator opens, but as Brady and Zaka step off and Thad and I follow, Thad grabs my hand and tugs me aside for a second.

"If I forget to tell you in all the chaos that this afternoon will be, I want to thank you for bringing me my first client."

I step into his arms and press my chest to his. "You're the one who was charismatic and friendly enough to catch his eye. He signed with you because of who you are, not who introduced you."

"Still. Thank you. Meeting you has changed my life, and ... I've been wanting to say something for a while now, and with the big things happening today, I can't hold it in anymore. I love you. I'm in love with you. And I know I wouldn't be this person without having had you in my life. No matter where we go from here, what happens with either of our careers, I just wanted you to know that you're loved."

And there's my moment. The moment of pure peace, knowing that the man I love feels exactly the same way.

"I love you too," I say. "You're the only man I've ever said that to, the only man I've felt it with, and no matter what happens, I want you to know that it's true."

"Even if I'm not living with you?" His concern over my rejec-

Chapter 40

tion sensitivity disorder is genuine, which is understandable, but he doesn't need to worry when it comes to him.

"My enemy—logic—knows if we do it too soon, we might implode. So between waiting for the right time or losing you completely, I'll wait forever if I have to. I don't want to, but I will."

"I never want you to feel like I'm half out the door or—"

"I don't. I promise."

He cups my face. "All I want is to do right by you. By us."

I breathe him in and revel in something even more powerful than the I love yous. Falling in love is easy. Keeping it is work, and Thad shows me every day that he's willing to do whatever it takes.

He moved across the country for me, left his family and friends behind, all on a maybe. Maybe we could make it work, maybe we could be together, maybe we have a future. He did that for me.

He came here to love me, support me, and be there for me the same way I want to be there for him. I have no doubt in the love I have for Thad St. James.

Epilogue
SIX MONTHS LATER

"I now know the real reason you're in a relationship with two men," I say to Brady as we watch his boyfriends move my boxes into Kelley's house.

"So I don't have to do any heavy lifting at times like this? It's exactly why. That, and the cost of living these days is so pricey, you need a three-income household really to survive."

"We can hear you," Prescott says.

"Wasn't trying to be quiet."

Brady's partners really are great, and from the couple of times Kelley and I have gone out with the three of them, they both treat Brady like a king. Maybe too much like a king.

"Are you sure we shouldn't be helping them? It's my stuff, and I asked you here to help me. Not them."

"They like showing off their muscles. I promise."

"I'll take your word for it. I'm going to start getting unpacked while they lug everything inside." Not that there's much. I left my furniture back in New York for whoever my roommates were going to fill my room with. It's basically all clothes, books, baseball crap I probably should've thrown out already, and knickknacks that I've collected over the years.

"Are you sure you should unpack? Maybe you should wait for Kelley to come home from his road trip, see that you've moved yourself in while he's been away, and then maybe ask if he even wants to live with you."

"Nah, it'll be all good."

If I was on the outside of this situation, I would agree with Brady. Someone secretly moving all their stuff in while their partner is away after only being together for six months? Totally presumptuous, controlling, and probably a huge red flag. But considering Kelley wanted me to move in with him as soon as I got to LA, and as much as he denied it that me rejecting the idea hurt, not to mention the countless times he's brought up my lease on my apartment and what I think I'll do when it's up, it's safe to say that when he gets home tomorrow night, I'm going to make him the happiest man in the world.

I practically live here already when he is home. I have a key to the place, and I only ever stay in my apartment when he's away. Which is a lot.

There was no real moment where I knew I was ready to move in with him. It's almost as if I've had it in my head that after my six-month lease was up, it was a given.

Because I never want to be away from Kelley. Our jobs keep us apart a lot of the time, so it makes sense to share our space.

I've always wanted to live with Kelley, but I didn't want to rush things. If we had, I have no doubt we'd still be as strong as we are today, but I didn't know six months ago if that would be the case.

We were new, and while we'd first hooked up over winter but didn't get officially together until summer, it's not like we can count those six months when we'd seen each other once or twice over that time.

But now ... Now I know I can be who he needs me to be. He might doubt who he is sometimes, he might get in his head, freak out about something he sees in the media—he's getting better at not looking, but slips happen—but he will never doubt me because I make sure of it.

And this step, this is just another way of me showing Kelley that he's my priority.

I might have been happy to be an okay baseball player. I might have been okay to coast through my internship. But if there's anything I'm sure of in this world, it's that I'm not okay with being a mediocre boyfriend. I want to be the best. Kelley makes me want to be the best because he deserves it.

On their way back out to get more boxes, Kit and Prescott are stopped by Brady.

"If I had moved in with you two when I was back in college and didn't tell you I was going to do it, would you have freaked out?"

This won't work. They're not going to rattle me. I won't let them.

Prescott answers immediately. "Restraining orders would've happened."

"See!" Brady says.

"I wouldn't have," Kit says. "It probably would've made me stay in California longer than I did."

I turn to Brady. "Kit's my favorite of your boyfriends."

Prescott huffs. "Just for that, any boxes that say fragile, I'm gonna throw against a wall by 'accident.'" He disappears out the front door, and I can't help but laugh.

"He does know most people would stop helping altogether?"

Brady smiles. "What can I say, they love me."

"And I love Kelley. He's ready for this. I know he is."

"I hope you're right."

"I am."

What if I'm not right about this?

I'm sweating. Kelley's on his way home, I have dinner in the oven, candles everywhere, and all I can think is that as soon as he sees all my stuff in his house, he's going to freak out.

Which is ridiculous because he's wanted this since I moved to LA.

It's not like he's suddenly changed his mind.

The Backup Plan

Shit, what if he's changed his mind?

I wonder if it's too late to call Kit and Prescott and ask them to come move my stuff back out. Though, my apartment's already gone, so I have nowhere to put it, and how did this romantic gesture go from being exciting to turning me into Kelley levels of anxious?

Before I have the chance to panic to the point of throwing all my belongings out a window, the front door opens, and Kelley's voice travels down the hall and into the kitchen. "Thad?"

My heart thuds, and I try to call out where I am, but only a rasp leaves me.

Kelley appears a moment later, wide smile on his face. "What's all this?"

"A welcome home."

He approaches me, wraps his arms around my back, kisses me softly, but then pulls away and picks a cherry tomato off his salad plate and pops it in his mouth. "You cooked. Should I be scared?"

"I'll have you know I'm getting really good at cooking, thank you very much."

"Uh-huh. So, what did you order in and put in the oven to pass off as your own?"

He knows me too well. "Your favorite. But I did make the salad."

"And it's not burned. Good job."

"Are ... are you supposed to cook salad?"

Kelley laughs. "No, but that was my joke. I guess it doesn't work when you have no idea how to cook."

"Oh." Any other day, I would've gotten that, but it went right over my head because I'm nervous as fuck.

"Are you okay?"

No. I'm being ridiculous. "I'm really not. I need to show you something."

I take his hand and lead him toward the bedrooms.

"I like where this is going."

"It's not sex. We'll have sex later, but that's not what this is." I stop at the guest bedroom door and take a deep breath.

"Ooh, who do you have in there? My parents. Your parents. Um, a therapist who wants to commit me for a seventy-two-hour hold?" He hesitates. "Maybe I don't want to know what's in there."

"Out of all of those options, I'm hoping you think it's better than all of them combined. If not, I'm kind of fucked." And homeless.

I open the door to put us both out of our misery, and when Kelley sees the stacks of moving boxes—which I haven't unpacked because Brady got in my head—Kelley's face lights up.

Like I knew it would. Definitely knew it would.

Wasn't freaking out at all.

He bounces on the balls of his feet. "Is this what I think it is? Are you finally moving in?"

"If you'll have me."

His arms engulf me. "If I'll have you? I've never stopped wanting you here. I don't think I've been too subtle about it. Were you really worried?"

"I wasn't! I had this big idea planned where I unpacked all my stuff and was just living here when you got back, and then Brady got in my head."

"He's fired. How dare he make my man think." Kelley is nonstop smiling, and being the one who's made him that happy makes any nervousness I had worth it.

"Can I please be there when you fake fire him in person?"

"Deal. We're really doing this though? You're here? With me? Living together and, you know, being all legit?"

"Legit? What, were we not as serious last week, having not been living together?"

"No, but you know what I mean. This is big."

"It's only as big as we make it out to be. We both struggle with change, so—"

Kelley shakes his head. "I don't mean big as in a big deal. It's the right amount of big. It's big big. Good big."

I can always tell how happy Kelley is by how little sense he makes.

"It's the beginning of everything else, you know?"

"Everything else?" I ask.

"Marriage. Kids—"

My face must give away my shock because he quickly backtracks.

"Before you start freaking out, I know these are things we need to work toward. We can't jump in as much as I want to. But this is a start."

"You ... you think about that stuff? With me? Without getting bouts of anxiety and second-guessing everything first?"

Kelley presses against me, where he belongs. Where I want him to be forever. We haven't spoken about this kind of thing before, so to hear he thinks that way too, it's everything to me.

And just when I think everything is falling into perfect place, he goes and says the one thing that cements my feelings forever. "Ever since that night you promised me I could be myself around you, I've believed it. I've lived it. Out of everything in my life I could get anxiety over, loving you isn't even on the list."

Thank you

Thank you so much for reading The Backup Plan.

King Sports has been an idea floating around in my head ever since I finished writing the Fake Boyfriend series and knew Damon was going to take on the world.

If you haven't read Damon's origin story, back before he had gray hairs from stress, you can do so here: https://mybook.to/FakeBoyfriendFakeOut

If you want to read Brady's book and how he came to fall in love with two men, it's available here: https://geni.us/cantsaygoodbye

King Sports 2 is in the works, but who could it be about?

Also by Eden Finley

Find all of Eden Finley's books here:

https://amzn.to/2zUlM16

FAKE BOYFRIEND SERIES

Fake Out

Trick Play

Deke

Blindsided

Hat Trick

Novellas:

Fake Boyfriend Breakaways: A short story collection

Final Play

FAMOUS SERIES

Pop Star

Spotlight

Fandom

Encore

Novellas:

Rockstar Hearts

FRANKLIN U: multi-author shared world series

Football Royalty

Twincerely Yours

MIKE BRAVO OPS

Iris

Rogue

Atlas

Zeus

BOOKS COWRITTEN WITH SAXON JAMES

Power Plays & Straight A's

Face Offs & Cheap Shots

Goal Lines & First Times

Line Mates & Study Dates

Puck Drills & Quick Thrills

Egotistical Puckboy

Irresponsible Puckboy

Shameless Puckboy

Foolish Puckboy

Clueless Puckboy

Bromantic Puckboy

Forbidden Puckboy

VINO & VERITAS *Sarina Bowen's True North Series*

Headstrong

STEELE BROTHERS

Unwritten Law

Unspoken Vow

Printed in Great Britain
by Amazon